HARD DOUGH
HOMICIDE

HARD DOUGH HOMICIDE

Olivia Matthews

St. Martin's Paperbacks

This is a work of fiction. All of the characters, organizations, and events portrayed in this novel are either products of the author's imagination or are used fictitiously.

Published in the United States by St. Martin's Paperbacks, an imprint of St. Martin's Publishing Group.

HARD DOUGH HOMICIDE

For information, address St. Martin's Publishing Group, 120 Broadway, New York, NY 10271.

www.stmartins.com

ISBN: 978-1-250-83906-0

Our books may be purchased in bulk for promotional, educational, or business use. Please contact your local bookseller or the Macmillan Corporate and Premium Sales Department at 1-800-221-7945, ext. 5442, or by email at MacmillanSpecialMarkets@macmillan.com.

Printed in the United States of America

St. Martin's Paperbacks edition / June 2023

10 9 8 7 6 5 4 3 2 1

To My Dream Team:

- My sister, Bernadette, for giving me the dream.
- My husband, Michael, for supporting the dream.
- My brother, Richard, for believing in the dream.
- My brother, Gideon, for encouraging the dream.
  - And to Mom and Dad always, with love.

CHAPTER 1

"Grace, how long you been coming here, you still don't know the menu?" My maternal grandmother, Genevieve Bain, looked at our bakery's customer in disbelief. Her Grenadian accent rolled out her complaint in waves. Granny called herself helping me process our patrons' orders early Friday morning. If she wasn't careful with her tone, she'd find herself chasing our guests away.

My family and I had opened our West Indian eatery, Spice Isle Bakery, in Brooklyn, New York's Little Caribbean neighborhood about four weeks ago. The shop was becoming a hub where the community gathered to get a taste of our culture, not only in the dishes we served but also in the décor, the music we played, and the stories we shared. Our customer base had grown quickly with a solid foundation of familiar faces and new customers discovering us every day.

The scents of confectioners' sugar, melted butter, warm chocolate, and fresh pastries mingled with the sharp aromas of bush teas. The soft chime from the bell above the bakery door had become a constant beat beneath the old-school reggae music bouncing from the bakery's sound system. Several of our customers shook their shoulders and rocked their hips to the captivating rhythm.

I loved the energy in the bakery, especially when it was crowded with guests. The banter, whether it was good-natured or grumpy, was like the exchange you'd find at any family gathering. That's one of the things I loved most about our shop. I also loved baking, a skill I was continuing to work on with Granny's help.

Grace Parke was one of our bakery's regulars. The middle-aged woman looked very professional in a soft gray skirt suit. "I'm in the mood for something different." She studied the menu as though she'd never seen it before.

A tearing sound came from the center of the line. A man who appeared to be close to my father's age leaned forward. "You're in the mood to hold up the line, you mean. Some of us have to get to work."

"Grace, you should do what Benny and I do." Tanya Nevis spoke from the dining area, where she sat at a table for two with her beau, Benny Parsons. The petite older lady had been friends with Granny for years. Her Grenadian accent flavored her words. "Come back when the line's not so long if you want to try something new."

Grumbles rose from other guests in the line, which extended out the door. If customers in the bakery were agitated, I didn't want to think about how annoyed patrons who waited in the crisp late-April-in-New-York weather were. How many of them had given up and left?

Desperate to avert an angry confrontation in the middle of our shop, I pasted an encouraging smile on my lips and offered Grace one of our printed menus. "Ms. Parke, why don't you come stand by me? You can look over this menu so we can help our other customers. As soon as you're ready, I promise to take your order."

"Oh, all right." Grace adjusted the strap of her brown purse on her sturdy shoulder before accepting the menu.

"Thank you, Lyndsay. Some people can't wait a few minutes."

An older woman toward the back of the line grunted. "We've been waiting a few minutes. But you were taking a few days."

Granny and I waited on other customers while Grace mulled over her choices. My grandmother refused to wear the Spice Isle Bakery "uniform," which consisted of a black chef's smock, matching chef's cap, and slacks. Instead, she was stunning in a sapphire-and-gold-patterned cotton dress that flowed over her slender curves. A matching head wrap protected the food from strands of her hair.

Tanya called across the customer line. Her tone was coy. A teasing smile curved her lips and brought a twinkle to her dark brown eyes. "Joymarie, are you going to see Devon this weekend?"

Joymarie Rodgers had just started dating my older brother, Devon. Dev was part owner of Spice Isle Bakery along with Granny, my parents, and me. He also was the youngest junior partner with a Brooklyn-based international law firm. I loved saying that. And I loved that, after months of Joymarie showing an interest in my brother, Dev had finally asked her out. I was certain they were meant to be together just like Mommy and Daddy, who'd been married for more than thirty-five years.

Tanya's question brought an explosion of attractive color to Joymarie's brown cheeks. She was a striking image in a figure-hugging violet-and-pink-patterned, knee-length dress beneath a tan spring coat. Soft ebony curls framed her heart-shaped face. "We hope to. He may have to work, though."

Grace looked up, straightening her rigid posture. "He may have to work? Shouldn't *you* be his priority?"

"Grace." Granny's tone was sharp. "Shouldn't *you* be studying the menu?"

I managed to smother my laughter, but several patrons didn't even try. Their amusement bounced around the shop. A few guests repeated the exchange for those who'd missed it. Grace shrugged carelessly before returning to the menu.

Another regular, the Knicks Fan, stepped to the counter. He was tall and slender, like a basketball point guard in a smoke gray suit. His skin was dark and smooth. Thick, tight black curls shaped his head. "Lemme get a banana bread and sorrel to go." He handed me his credit card as Granny turned to get his order from a batch of pastries fresh from the oven. "Enzo Fabrizi sold his father's bakery."

Enzo's father, Claudio, had owned and operated Claudio's Baked Goods.

"I saw that a couple of days ago." I processed his order and returned his card. "It was sold to a fast-food chain." The idea of Claudio's shop becoming part of a fast-food franchise seemed unreal.

Even before we'd opened, Claudio had vowed to shut down my family's shop. Instead, he'd been murdered the day of Spice Isle Bakery's soft launch and his business was the one to close. His killer had tried to frame me for his murder based on the fact that Claudio and I'd had a heated argument in front of a dozen customers in the middle of Spice Isle Bakery.

"Claudio's probably spinning in his grave." José Perez, the *Brooklyn Daily Beacon* crime reporter, stepped into the bakery as the order line advanced, letting additional customers in. His Puerto Rican heritage was present in his voice. He was tall and lean in straight-legged faded blue jeans and a pearl gray fisherman's sweater. A lock of his thick, wavy raven hair fell across his forehead like Superman.

The reporter was probably right. Claudio would hate the idea of his beloved bakery turning into a chain fast-food restaurant, but Enzo didn't have a choice. Claudio's bakery wasn't the only business affected by his death.

Grace returned the menu to the stand in front of the cash register. "I know what I want now, Lyndsay. May I have a currant roll, please?"

Granny gaped at the other woman. "All that and you get currant rolls all—"

I cut my grandmother off. "One currant roll coming up. Thank you, Ms. Parke."

I ignored the sound of my grandmother kissing her teeth.

On his way out, the Knicks Fan stopped beside José. "What's the latest on Claudio's murder trial?"

José seemed happy with himself. His lean, tanned features shone with excitement. "The defense's still trying to negotiate a plea deal."

I shifted my shoulders to release the tension. "I hope they're able to come to an arrangement, because I don't want to have to testify."

Granny hummed her agreement. "I don't want you to have to get on the stand in a murder trial, either. No, sir."

"Neither do I." The comment came from my mother, Cedella Bain Murray. She and my father, Jacob Murray, were busy in the kitchen, working to keep up with the volume of orders. Obviously, they weren't too busy to pay attention to the conversation that carried into the passthrough behind the customer service counter.

"It's unanimous." Daddy's voice was dry but firm. Both of my parents' accents revealed their Grenadian roots.

I struggled to hold back a smile. Under New York's

criminal justice system, I didn't think a note from my father would outweigh a subpoena, if it came to that. I'm just saying.

Detective Bryce Jackson of the New York Police Department's Homicide Division entered the bakery late Friday morning. The breakfast rush had just ended. We were in the lull before the lunch crowd. Had he timed his arrival deliberately?

In the almost three weeks since I'd proven my innocence in the investigation into Claudio's murder, which he and his partner, Detective Stanley Milner, had led, Bryce had stopped by the bakery nearly every day. Sometimes Stan was with him. His partner had a fondness for our currant rolls. Usually, Bryce came alone. He seemed to be trying to make amends for suspecting I'd killed Claudio. He should try harder.

I glanced at Granny seated at her table across from the checkout counter. She was working on her latest crocheting project, a green-and-gold doily.

Bryce crossed to the counter. "Good morning, Lyndsay." His voice was a warm baritone as smooth as a musical instrument. His accent tagged him as a native Brooklynite.

"Good morning, Detective." I set aside the container of disinfecting wipes I was using to clean the counter. "What can I do for you today?"

"You can call me Bryce." This wasn't the first time he'd invited me to do so. He'd lowered his voice, probably hoping Granny wouldn't hear him. His hopes were in vain. Granny might appear to be ignoring us, but she heard everything.

The detective and I'd met my sophomore year at Flatbush Early College High School. He'd been a senior and he'd been fine. Tall with a lean swimmer's build, beautiful hazel brown eyes, and cornrows that shaped his head and emphasized his tawny, angular features. Fast-forward twelve years. We'd been reunited when he'd suspected me of being a remorseless, bread-knife-wielding murderer. Hence he wasn't in my cell and didn't have my number. But don't call it a grudge.

"Where's your partner?" I glanced toward the door even though I knew Stan wouldn't be there.

"He's at the station." Bryce paused. "I offered to get the currant rolls today. Could we have three? I'm sure his wife would appreciate one."

"Sure." I searched his eyes. I was pretty sure that wasn't what he'd intended to say.

With Granny comfortably seated at her table, I completed Bryce's order on my own. Part of me wanted to rush him on his way. This was the part of me that didn't understand how he could've considered me a viable suspect in a homicide case. But another part of me wanted to find a way to delay his leaving. This was the dangerously vulnerable side that, if given a chance, would pretend Claudio's murder investigation had never happened.

I handed him his receipt and the bag of currant rolls. "Thank you for your business. I hope you enjoy the pastries."

"We always do." Bryce's smile seemed distracted. "Lyndsay, I was wondering if you'd want to go to that soca club near your house with me tonight?"

Was he asking me out? My high school crush was asking me to go dancing with him. Fifteen-year-old me wanted to faint. So did twenty-seven-year-old me. Bryce Jackson was a catch: handsome, intelligent when he wasn't making poor judgement calls, and ambitious. I won't lie; I'd like to get to know him better. But . . . "Thank you, but I'm busy tonight."

"Doing what?" Granny's question wasn't welcome.

I slid her a look. There wasn't any way on earth I was going to convince her to give us some privacy. And taking Bryce aside would just delay his leaving. Part of me didn't want that.

I turned back to him. "There's something I've wanted to ask you."

"What is it?"

I looked him straight in the eye. "Did you really think I was capable of killing Claudio?" He hesitated. My heart sank. I gave a humorless chuckle. "That, Detective Jackson, is the reason I'm busy tonight. I'll be busy every night until you can answer that question for me without hesitating."

His sigh was heavy with resignation. Regret dimmed his bright hazel eyes and threatened my resolve. I squared my shoulders and stood firm.

"Understood." He gave me a half smile and nodded at Granny before he left.

"Lynds, let me ask *you* something." Granny's voice pulled me from my thoughts. She shifted on her chair to face me. "How was the man supposed to know you weren't a killer without investigating? You hadn't seen each other in twelve years. And even when you went to school together, you weren't friends. So how was he supposed to know?"

"He just was." My expectations may seem unreasonable to some, but they didn't feel that way to me.

Not long after Bryce left, I went to the kitchen to help Mommy and Daddy prepare for the Friday lunch rush. Granny remained in the main part of the shop, crocheting when she wasn't greeting guests.

The office phone rang as I loaded the dishwasher. I hustled to answer it before the call rolled into our bakery's voicemail. The caller identification displayed a Kings County Early College High School number. *Not this again.*

I swallowed a groan before forcing myself to take the call. "Good morning. Spice Isle Bakery. May I help you?"

"Good morning, Ms. Murray. This is Guy Law, administrative assistant to Principal Emily Smith at Kings County Early College High School."

Guy had called the bakery three times in the past two weeks. This was his fourth call. Each time, he identified himself the same way. I couldn't understand why. "I remember who you are, Mr. Law. And you already know my answer. Our bakery is very busy. As I've explained before, we aren't able to cater Principal Smith's retirement dinner. I'm sorry. But there are several other West Indian restaurants that might be able to meet your schedule."

Mommy's stage whisper carried from the office's doorway. "Lynds! Lynds!" She waited for me to turn to her. "Is that Guy Law?"

I nodded, looking from Mommy to Daddy standing behind her. Mommy rolled her eyes. Daddy shook his head with a look of annoyance.

They must have heard me say Principal Smith's name and realized Guy had called. Again. They also knew I was lying to him. We weren't too busy to cater the principal's retirement dinner; we just didn't want to.

Mommy had taught high school math for thirty-one years. During the final nine or ten years, Emily had been her boss—and a big reason my mother had taken early retirement. To put it mildly, the principal had driven her crazy. That's why her former supervisor's request had surprised Mommy when I'd told her about Guy's first call.

At the time Emily had become the high school's principal, Dev had been attending the University of Michigan Law School, but I was living at home while attending Brooklyn College. Mommy had done her best to hide her frustration from me. But I could feel her tension. She and Daddy would vent to Granny about their workdays when they thought I couldn't hear them. Of course, I'd reported all of this to Dev. That's what families do.

Although Mommy had taught at Kings County Early College High School, Dev and I had attended its rival, Flatbush Early College High School. Our school had been just as good if not better than Kings County Early, and it was closer to home. Could you imagine if we'd attended the school where our mother had been a teacher? The harassment I'd've endured would've been so much worse. Or maybe not. Maybe being a teacher's daughter would've given me immunity from the school bullies, if not the neighborhood bullies. I doubted it, though. And anyway, that was in the past.

I understood what Mommy had gone through. I hadn't had a great relationship with my last boss, either. The thought of hosting an event in his honor left a bad taste in my mouth. I'd almost rather do anything else. So out of consideration for my mother, I'd turned down Guy's requests for a catering proposal. But the school wouldn't take no for an answer. Emily was adamant about having us host her retirement dinner. So Guy kept calling. It was annoying.

"What's going on?" Granny had entered the kitchen.

Mommy and Daddy updated her in hushed tones while Guy continued pleading his case over the phone.

"The thing is, Ms. Murray, Principal Smith has her heart set on having her retirement dinner at your restaurant. She doesn't want to go anywhere else." Guy's voice had once again become wheedling. "The principal admires and trusts your mother. She believes Cedella Murray is a woman of integrity and has the courage of her convictions."

Tell me something I don't know.

The compliments made me proud, but I didn't see a connection between Emily Smith's admiration of and trust in my mother, and her wanting to have her retirement dinner here. What was she expecting would happen at another shop? "I appreciate Principal Smith's kind words. I'll share them with my mother, but we still aren't able to host her dinner."

Mommy, Daddy, and Granny exchanged curious looks. They probably were wondering what Principal Smith had said about Mommy.

"Are you sure?" Guy sighed his disappointment. "It's a small dinner party, five or six people at most, including me and Principal Smith."

I squeezed my eyes shut as irritation overwhelmed me. I should just hang up, but he would only call back. My eyes popped open as an idea came to me. "Your event is less than two weeks away. You'd incur a rush charge. You also want to hold it on a Monday, which is one of the days we're closed, so that would be an additional cost." Hosting events on Mondays or Tuesdays when we were closed to the public would give our clients privacy. We could take this same approach for other celebrations like birthdays, graduations, and anniversaries. It was something to think about. "Let me do the math." The amount I quoted caused Mommy's, Daddy's, and Granny's jaws to drop.

"Um, Ms. Murray, could you hold while I check with Principal Smith, please?" Guy sounded uncertain.

I cleared the amusement from my throat. "Of course." I covered the mouthpiece and whispered, "He's checking with Principal Smith."

Granny nodded her head decisively. "That was good thinking, love. Give them a cost they can't afford and they'll go away."

Daddy chuckled. "I agree. The price will get them to stop calling."

Mommy grinned, pressing a hand to her chest. "That's true, you know. There's no way Emily will be able to justify spending all that on her retirement celebration."

I continued to whisper. "That's what I'm hoping—"

"Ms. Murray." Guy had returned to the line. "Principal Smith has approved your estimate. If you email us the contract by end of day today, we'll sign it and have it back to you by Monday morning at the latest. Does that sound acceptable?"

I froze in shock. I'd never expected them to agree to our pricing.

"Ms. Murray?" Guy prompted.

I shook myself to snap out of my trance. "Could you give me a moment to check with my family, please?" I put the call on hold without waiting for his response. "They've agreed to the price and want us to email a contract to them tonight."

"What?" they responded in unison at a volume that hurt my eardrums.

I still felt a little dazed. "That's a lot of money. I don't think we can turn it down. But, Mommy, I feel the final decision should be yours. Would you be comfortable doing this event for your former boss?"

Granny turned a wide-eyed stare from me to Mommy. "That's a lot of money. We should have asked for more."

"Genevieve." Daddy's tone was almost scolding.

"Whadayou?" Granny spread her hands. "We have loans to repay, you know."

"Lynds's right." Daddy rested a hand on Mommy's shoulder. "The decision should be Della's. Emily Smith was a miserable supervisor. If Della's not comfortable doing this event, we shouldn't do it."

"I agree." Granny gave another decisive nod. "But I just want you to have all the facts, Della. The money and experience from this job will help us."

"I understand." Mommy looked from Daddy, to Granny, then to me. "And I think we should do it. This is a business. We have bills to pay, and this is too much money to turn down."

Daddy watched her closely. "Are you sure, Della?"

Mommy put her hand over Daddy's where it rested on her shoulder. "I'm sure. Besides, I'd only have to see her for a couple of hours that one day."

"And you won't be alone." I searched Mommy's dark eyes, looking for indications of hesitancy or second thoughts. I didn't see any. I took Guy off hold. "Mr. Law, we have a deal, pending the signed contract."

CHAPTER 2

Planning a retirement dinner party for six in less than ten days while running the bakery was hard. By Monday evening, I felt like a tsunami wave had rolled over me.

"Dev, stop apologizing for not being able to help with tonight's event." I interrupted my older brother, Devon Murray, as I strode back to the long, rectangular blond wood island in the center of our family bakery's industrial kitchen. "It would've been great if you could've been here, but we know you have a demanding job. And everything's under control, so stop worrying." Dev had called my cell phone while my mother, father, grandmother, and I rushed around the kitchen like our pants were on fire, preparing for our first-ever catering event.

"I'm sure you have everything running smoothly, but I'd wanted to be there." Dev was working late. Again.

I understood his disappointment. If the situation were reversed, I'd feel the same way. This booking was a big step for our growing business. "We'd wanted you to be part of it, but I'm sure your client's glad you're staying to finish his company's report."

Tonight's event was the retirement dinner for Emily Smith, the soon-to-be former principal of Kings County Early College High School.

"I'm looking forward to hearing about the dinner and Mom's ex-boss." Dev's forced cheer didn't mask his fatigue.

I felt a twinge of concern. Was he working too hard? "How're you?"

"I'm fine. Just tired." His voice was strained.

That sounded like an understatement. After spending long weekdays and most weekend mornings at his office, he showed up to help at the bakery every weekend afternoon, into the evening. We enjoyed his company and appreciated his help, but when he'd offered to invest in the bakery I hadn't expected him to make it another full-time job. I'd warned him he was doing too much. Did he think I was talking just to hear myself speak?

My brow furrowed with concern. "I should let you go so you don't have to work too late."

Our goodbyes were almost as long as our conversation. I checked the time on my cell phone before pocketing it. Our guests would arrive in about thirty minutes. Plenty of time. Granny had prepared the dining area. All we had left to do was put the final touches on the meal, then tidy up before greeting them.

My father stood to my right at the top of the blond wood center island. He was singing along with Bob Marley's "No Woman, No Cry" as the music swayed from the CD player on the front counter. It was one of the legendary reggae artist's famous love ballads. Daddy played it when he needed to soothe his nerves. From the tension simmering in the kitchen, he wasn't the only one who could use some calming. We were all uneasy about hosting our first catered event.

Floating just above the smell of fear were the savory, spicy aromas of the evening's main entrées. The scents stirred both pride and hunger. We were serving plated dinners of fried sweet plantains, and rice and peas. The main entrée was an option of curry or jerk chicken. More of the guests had requested the jerk.

Daddy stopped his duet and glanced up at me, holding his chopping knife above the ripe plantain he was cutting. "How's your brother?"

My father was tall and fit in his black slacks with matching chef's smock and cap. He and Dev looked so much alike with their chiseled sienna features. Looking at him was like seeing Dev twenty-seven years in the future. Like Mommy and Daddy, Dev was tall and slender. I took after our grandmother, shorter and curvy.

I crossed to the sterling-silver-and-black oven to check the jerk chicken. "He's tired. And he seems preoccupied."

"He's been that way for a while now, eh?" Granny's voice was taut with worry. She stood to my left at the foot of the table, chopping vegetables for the garden salad. She reached for another stalk of celery, deftly slicing it on the chopping block. Lettuce, tomatoes, cucumbers, carrots, and onions already waited in the yellow-and-red porcelain bowl.

Mommy stood behind Daddy at the silver-and-black stove. She stirred the curry chicken in its skillet before checking on the pot of rice and peas. "He needs to take time off from the law firm and the bakery. He works too hard." Her Grenadian accent added a bounce to her fussing.

"Our children have always been hard workers." There was pride in Daddy's voice. "But he's seemed off this past week."

"Once we're past this dinner, I'll corner Dev and make him tell me what's wrong." I put my hand on Mommy's shoulder. Her muscles were tight beneath my palm.

"How're you holding up? Are you still OK about seeing your former boss again?"

She gave me a restless shrug. "I want this evening to go well."

Granny grunted. "Everything will be top notch, which is better than that woman deserves."

I smiled at Granny's protective tone before turning back to Mommy. "You never told me what Principal Smith used to do that would make you so angry."

Mommy kissed her teeth. "It wasn't just me. All you need to understand, she got on *everybody's* nerves. Her staff must be counting the days until she's gone."

I had a flash of memory of Mommy coming home from work, her heart-shaped face swollen with anger and her bow-shaped lips thin with temper. Seeing her that way had upset me. At the same time, I'd wanted to protect her from whatever or whoever had caused her distress.

"Who all's coming again?" Granny's question drew me from the past.

I visualized the list Guy had emailed to me with each person's food request. "It's a small group, just five people, plus Emily: her admin, the librarian, nurse, assistant principal, and a guidance counselor."

Daddy glanced over his shoulder at Mommy. "How'd they make the short list, eh?"

Mommy chuckled. "Better yet, how do they feel about being singled out?"

The look that passed between them was a silent, *I love you*. According to Granny, they'd been looking at each other that way since childhood. I wanted someone who looked at me that way—in time. Right now, I was in an exclusive relationship with our bakery.

I held up my hands, palms out, to get their attention.

"For tonight, we'll leave the past in the past and focus on what we do best."

Granny gave me an approving look. "Cooking Caribbean cuisine with love."

"That's right." I sent her a smile. "The meal will be so good Principal Smith won't know what happened to her."

We'd decorated the dining area with a few accents that were in keeping with our shop's Caribbean theme. Granny had sewn a festive yellow tablecloth with red and green embroidery to reflect the colors of the flag of Grenada. It was subtle and matched the wall tapestries she'd sewn and displayed around the room. It also perfectly covered the three tables we'd pushed together to accommodate Emily and her five guests. The result made the arrangement for the Monday evening retirement dinner seem like one long table.

For centerpieces, Granny and I had filled glass bowls with beds of red potpourri petals and added blue and yellow glass marbles, then circled them with seashells. The effect was elegant and understated. If we were careful, we could store those items for future events, please God.

It was quarter to six. Our first guests should be arriving soon. Granny and I waited for them in the customer service area. Every now and again, a soft "click-whirr" would interrupt the music coming from the bakery's speakers as my grandmother operated Dev's camera. He'd loaned it to us because Emily had requested photos of the event. She was paying extra for them.

"Granny, you don't need to take photos yet." I smoothed my baker's smock and my braids. Did I have time to rush into the restroom to check my appearance? Probably not. "The guests haven't arrived."

"These aren't for the client." She snapped a photo of the

empty dining area. "They're for the website. You can add them to the page about our catering services."

My eyebrows rose. Why hadn't I thought of that? "Great idea, Granny. Thank you."

She grunted. "I'm not just good looks, you know."

I gave her a cheeky smile. "Brains as well as beauty."

Granny's scolding look contradicted the humor sparkling in her dark eyes and twitching her full lips.

She refused to wear our Spice Isle Bakery uniform, which was really just a black chef's smock and matching cap. Perhaps after working for the Grenadian postal service she'd had enough of dressing like other people. So today, she made her personal statement in a formfitting seafoam blue dress. The hem ended below her knees and the sleeves were capped at her elbows. She kept in shape with almost daily Zumba classes and swimming sessions at the neighborhood gym.

I felt dumpy standing beside her, but the uniform underscored my professional position with our bakery. We needed to make a good impression, and our guests wouldn't judge us only on the food. Ambiance and customer service mattered, too. I wasn't worried about whether they'd enjoy the meal. As Granny often said, our food was exceptional. We needed to make sure they also enjoyed the experience.

Daddy pushed through the swinging door from the kitchen. He held it open to let Mommy precede him. "Everything's ready in the kitchen."

"Great. Thank you." I checked my cell phone for the fifty-leventh time. Three minutes had gone by. My palms were sweating.

I wasn't the only one who was nervous. Behind me, my father was humming, "No Woman, No Cry." Granny and I exchanged wide-eyed looks. How could a person who'd held a high-stress management position in the city's finance department for more than a decade be so nervous over a dinner?

Mommy squeezed his upper arm. "Jake, give the song a rest, nuh?"

Daddy started. "Was I humming?"

The bell chimed above our entrance, interrupting Mommy's response. A twentysomething-year-old man and a middle-aged woman entered the shop. Granny snapped their picture.

The man looked ready to suit up with the New York Giants football team's offensive line. His wealth of thick red hair was an arresting contrast to his pale, freckled complexion. Cautious brown eyes swept the room before settling on Mommy, Daddy, Granny, and me.

The woman gave us a warm smile as though we'd been friends for years. Her conservative blue-gray coatdress contradicted the edgy lime green streaks in her long, bone-straight raven hair.

"Looks like we're in the right place." Humor warmed her voice. She extended her arms and strode straight to Mommy. "Cedella, the school's not the same without you."

"It's good to see you, June." Mommy's smile was genuine.

The warmth of their greeting eased some of the knots in my neck and shoulders. Maybe this event wasn't a complete mistake if it allowed Mommy to see old friends.

Turning to our other arrival, I stepped forward with a friendly yet professional expression. "Welcome to Spice Isle Bakery."

Some of the tension that wrapped him like *dhalpuri* around curry beef eased. He stuck out his chest. "You must be Lyndsay Murray. I'm Guy Law, Principal Emily

Smith's administrative assistant. Thanks again for hosting her retirement dinner. Principal Smith loves Caribbean food."

Granny tilted her head in confusion. "Who doesn't?"

I extended my left hand toward Granny to begin the introductions. "This is my grandmother, Genevieve Bain." I switched arms to gesture toward my parents. "My mother, Cedella Bain Murray, and my father, Jacob Murray."

"It's nice to meet you." Guy adjusted his jacket. His navy suit could use a bit of tailoring. It was an inch too short and a size too small. "As I stated, I'm Guy Law, assistant to Principal Emily Smith. And this is—"

"I'm June Min-ho, the school's librarian." She sent Guy a quashing look before resetting her smile. "It's a pleasure to finally meet all of you. Cedella spoke so often about her family. I feel like we know each other. Although, Jacob, we met once or twice when you came to take her to lunch." She turned to Mommy. "Is Devon still with the law firm?"

The power struggle between June and Guy was like a hot pink neon sign flashing: "Cross at Your Own Risk." I recognized the office politics from my years with the marketing agency. I didn't miss it.

Guy interrupted June and Mommy's exchange. "Ms. Bain Murray, I think I started right after you left." His tone was riddled with self-importance and condescension.

"That's right." Mommy's reserve was subtle, but I was sensitive to her moods. She was happy to see June, but that didn't make her any more enthusiastic about this dinner to honor Emily Smith. She was only doing it for the family business. Catholic guilt was choking me.

Guy continued his attempts to monopolize the conversation. It felt like he was doing it on purpose. "Well, thank you for catering this event. You made everything so easy for me."

"Make sure you tell all your friends." Granny gave him a measuring look.

Guy either hadn't noticed my grandmother's scrutiny or chose to ignore it. "I will."

Daddy gestured toward the dining area. "Would you like me to show you to the table?"

"Go sit down, June." Guy checked the time on his cell phone, then pulled a sheet of paper from an inside jacket pocket. "I'll stay to check the arrivals against the guest list."

There were six people on that list, including Guy. I was certain my family could handle greeting four more people, but I kept my thoughts to myself.

The temperature in the shop dropped at least fifteen degrees. June's dark eyes hardened and her smile grew stiff. "I'm fine where I am, thanks, Guy." She turned her back to him. "This place is fabulous. And the smells." She interrupted herself with a laugh. "I'm suddenly very hungry. I love it. Congratulations. Is that your artwork, Cedella?" She pointed at the three wood-framed paintings on the wall behind the customer counter.

My mother had painted images from our birthplace, Grenada, West Indies, which we were proud to show off in our bakery. Her talent had brought to life a few of the island's signature scenes: Grand Anse Beach's blue-green bay and soft white sand, steelpan bands leading a parade of Samba dancers in jewel-toned costumes, and the Port of St. George's with the azure waters of the Caribbean Sea in the foreground and the grandeur of the emerald mountain range rising in the background.

The shop's bell rang again, drawing our attention back to the doorway. Two men, one middle-aged and the other several years younger, stopped just inside the customer service area. Granny snapped another photo. She was taking her role as event photographer very seriously.

"Jeez." Daddy muttered the interjection beneath his breath.

I frowned, studying the men more closely. Why had my father had such an immediate and negative reaction to them?

The one to the right was taller. His three-piece brown suit, red silk tie, and Italian dark brown shoes looked expensive. Fluorescent lights captured the gray hairs sprinkled among his tight dark brown curls. He raised both arms as though in victory. "Cedella, it's so good to see you again! You look fantastic."

"Daniel." Mommy was cool.

"Who's that?" Granny whispered her question to Daddy.

"Daniel Rawson." Daddy sounded like he'd swallowed spoiled milk. "Assistant principal. He's had a crush on Della since he started working at the place three years ago."

"Oh-ho." Granny sounded amused. "Perhaps we should've asked to approve the guest list."

"We knew he'd be here." Daddy's spare features were tight. His dark eyes tracked the other man's approach with a warning glare. "But knowing is one thing. Seeing him is another."

I looked at Daniel with fresh eyes, seeing him for what he was now: a wannabee home-wrecker. He knew my mother was a married woman. One wrong move and I'd gladly help my father show him the door.

Granny patted Daddy's shoulder. "Don't tense up so. My daughter can manage this herself."

Daddy grunted. "She's not the one I'm worried about."

I'd never seen this side of my father before. Not for the

first time, I wished I could find someone who loved me as completely and fiercely as my parents loved each other. That is, when the time was right. For now, I had a business to build.

The man who'd followed Daniel into the bakery wore an uncertain smile along with an understated jacket, slacks, and tie. His wavy dark brown hair gleamed under the bakery's lights.

Guy made a show of checking their names off his list while sharing their identities with me. "Daniel Rawson is the assistant principal and Miguel Morales is our newest guidance counselor."

Miguel nodded before returning his attention to Mommy. "It's nice to meet you, Cedella. I've heard a lot of great things about you. You're the only other person Emily's ever respected."

Mommy's eyes widened in surprise. "Who told you that?"

Miguel's smile widened into an amused grin. "Everyone."

Daddy put an arm around Mommy's waist. "Who's the other person Emily respects?"

"Herself." Miguel chuckled. My parents, Granny, and I laughed with him.

Guy cleared his throat, interrupting our moment of amusement. He didn't look like he got the joke. "The only people missing are the guest of honor, Principal Smith, and our school nurse, Meera Singh. It's getting late." Tension was building around him.

Pulling my cell from my right front slacks pocket, I noted the time. "It's only a few minutes past six." But I understood his agitation. I didn't like to be kept waiting, either.

"I know, but I'd asked everyone to arrive before six PM

to be here before Principal Smith." Guy sighed. "She'll want to make an entrance. She's going to be . . . upset . . . if everyone's not here when she arrives. I don't—"

The door chime announced another newcomer. Guy turned toward the entrance. The blood drained from his cheeks. His features froze.

A tall, middle-aged woman posed in the threshold as though preparing for a *Vogue* photoshoot. Her scarlet dress skimmed her full figure. Its hem ended just above her knees. The material emphasized her blue eyes and set off the torrent of dark amber tresses that settled on her broad shoulders. She'd hooked her left hand on her hip and stood with her right leg in front of her left.

I leaned toward him to whisper, "Is that Principal Smith?"

His throat muscles worked as he swallowed. "Yes."

Time's up.

CHAPTER 3

"Good evening, everyone." Principal Emily Smith's red lips curved into a smug smile when she noticed Granny taking her photo.

Guy jogged forward to greet her. "Principal Smith, we're all so happy to help you celebrate this momentous occasion, capping your sterling career."

My eyebrows took flight. I wasn't the only one wondering why Guy was being such a *bababooy*. His coworkers looked disgusted. Mommy and Daddy seemed startled. Granny took another picture.

Emily's eyes darkened with irritation. She pinned Guy with her displeasure. "There are only four other people here. The reservation is for six." Although she kept her voice low, her words still carried to us. "Where. Is. Meera?"

Guy's throat worked as he swallowed. "She hasn't arrived yet."

"Urgh! That woman has no concept of time." She grumbled her outrage.

"I'm sure she's on her way." Guy's voice was breathy with nerves.

"I specifically directed you to have everyone here

before me." She sounded as though she was speaking through clenched teeth. "*They* were supposed to wait for *me. I* do not wait for *anyone.*"

Guy nodded vigorously. "I know, Principal Smith, but—"

She interrupted. "Spare me the excuses. What do I always tell you?"

Guy inclined his head. "You don't want excuses. You want results."

"Right." She pulled a small mirror and her lipstick from her purse and reapplied her makeup.

Guy's cheeks flushed. His brown eyes wavered before settling on her lightweight silver spring coat. "May I take your coat, Principal Smith?" He reached for it. Emily shoved her purse at him as well, as he turned to me. "Where's your cloakroom?"

Ignoring Granny's snort of disdain, I pointed a finger over my shoulder. "We don't have a cloakroom. Our guests usually hang their coats and purses on the backs of their chairs."

"Oh?" Emily's carefully arched amber eyebrows hopped in surprise.

We never claimed to be anything other than what we were: a neighborhood bakery that served affordable meals; not some trendy, high-end restaurant with a months-long waiting list and a cloakroom. There was no reason for me to be embarrassed.

So why was I?

Guy cleared his throat. "I'll put your coat on your chair, Principal Smith."

Emily waved him away. "Go ahead, Guy. You don't have to announce your every move."

Stepping around me, Guy speed walked to the dining

area, then took his time settling Emily's coat around the seat at the head of the table.

The principal's arrogance was wearing everyone thin. How could anyone have a pleasant experience in her company? Her staff must be ecstatic she was finally leaving. I looked at them. Their expressions ranged from dislike to disgust. They were probably planning their own celebration for the day after Emily's retirement. Maybe the bakery could get the contract to cater it.

Emily's demeanor as she gazed around the bakery brought back unpleasant memories of the county's health inspector. "Your bakery's very nice, Cedella. And the food smells wonderful. But I'm not surprised you've done well for yourself in your second career. Everything you touched was always a success. I wish I had that ability."

"Thank you, Emily." Mommy seemed dazed. I couldn't blame her. So was I. "And congratulations on *your* retirement. Have you made any plans for how you're going to spend your time?"

"I haven't decided yet." Emily continued wandering the customer service area. "But nothing as ambitious as starting a business from scratch. You know I prefer taking shortcuts."

Mommy's features tightened as though remembering an unpleasant exchange she'd had with the principal. She returned Emily's amused regard with defiance. The chime indicating a new arrival filled the awkward void.

Emily turned toward the door. "Meera! Thank you for fitting us into your busy schedule."

The tall woman's dark eyes widened and her round cheeks flushed. Her straight raven hair swung above her narrow shoulders as though continuing the momentum that had propelled her into the shop. She adjusted her purse strap on her shoulder with her left hand and raised her right hand, palm out. "I'm so sorry, Emily, I—"

Emily cut her off. Her tone was cool. "The fact is you're always late. Why would today be any different?"

I winced. *Good grief.* Principal Smith could challenge my former boss for the title of worst person ever.

June gasped. "Emily, you've gone too far."

"Oh." Emily's thick waves of amber hair swept over her shoulders as she spun toward the librarian. She feigned surprise as she crossed her arms beneath her ample bosom. "Perhaps you'd rather talk about your fundraiser."

"That—" June pressed her lips together. Her eyes blazed with anger as they bore into the older woman.

"I didn't think so." Emily turned back to Meera. "You would've gotten a marginally better employee review if you had more respect for other people's time. Now you've kept us waiting long enough."

A dark energy slammed into the bakery. The mood had shifted from reluctance to revolt. Daniel, the assistant principal, and Miguel, the guidance counselor, stared at the door as though considering whether they could make their excuses and leave. I wasn't worried about being paid. We'd fulfilled our contract in cooking for, staging, and photographing the event. But if the guests started leaving, who was going to eat all the food we'd prepared? I had to figure out a way to dial down the tension crackling in the air or kiss any hope of referrals goodbye. We needed that positive word-of-mouth marketing, especially after all the hard work that went into preparing for this event. If things kept going this way, instead of the exceptional food, beautiful décor, and excellent customer service, the only thing this group would be talking about for a long time to come would be caustic comments and hurt feelings.

"Emily, there's no need for you to be so cruel." Mommy's voice dripped with ice. Her stony, tight-lipped scowl of displeasure was one Dev and I remembered well.

Emily's eyes sparkled with mockery. "Cedella, you can still put me in my place. Fine. Could you please point me toward the women's powder room? I need to put on my face, especially if someone's going to be taking pictures."

Mommy pointed Emily in the direction of the restrooms in the hall at the back of the dining area. Emily stopped at the table we'd prepared for the dinner and collected her handbag before continuing on to the restroom. The other guests moved with slow and heavy footsteps to the table.

"I wonder which face she's going to put on." Mommy's voice was low. "She has so many of them."

I arched an eyebrow. "She should choose wisely. She's already pushed a lot of buttons. I don't think people are going to put up with much more of her foolishness."

Already the guests looked more like mourners at a wake than celebrants getting ready for a party. Not for the first time, I wondered why Emily had chosen these five individuals for her retirement dinner—and why they'd agreed to attend.

"Granny, how many pictures are you going to take?" I kept my voice low as I drew my grandmother aside to consult in private.

She studied our guests with narrowed eyes as though arranging future photo compositions. "We need to catch everything, you know. Some of these photos are for our website. I'm not including faces for those."

It was minutes after six o'clock Monday evening. We needed to start the first course, Granny's garden salad. But her zeal with the camera was getting a little scary. It screamed for ground rules.

"I don't want to make any of the guests uncomfortable." I tried to appeal to her sense of fairness. "Not everyone wants to be photographed with their mouth full."

"OK. OK. No pictures with people feeding themselves or chewing." She sounded disappointed.

I started to say something comforting, but a male voice interrupted me.

"Excuse me. It's Lyndsay, right?" Assistant Principal Daniel Rawson approached us. He was a few inches shorter than Daddy, perhaps an even six feet. His expensive suit seemed tailored to mask a soft midsection. Tight brown curls receded from his round face.

I gave him a courteous smile. "That's right, Mr. Rawson. How can I help you?"

He folded his hands together at his hips. His dark brown eyes seemed curious. "You look so much like your mother. I enjoyed working with her. She's a smart lady and very self-assured."

I was warming to him. "I know."

He glanced toward Granny and shook his head. "It was a great loss for the school when she took early retirement, but this bakery is impressive."

"We know." Granny's eyebrows knitted. She looked Daniel over as though searching for answers. "Is there something we can help you with?"

Daniel's laugh was awkward. "Where are your restrooms?"

I pointed to my right, directing his attention to the back of the room. The sign above the threshold leading to a narrow hallway read: "Restrooms."

Granny tilted her head. "You couldn't see that?"

I sent her a warning look. We needed to make a good impression with this group if we wanted our hard work, time, and attention to result in quality referrals. That meant

Granny needed to avoid saying anything potentially insulting to our guests.

Daniel chuckled again. "I must've been distracted. Thank you."

As he turned to leave, the sound of raised voices caught my attention. I exchanged a concerned look with Granny. "It sounds like Emily's arguing with someone again."

Granny sighed. "She'd better mind herself or she'll be sitting at that big table alone."

"You're right." I groaned as the voices got louder. I noticed Daniel hesitate halfway to the threshold as though reluctant to get too close to the battleground. "I'd better check it out."

I forced a smile as I hurried past the dining table where three of our six guests were waiting. They'd taken the chairs at the opposite end from Emily's place setting at the head of the table. It appeared no one—not even Guy—wanted to be near her. They slouched on their seats with their faces crumpled in various expressions of discomfort and discontent. Guy was reading his cell phone. Miguel checked his watch. June was studying the bakery as though looking for places to hide before Emily returned. A cloud hovered over them, growing fatter and darker every minute.

This was *not* going the way I'd hoped. It felt like all of our time, talents, and efforts were going down the drain. I kept moving forward, gritting my teeth as I offered a prayer: *Please, God, help us to at least get through the salad course before the guests run out the door. Amen.*

I slowed as I approached the archway where Daniel still hovered. The words in the heated exchange were now clear.

"You were so cruel." That was Meera's voice coming

through the door of the women's restroom. Her East Indian accent had deepened. "Why are you always so cold and callous?"

My heart hurt for her. I could imagine how humiliated she must have felt when Emily had insulted her in front of her coworkers as well as my family, most of whom she was meeting for the first time. But she also impressed me. It took a lot of courage to confront a bully. I'd know. I'd never been able to gather the confidence to do something like that, at least not for myself.

"He'll get over it." Emily's tone was mean and dismissive.

What did she mean, *He'll get over it*? Who was "he"? What will he get over?

And how was I going to keep Meera and Emily apart for the rest of the evening?

"You don't know that." Meera raised her voice. "He told me what you said. You're reprehensible. Why must you always be so cruel?"

"Drop it, Meera. It's done." Emily slammed through the door—and stumbled into Daniel.

The assistant principal caught her, steadying her with his hands on her hips. A look of concern tightened his friendly face. "Are you OK, Emily?"

"Yes, of course." She slapped his arms away.

Raising his hands, Daniel stepped back. "I was trying to help. You were a little unsteady on your feet."

"That's you. Mr. Helpful." Her blue eyes shot daggers at him. "Are you that anxious to secure your position as my successor?"

Daniel lowered his arms. Tension vibrated from him. His smile tightened. "No one could replace *you*, Emily."

My eyes stretched wide as I watched Daniel continue

on to the men's room. Goose bumps rose on my skin and ice tumbled down my spine. But Emily's expression was smug as though she hadn't recognized the insult in Daniel's tone. I clenched my teeth to keep my jaw from dropping.

"You see?" Meera stood at Emily's back. Her voice was gruff. "You're cruel. You'd better tread carefully, Emily. One of these days, your words and actions will come back to haunt you."

"Excuse me." I raised my hands, trying to get their attention. These conflicts were inappropriate and had already gone on too long.

Ignoring me, Emily turned on Meera. "Are you threatening me? I'm still your boss for the next two weeks."

"Excuse me. Hello?" I raised my hands chest high and waved them, trying to get Emily and Meera's attention without shouting.

Meera squared her shoulders and stared Emily down. The two women were about the same height. "No, it's not a threat. It's a prediction."

It was no use. I had to raise my voice. "Excuse me!"

Meera flinched at my tone. Startled, her eyes flew to mine.

"What is it?" Emily scowled.

I gestured behind me. "We can hear you in the dining room. Your argument's making the other guests uncomfortable."

Meera's cheeks turned red. She slid a look toward her coworkers, then back to me. "I apologize."

Emily patted her hair and straightened her dress. "Yes, I'm sorry, too."

Relieved, I offered a professional smile. "I'll see you ladies in the dining room. We'll start serving the garden salads in five minutes."

Without waiting for a response, I turned on my heel and strode back to the dining area. Tension spread from the nape of my neck, over my shoulders to my upper back. Were there enough referrals in the world to make this amount of stress worth it?

CHAPTER 4

While I'd been dealing with the conflict near the restrooms, Granny had convinced the other three guests to pose for pictures. It was amazing how mugging for the camera had helped ease their tension. With luck, their good mood would be contagious and the retirement dinner would be rescued. I started toward the kitchen to get the salads.

"Are you afraid to sit near me, Meera?" Emily's voice was mocking.

I looked over my shoulder to find Meera dubiously eyeing the last two available seats—one on Emily's left and the other on her right.

Meera lifted her chin. "I'm not afraid of you, Emily."

I stepped forward, trying frantically to think of some way to prevent another battle. Before I could speak, Emily gestured toward June.

She patted the chair to her left. "June, sit here. Miguel, you take the other chair."

With visible reluctance, June and Miguel left their seats toward the foot of the table to join the high school principal.

Granny stopped beside me and lowered her voice. "It didn't take her long to ruin the mood again."

"No, it didn't, but thank you for trying." I led us into the kitchen. "Let's turn up the music and start serving the meal."

Mommy and Daddy looked up as we entered. They must have seen signs of stress on our faces.

"That bad, eh?" Mommy asked.

"Everybody's face swell up just so." Granny did an imitation of some of our guests' scowls. "I can't see how anyone's eating anything tonight. All this food. What a waste."

"Why would she sabotage her own retirement dinner?" I crossed to the shelves to collect two serving trays.

Daddy turned away from the pan of curry chicken to face Mommy. His brow was furrowed in confusion. "There isn't one person in the entire school who she liked?"

"I don't think so." Mommy added a quarter cup of water to the rice and peas, then turned down the burner beneath the pot. "And I can't think of a single person who liked her."

Granny took the individual salad bowls from the fridge. She'd arranged them beautifully, filling the small gold porcelain dishes with lettuce, carrots, red onions, and celery, then topping each with a circle of thinly sliced cucumbers and a scoop of diced red tomatoes. "Then why'd she make a big puppy show out of organizing this retirement dinner?"

"Everything she does is for attention." Mommy spread her arms with a shrug. "I think this is another chance for her to be in the spotlight."

I placed three of the six salad bowls on my serving tray. "Guy said the dinner was Emily's idea and that she made the guest list."

Granny arranged the remaining bowls of salad on her tray. "Well, I hope she's happy making everyone miserable."

"I'm surprised they agreed to come. They know what she's like." Mommy opened the oven to check on the jerk chicken.

Daddy turned back to the curry chicken. "Maybe they didn't feel as though they had a choice."

I crossed to the stereo system as the fourth rendition of Bob Marley's "No Woman, No Cry" was coming to an end. "Daddy, let's try something different. We need a playlist of songs that will cheer people up and get them dancing on their seats." I flipped through his CD collection and found Harry Belafonte's greatest calypso hits. I started us off with "Kwela (Listen to the Man)." The song's bounce and its pivotal crescendo seemed perfect.

Twenty minutes later, the salad course was over and the mood among our guests had improved. I gave most of the praise to my grandmother's garden salad, but some of the credit belonged to Harry Belafonte. "Jump in the Line" had been a particular hit. But the conversation was still sparse and forced. As Granny and I served the main course, "Mathilda" faded and the opening strains of "Jamaica Farewell" came through the dining room's speakers.

"It's a pity the school board won't approve another fundraiser for the library." Emily leaned back as I placed her curry chicken entrée in front of her. She and Meera were the only ones who'd requested that dish. The other guests had selected the jerk chicken.

"I agree." Guy nodded vigorously. "It was a successful event. I think the parents, students, and staff really enjoyed it. I know I did, despite the hard work involved."

Emily forked up some of the curry chicken. "Well, at least until the end."

June's face turned pink. Uh-oh. Was the jerk chicken

too spicy? She lowered her fork and sent me a tight smile. "The food's delicious. My compliments to the chefs."

"My compliments as well." Miguel raised his glass. "The food's fantastic. I'll definitely be back, and I'm bringing friends."

My muscles eased with relief. "Thank you so much. That's wonderful to hear."

We were going to get recommendations!

I exchanged a look of triumph with Granny. All of our hard work, time, and efforts were paying off. I was as exhilarated as I'd felt when we'd first launched the bakery to great success, or when I'd proven my innocence in the murder investigation last month. That's another story.

My mental victory celebration came to an abrupt end. Someone was wheezing. My eyes flew to the head of the table. My heart raced in fear. Emily struggled to her feet. Her pale cheeks were darkening to an angry red. Her eyes were wide with panic. She clutched at her throat.

The five other guests stared at her, frozen in shock. I felt their confusion. Without stopping to think, I dropped my serving tray on the table behind me and ran to help her. Before I could reach her, Emily's eyes rolled back in her head. She stumbled backward, knocking over her chair and falling to the floor.

"Emily! Someone call an ambulance!" Kneeling beside her, I rolled her onto her back.

Granny stabbed numbers into her cell phone. "Is she breathing?"

My hands shook as I checked her pulse. "Barely."

Nervous energy had kept me on my feet when the paramedics had arrived minutes after Granny's call Monday evening. As soon as they'd walked through the doors, everything had shifted into high gear. Their rapid-fire questions were a blur now. Granny and I had done our best to keep up, giving them as much information as we could. But the truth was no one—neither my family nor our guests—had a clue what had triggered Emily's attack. Her sudden convulsing and faint had come out of nowhere. Now that the emergency medical team and dinner guests were gone, my physical, mental, and emotional exhaustion hit me like an ocean wave. I was trying to process this terrible situation while gathering the energy to clean the bakery.

"Should we have gone to the hospital with her?" I sat with my mother, father, and grandmother at the tables we'd arranged for Emily's retirement dinner.

"The hospital will get in touch with her family." Daddy removed his chef's hat and smoothed his long, blunt fingers over his still-dark, tight curls.

Seeing the barely touched plates of food at each of the six table settings depressed me. Well, at least they'd gotten through the salad course. I was grateful for that, but for health and safety reasons we'd have to dispose of the meals we'd served. That broke my heart. None of our guests had wanted to take their leftovers. They hadn't given reasons, which made me worry. Did they think the food had made Emily sick?

Emily's guests had sat like stones before the paramedics had arrived. But once the medical professionals had taken the principal away, Daniel, Guy, Meera, June, and Miguel had crawled over the floor, repacking the contents of Emily's handbag, which had spilled after her chair had toppled. It had been weird. It was as though they all wanted credit for doing something to help their boss.

"Does Emily have family in Brooklyn?" I pushed myself to my feet and stacked the barely touched plates onto a serving tray to carry them back into the kitchen. I examined Emily's plate, dragging a fork through the chicken, rice, and peas. There didn't seem to be anything wrong with it, no weird colors or odors. Although to be fair, all I could smell was the curry.

"I don't know." Mommy loaded a second tray with plates. "In all the years I worked with her, she never mentioned her family and I never asked."

Daddy placed the silverware, glassware, napkins, and pitcher of water onto the third tray.

Granny led the way to the kitchen, holding the swinging door for us to walk through. "I'm upset none of the guests wanted to take the food home with them. It was exceptional."

The white laminate kitchen counter was stacked with pots, pans, and baking trays. Daddy went to the sink to wash the cutting board and knives. "They must suspect the food made Emily pass out. Why else wouldn't they take the leftovers? It's free food. The school's paying for it."

My thoughts exactly.

I set my tray on the center island beside Granny's and Mommy's. "I really regret that Principal Smith passed out during the dinner. It's a horrible thing that happened to her. I hope she'll make a speedy and complete recovery. It's also a terrible way for our first catered event to end."

Granny gave a solemn nod. "Yes, it is."

I thought of all the potential new customers and events this dinner could've brought us and my heart wanted to break all over again. Perhaps I was being too impatient and trying to grow the bakery too quickly. I was anxious to make this venture a success, but we were still in the first few months of our business. My five-year plan was based on using this first year to build and attract a loyal customer base. It wasn't until years two or three that I'd planned to hire more staff and start catering. But Emily had insisted on our hosting her retirement dinner and wouldn't take no for an answer.

I may have done our business irrevocable damage by not turning down the job. Having the honoree hospitalized during the event couldn't be good.

"I hope she recovers quickly, too." Mommy got the dish towel and stood beside Daddy, preparing to dry the dishes as he washed. "Knowing Emily as I do, she's bound to be embarrassed by this whole thing, so it's just as well she's retiring soon. She won't have to worry about seeing the people who witnessed her shame."

Daddy hummed his agreement. "I hope somebody tells us what happened to her. We ought to know what caused her to be taken to the hospital."

"It couldn't be the food." Mommy was adamant. "We tasted all the dishes before serving them. We didn't get sick. And none of the other guests got sick, either."

"Maybe it was her meanness that upset her stomach." Granny wiped down and dried the trays before storing them. Apparently, I wasn't the only one putting off the moment we'd have to throw out all of that food.

"You have a point, Genevieve." Daddy met Granny's eyes over his shoulder. "Emily's one sour, combative person. But it's much more likely she had an allergic reaction to something in the dish."

I shook my head, almost too tired to think. "But, Daddy, I'd asked about food allergies when I was finalizing the purchase order with the school. Guy specifically said Emily didn't have food allergies. In fact, he said she'd had curry many times before. It's one of her favorite dishes."

"Then I don't know what to tell you." Daddy shrugged his broad shoulders under his chef's smock. "I hope this doesn't turn the other guests away from the bakery. It would—"

The pounding against the bakery's front door made everyone jump. Granny, Mommy, and I gasped with fright. Who would bang on the store like that? Had one of the guests left something behind? Daddy marched into the customer service area like a man on a mission. Mommy, Granny, and I followed close behind him. Strength in numbers and all that. We didn't know what to expect, but it seemed I wasn't the only one who had a bad feeling.

Bryce and his partner, Stanley, stared back at us through the glass entrance. Their grim expressions stirred the small hairs on the back of my neck. Why were they here? They knew the bakery was closed Mondays and Tuesdays.

Daddy unlocked the door, pulling it wide as he stepped back to let the two men in. "Detectives, good evening. How can we help you?"

"Good evening, Murray family." Stan's dark gray eyes twinkled with warmth. His everything-is-right-with-the-world attitude was strange coming from a homicide detective in a city that averaged a murder a day. "Something smells good."

He inhaled deeply, seeming to lose himself in the aromas drifting into the bakery's customer service area from the kitchen: savory curry, spicy jerk, sweet fried ripe plantains.

Bryce followed Stan across the threshold. His eyes met mine. The pulse at the base of my throat jumped. I swallowed it back down.

"Good evening." He inclined his head, greeting my family before settling his attention on my father. "Emily Smith had dinner here today." He wasn't asking.

"That's right." Daddy's tone was curious, concerned. "How is she?"

"She's dead, Mr. Murray." Bryce's tone was somber.

"What?" Daddy's eyes widened with shock.

"Emily's dead?" I'd been afraid of this. My heart was heavy in my chest.

"What happened?" Mommy demanded.

"Oh, Lord." Granny's hands shook. The tray she'd carried from the kitchen started to fall. I caught it before it hit the floor.

Bryce continued. "We need you to preserve the food and the scene. We're treating this as a homicide."

Blood drained from my face, feeling like scores of needles stabbing my cheeks. Tightening my grip on the tray, I exchanged looks with my family. Their eyes were wide and their lips were parted in identical expressions of dismay.

Speechless, I turned back to the detectives. Not this again.

CHAPTER 5

"Maybe we should sit down." Stan's attention settled on the tables we'd arranged for Emily's retirement dinner.

We hadn't had time to put the furniture back where it belonged. Daddy led the way to the table. Mommy, Granny, Bryce, and Stan followed. I locked the door before joining them. There were just enough chairs to accommodate us, but it was a little creepy sitting in the midst of a crime scene. Stan looked like who he was: an overworked, underpaid public servant. He was a little overweight for his average height. And his wealth of bed-head gray hair could benefit from a comb and haircut. It was hard to guess his age. His soft, pale, round features were practically wrinkle-free, but he seemed close to retirement. Despite his rumpled appearance, his hands were always smooth and his nails well manicured.

On the other hand, Bryce looked like an aspiring actor who was working homicide until he caught his big break. My adolescent crush hadn't changed much over the years. He'd given up his cornrows for a more conservative haircut. Still my stomach muscles did the same foolish flips they'd done back in high school.

My eyes dropped to the badge suspended from a chain around his neck. Would things have been different if when we'd met again he hadn't accused me of being a cold-blooded killer? Probably. Yet here he was, returning to my family's bakery in connection with another suspicious death. Was it any wonder I was feeling some kind of way?

Bryce took the seat beside Stan on the left side of the table. "A preliminary examination of Emily Smith's body shows she died of poisoning."

Seated beside me on the right side of the table, Granny scowled. "Food poisoning? But she barely ate anything."

Stan held up a hand, palm out. "No, Ms. Bain. It wasn't food poisoning. The coroner's still doing tests, but it appears the victim ingested a toxic substance."

I caught the concerned look my parents exchanged from the opposite ends of the table. "I guess that could explain Emily's seizure."

Bryce's thick black eyebrows knitted in a frown. "She had a seizure after eating your food?"

"She'd barely touched her meal." I was so offended, I needed a moment to collect my thoughts. "Seconds after I served her, she started wheezing. She stood. Her body was shaking. Her eyes rolled back in her head, and then she passed out."

I'd read about certain poisons in mystery novels. Curiosity had prompted me to do more research. There were several fast-acting poisons that were so potent and their effects so painful that muscle convulsions and seizures overtook the person who'd ingested it before they died. I wasn't going to share my knowledge with the detectives, though. They were already looking at me as though they wanted to take me back to the precinct for an interrogation. Bryce finally looked away. I released a breath I hadn't realized I'd been holding.

Who could've poisoned Emily? It must've been one

of her guests. But how would they have administered it? I didn't recall seeing anyone—other than her—touch her food. I suppressed a shiver.

Stan continued. "Ms. Smith appears to have ingested some type of poison."

"*Bonjay!*" Granny gasped. "And you want to question us because our bakery was the last place she was seen alive."

Bryce's eyes swung to her, searching her features in a way that made it clear Granny was under suspicion. We all were. Again. "What can you tell us about the dinner?"

Granny straightened her shoulders and puffed out her chest. "It was exceptional."

Stan chuckled. "I'm sure it was, Ms. Bain. My wife's loved everything I've brought home for her from the bakery, the currant rolls, hard dough bread, coconut bread. She can't believe I know people who can bake like that."

Mommy leaned forward, smiling at the rumpled detective. "Does your wife cook?"

Are you kidding me right now? I wanted to shout, *Don't smile at them. They're not our friends!*

Stan shook his head with a crooked smile of regret. "No, ma'am. My wife's not much of a baker. Or cook. But she's a fiend at keeping our bank accounts balanced."

Daddy inclined his head toward Mommy, seated at the foot of the table. "Cedella handles our finances, too. She's very good."

Had everyone forgotten what we were supposed to be doing here? I looked in disbelief at my family seated around the table. This wasn't drinks with friends at the end of a tough week. This was a *murder investigation* and unless I was mistaken—which I wasn't—we were under suspicion. Again.

"Detectives." I lifted my voice to prevent any other distractions. "What do you want to ask us about Emily Smith's death?"

Bryce gave my features the same scrutiny he'd given Granny's. I returned his examination with a stony expression. "The EMTs said this was a retirement dinner for her. How did you come to host it?"

Granny, Mommy, and Daddy answered Bryce's and Stan's questions about the event: Who'd contacted us, how, and why? Who'd handled the arrangements? How was the menu determined? Who arranged the seating assignments?

What would Dev think of the detective's questions? Why were they asking these particular ones? Were our answers giving away too much information? Not enough? Could they be twisted to incriminate us? I didn't want the bakery to be at the center of another homicide investigation. I didn't want to go through that again. The first one had been horrible. A second one could ruin us.

But Fate hadn't given us a choice.

Bryce looked from Granny to me. "Aren't you usually closed Mondays and Tuesdays?"

I ended my silence. "We made an exception for this event."

"Why?" Stan asked. His tone was casual enough, non-threatening. *Ha!*

Granny shrugged. "They paid extra."

I elaborated. "Principal Smith wanted the space just for her celebration. She didn't want other customers here. Hosting it on a day that we're usually closed allowed us to focus on them."

Bryce wrote down my answer. "So you usually do paperwork or something Mondays and Tuesdays."

"That's right." Why was he writing that down?

"When do you take time off?" he asked.

I scowled. What was he getting at now? "I haven't figured that out yet. Why?"

"Just curious." Bryce glanced at me, then turned away.

"Something sure smells delicious." Stan's smile was disarming. "What was on the menu?"

Daddy answered that question. "We offered a choice of either jerk or curry chicken to go with the rice and peas, fried plantains, and garden salad."

Bryce wrote that information as well. "Who did the cooking?"

"We all did." I glanced at my parents and grandmother. "We always help each other in the kitchen."

I was solid on the entrées: chicken, beef, fish, veggie. You name it. My cooking was as masterful as Harry Belafonte's singing. I was still working on my baking, though. I'd mastered the currant rolls, and my coconut bread was coming along. Granny said my hard dough bread needed more finessing. And she was right.

Bryce was still taking notes. "What did Principal Smith have?"

An image of Granny and me serving the dinner crossed my mind. "She and another guest had the curry. Everyone else had the jerk."

Stan looked up from his notepad. "Who served the meals?"

Granny touched my arm. Her hand was soft and warm through the sleeve of my black chef's smock. "Lynds and I did."

The whole situation was a puzzle. Between our cooking the meal and serving it, the food never left our sight. Then how had the poison gotten into Emily's meal?

Bryce turned to my mother. "Ms. Murray, you mentioned you used to work for Principal Smith. You thought that was one of the reasons she wanted the bakery to cater her retirement dinner. What kind of relationship did the two of you have?"

Warning bells pealed in my mind. It was a déjà vu moment. Just as circumstantial evidence had pointed the detectives in my direction during the murder investigation of a rival baker, it seemed as though they were trying to use the same tactic, but this time with Mommy.

"My mother and father were in the kitchen, cooking." My voice was rough with anger. I couldn't help it. "They had no idea which plate, much less which meal, would be served to which guest. They didn't have any reason to know. Only three people had that information: me; Principal Smith's administrative assistant, Guy Law; and the person who'd chosen the meal."

Stan scanned the dining room, then looked over his shoulder toward the customer service area. "Mind if we have a look around?"

Daddy waved his hand to encompass the bakery. "You can—"

What!?! Oh, no, no, no.

I interrupted my father before he could get another word out. "Do you have a warrant, Detective Milner?"

Stan gave me a rueful smile. "No, Ms. Murray, we don't have a warrant."

I could just imagine Dev's reaction if I were to allow the police to search our bakery without a warrant. He'd put spy cams all over the store, never trusting me to act on my own again. I was willing to cooperate with the investigation. I wanted to know what happened to Emily and how. But I wasn't going to allow law enforcement to take advantage of my family.

"Detectives, we're as eager as you are to find out what happened to Principal Smith." I spread my arms with a shrug. "She was our client and this is a tragedy. But we're not going to let you use those two truths to get around our constitutional rights. When you have a warrant, come back with it and we'll let you search our bakery."

"Fair enough." Stan rose.

I escorted him and Bryce out of the bakery, then locked the door again.

"Good thinking, Lynds." Daddy's voice came from behind me.

I turned to face my parents and grandmother. Various levels of concern clouded their features. I gave myself a mental shake. This wasn't the time to bury my head in the sand. I had to get ahead of this situation before the police listed us as suspects in a homicide investigation. *Again*.

I stepped away from the door. "We'd better call Dev."

"The police are investigating you in connection with *another* homicide?" Dev was doing his best to keep his voice down. I heard the strain in his tone.

We were using the video conference feature on my cell phone to speak with my older brother before leaving the bakery. It was almost 8:00 PM Monday. Why was he still at the law office? Dev's work hours were another item to add to my growing list of things to worry about.

"No, they're not investigating *me*. At least not yet." I clenched my fist to keep the tremors of anger from spreading all over my body. "But I could tell Stan and Bryce suspect Mommy—or maybe all of us—of Emily's murder."

"I can't believe this." Dev narrowed his eyes at me as though he suspected I was pranking him. I wish I was.

The detectives had just left Spice Isle Bakery. Tension was building in my neck and shoulders. I wasn't the only one shaken by Bryce's and Stan's questioning. Granny's eyes were cloudy with concern. Mommy was wringing her hands, and Daddy had started humming "No Woman, No

Cry." We really had to get him away from that song, at least for a little while.

Having another perspective on what had happened tonight might help us see the situation and the potential trouble we could be in more clearly. Besides, Dev was a lawyer. We caught him up on the events, starting with Emily collapsing at the table and ending with our declining the detectives' request to search the bakery without a warrant. Of course, Emily's poisoning had shocked and disturbed Dev. He'd been even more worried about the detectives' interrogation. He had a lot of questions about what they'd wanted to know and how we'd responded. Once we'd shared everything with him, he looked as tense and anxious as I felt.

Oh, brother. We were in trouble.

Dev's voice was tinny coming through the cell phone's videoconference feature. "Lynds, I'm glad you told them they'd need a warrant to search the bakery. The warrant specifies where they can look, which means they can't search all over the place."

Despite his praise, I felt helpless and unsure. "I don't know how long it'll take for them to get a warrant." I looked around at Mommy, Daddy, and Granny before returning my attention to Dev. "For all I know, they'll be back in the morning. What should I do?"

"We have to cooperate with a legal search warrant. Read it carefully. Pay close attention to where the warrant states they're allowed to search." Dev's voice was firm and comforting. "Then call me."

Some of my tension eased, knowing my brother was always just a phone call away if I needed him. "I'm willing to cooperate with the investigation. We all are. We want to know who killed Emily, but we don't want to be accused or even suspected of something we didn't do. I don't want to go through that again."

"Neither do I." A cloud of concern shifted across Dev's lean sienna features as I watched him on my cell phone screen. He must be swamped with cases and briefs to be working twelve-hour days. I hated adding to his stress, but I needed his advice.

"This doesn't look good, you know." Daddy had stopped humming. Now he was pacing behind my chair. "We just got out from under one murder and now the bakery's right back in the middle of another."

And I was the reason our family and our bakery were linked to both cases. My heart hung like a stone in my chest. I struggled to fight my way out of the twin shackles of panic and dread. "I should never have agreed to host this event."

"Stop that, nuh?" Mommy sat on my left at the table. She put her hand on my shoulder and gave it a comforting squeeze. "We all agreed to do it."

We were gathered around a table that seated four. Through silent consent, we'd decided to give the table arranged for Emily's retirement dinner a wide berth. Someone had poisoned a guest at that table today. It seemed wiser not to tempt fate.

Granny sat on my right. "We made the decision as a family, just as we make most of our decisions."

"You can't blame yourself, Lynds." Dev's voice was firm. "You didn't do anything wrong."

"There's no sense moaning about the past anyway." Daddy's voice was tight with tension. "We have enough to worry about in the present. For example, how are we going to handle the media?"

"Oh, Lord." Granny pressed a hand to her chest as she

turned to me. "Suppose the papers call? Last time, that *Beacon* reporter was always coming around, trying to get you to talk to him."

José Perez, the *Brooklyn Daily Beacon* crime beat reporter, had been a thorn in my side during the last homicide investigation. Granted, in the end, he'd been somewhat helpful in identifying the real killer. But I wasn't looking forward to finding ways of avoiding José in my own bakery again.

Before opening the bakery, I'd been a marketing and public relations professional. I relied on that experience again. "We'll limit responses to whatever the reporters ask. Just say we're cooperating with the police to help find out what happened to Emily Smith. That's all we'll tell them." I waited for their nods of agreement.

"What about the customers?" Mommy asked. "Some people will hear someone was poisoned in our bakery and they won't come back."

Granny grunted. "They're probably hearing about it right now."

Knowing the community's grapevine, I was sure Granny was right. To make matters worse, our bakery had only been open a little more than five weeks. We hadn't had time to develop much of a track record. "We've been a part of this community for decades. Our neighbors know us. But to help encourage people to keep coming in, I'll also plan some promotions, like a buy one hard dough bread, get a second one free." I'd better get in some extra baking practice.

"Looking at the evidence, I can see why the police are suspicious of us." Daddy's voice came from behind me.

I snapped my head around to meet his eyes. "How can you say that?"

"It makes sense, Lynds." Daddy gestured toward the floor. "Emily went into convulsions and collapsed here."

Granny kissed her teeth. "You're starting to sound like your brother, Roman, finding a dark cloud in every silver lining."

"No, it doesn't make sense, Jake." Mommy shook her head so hard I almost got dizzy watching her. "The only people who handled that food before Emily were you, me, Mommy, and Lynds."

Dev rubbed his forehead. His movements shifted his image on the screen. "The fact that only Emily was affected means only her food had been tampered with. But no one could've gotten to her food before you fixed her plate. Granny, Lynds, are you sure neither of you saw anyone do anything to her meal before she started eating?"

"I'm positive no one touched it after I set the plate in front of her," I said.

"I didn't see nothing," Granny confirmed.

Mommy wrapped her arms around herself as though she was cold. "But how could Emily have been poisoned at the bakery and no one see it happen?"

Daddy started pacing again. "Then the question is how did the killer get the poison into her food if they didn't cook it, serve it, or touch it?"

I threw up my hands. My frustration had boiled over. "Maybe she poisoned herself."

They looked at me as though I was speaking in tongues, which was understandable. My theory was ridiculous. Why would Emily insist on having the school give her a formal retirement dinner, then take her life during it?

"You mean suicide?" Mommy shook her head. "No, that woman loved herself too much to do that."

"At that table, Emily had been surrounded by people

who didn't care for her." I gestured toward the principal's table. "They're the ones Bryce and Stan should be looking at. I'll be sure to tell them that when they return with their warrant."

My reminder caused fear to widen Granny's, Daddy's, and Mommy's dark eyes. I felt the emotion's cold fist as well. The image of the police searching our bakery would keep me awake tonight.

CHAPTER 6

meet @ beacon's office we'll demand retraction!

I frowned at the text my older cousin Serena Bain just sent me early Tuesday morning. She was referring to the news story about the suspicious death of Kings County Early College High School Principal Emily Smith that José Perez, the self-proclaimed celebrated crime beat reporter, had written for the *Brooklyn Daily Beacon*. Unfortunately for us, he'd put Spice Isle Bakery front and center of another homicide.

Thank you, José!

I'd read the article to Granny, Mommy, and Daddy what felt like hours ago but must've only been minutes. Right before our phones blew up. My muscles were still shaking with anger, outrage, and yes, fear. I clenched my fists on either side of the paper until my knuckles showed white. There was no way the *Beacon* would retract its story.

I responded to my cousin's text: *Aren't you working???*

Reena was a women's clothing buyer for a high-end department store chain, a career the fashionista had been born for.

I stood at the blond wood center island in our bakery's kitchen, watching Granny, Mommy, and Daddy around me. We wore casual clothes instead of our usual bakery uniform of black chef's smock, pants, and hat. I'd come to catch up on tasks I usually saved for Mondays and Tuesdays, mostly administrative stuff. Since the bakery was closed, my family usually took those days off, but today they'd offered to help. The *Beacon*'s story had derailed our plans at least temporarily.

I wasn't the only one headed toward a meltdown, though. Our extended family, who also subscribed to the *Beacon*, was flooding our cell phone with texts and calls.

"Roman, the bakery's not cursed." Beside me on my right, Daddy was on his cell phone. He was dressed in baggy navy pants and a nutmeg brown jersey. His voice was tense as he did his best to convince his older brother, my uncle Romany Murray, that supernatural forces were not involved.

Uncle Roman's response carried to me: "Being in the middle of two homicide investigations in less than two months is two murders too many, you know."

Yes, we knew that.

My phone buzzed as Reena's reply arrived: *i'll take today off let's go!*

Tempting. *Ree, it'll be fine. Gotta get back to bakery. Thx!*

I put my cell on Silent Mode and turned it facedown on top of the newspaper folded open on the center island. The story on Emily Smith stared back at me.

Keep it together! I couldn't let my family see me worrying. That would make the situation worse.

For once, our CD player was silent. Without the comforting and familiar sounds of our favorite reggae, soca, and calypso musicians, the kitchen was depressing. Even the smell of the lemon-scented solution we'd used to clean before leaving last night seemed oppressive.

Mommy was across the center island. Her shoulder-length raven hair was styled in a simple flip and parted on the side to frame her heart-shaped face. She was dressed in peach culottes and a scarlet blouse with elbow-length sleeves.

Her voice was strained as she spoke with her older brother, Alrick Bain, over the cell phone. Uncle Al was Reena's father. "We're not closing the bakery until the investigation's over. Well, first of all, we don't know when that would be."

I gaped at Mommy. I knew Uncle Al meant well, but . . . wow. What was he thinking?

"Gimme that." To my left, Granny waved her fingers demandingly as she waited for my mother to give her the phone.

Granny put us all to shame in an emerald green wraparound, knee-length dress. She'd accessorized with a matching sterling silvery jewelry set: several bracelets, earrings, and a necklace. Her long silver hair was swept into a bun and balanced on her head like a crown.

"Al, Mommy wants to speak with you." My mother passed the phone to Granny.

Without a word, Granny disconnected the call and put Mommy's cell on Silent. The sterling silver bracelets on her arm clinked together as she turned the phone facedown beside mine on the center island. Next she addressed Daddy. "Jake, hang up now, eh."

Daddy nodded. "Roman, I have to go . . . Yes, Roman, we pray every day. Several times a day . . . All right. Bye."

I couldn't tell whether Uncle Roman had said goodbye or if, like Granny, Daddy had disconnected the call.

Granny turned to me. "Lynds, what do you want us to do?"

My pulse beat so loudly it echoed in my ears, muffling Granny's question. I scanned the kitchen's black and sterling silver appliances and the white countertops, cabinets, and tiled flooring. "We know the detectives are returning today with a search warrant."

Mommy's delicate brown features tightened with strain. She exchanged a look with Daddy. "Better they do that today when the shop's empty than in front of customers tomorrow."

"I agree." Daddy crossed to Mommy, wrapping a supportive arm around her slim waist. "But how do we handle the story in the paper? José makes it sound like there was something wrong with the food."

"He's drawing conclusions about Emily's death without having any proof the food was tainted." Granny's bracelets clacked again as she gestured toward the newspaper. "Our *food* didn't kill her. Someone *poisoned* her."

I refolded the newspaper to hide José's story, concentrating on not balling it up and throwing it into the wastebin. "Why didn't José call us for a quote? At the very least he could've warned us."

The last time he'd covered a homicide investigation that the police had dragged the bakery into, José had pestered me for an interview. Why hadn't he reached out to me for this story? Instead, he'd basically written a hit piece on our business, which was sure to cost us customers. On top of that, he'd implied my mother was a person of interest by including her work history with Emily.

Mommy rubbed her hands over her upper arms as though trying to get warm in the comfortably cool kitchen. "The man's trying to do his job, Lynds."

Granny kissed her teeth. Her voice was thick with anger. "But eh, eh. Is his job to close our shop?"

Daddy raised his hands, palms out. "The person we should be blaming is the one who poisoned Emily. They're the one who put us in this situation."

"That's right." Mommy nodded. "Now we have to figure out how this murder in our shop's going to affect our business."

I swallowed to ease my dry throat. "It's going to be rough for a while. We're building a strong customer base, but we've only been open a little more than a month. Fortunately, a lot of our customers know us from the neighborhood and from school. They also know us from the Caribbean American Aid Society."

Mommy, Daddy, Dev, and I were members of the society, and Granny was on its board.

"That's the problem." Granny looked around the center island at us. "We've been open such a short while, but in that time, we've been in the news for two murders, you know. *Two*."

Daddy nodded. "That's right. The article doesn't put us in a good light. And this is after things had settled down from the investigation into Fabrizi's homicide. This can't be good for us."

We owed our banker too much money in the form of business loans to suffer any setbacks in our income. We had to keep the customers coming in. We had to grow the bakery. There was too much at stake. Was this the beginning of the end of my dream? It had barely started.

"We need a plan." I raised my voice above Granny's and Daddy's continued commentary about the end of the world. "We need a way to entice our customers and keep them connected to the bakery."

Granny turned to me. "Like what?"

I called on my marketing experience. "A buy-one-get-one-free incentive like I mentioned yesterday." BOGOs as they were known had proven very effective for many of my retail clients.

"All right." Daddy's frown cleared. His posture straightened. "We can offer that for the currant rolls, the coconut bread, maybe even the fish cakes and beef patties."

Granny nodded her approval. "That will work to bring people back, if the newspaper scares them away."

"I knew you would come up with something." Mommy flashed a grin. "How are we going to promote this?"

My thoughts raced. The time on my cell phone showed it was just after eight in the morning. And we were expecting company in the form of New York's finest. There wasn't a moment to lose.

"I'll print fliers to distribute around the area, and notices to post in our windows." Circling the center island, I strode toward the office. "I'll use the same graphics and text from the fliers for our social media."

The sound of banging on the bakery's front door carried into the kitchen, turning my whole body to ice. I snapped my head around to look at my parents and grandmother. Their frozen features and fixed stares reflected the anxiety I felt. We'd had the bell system installed to alert us to deliveries, but those came through the back door. Today's visitation could only mean one thing: The search warrant had arrived.

We left the kitchen together. Through the glass in the front door, I recognized Bryce and Stan. Knots of anxiety tightened in my stomach. I exchanged a look with Daddy.

"I'll call Dev." He pulled out his cell phone and took one of the seats at Granny's table.

From her table placed between the customer checkout counter and the entrance, my grandmother could observe our guests in the dining room while still being plugged into what was happening in the customer service and kitchen areas during business hours.

I crossed to the door to greet the detectives. How many scandals could our newly opened bakery withstand?

We were going to find out—whether we wanted to or not.

"Good morning, Murray family." Stan led Bryce and four uniformed police officers into our bakery shortly after 9:00 AM Tuesday. His steps didn't have their usual bounce. His smile wasn't quite as bright, and his gray eyes didn't meet mine.

"Good morning, Lyndsay." Bryce nodded at me before turning his attention to my parents and grandmother. "Mr. and Ms. Murray. Ms. Bain. We parked the patrol cars in your back lot so we wouldn't draw attention to your bakery."

I knitted my eyebrows. "Thank you?"

"We're not your enemy, Lyndsay." Bryce gave me a thick packet of white papers. "Here's the warrant you requested."

I caught a movement in the corner of my eye. "Hold on, Officer." Sidestepping Bryce, I put myself in the path of an overeager policeman, halting his advance on our kitchen. The twentysomething public servant was built like a boxer and carried what must have been an evidence collection kit. I set my shoulders and stared him down. "I have a right to review this document before you tear apart my place of business."

"She's right, Officer Blue." Bryce's voice sounded beside me. "Give her some time."

I gave the wannabee pugilist one last glare before turning my attention to the stack of papers Bryce had given me. For pity's sake. They'd packed the warrant with legalese, repetitions, and run-on sentences. *Urgh!* I skimmed the pages. It was a struggle to concentrate, though, with Bryce hovering to my right and Rocky Balboa's evil twin fidgeting in front of me. The document gave the detectives and officers permission to search the kitchen, office, customer service area, and bathrooms. Tension seized the muscles in my neck and shoulders.

"Get away from there!"

I spun in the direction of Mommy's shout, ready to run to her if she needed help. She was glaring at the shop's front right window. My breath caught in my throat at the size of the crowd on the sidewalk, staring in. That many people didn't just happen to come across the police vehicles in our rear parking lot. Some of them must also have read José's article in the *Brooklyn Daily Beacon*.

What a nightmare!

Granny joined Mommy, waving her arms. "Get away! You want I bless you up?"

When they continued to ignore my mother's and grandmother's angry words, I marched to the window and closed the cream venetian blinds, shutting out our nosy neighbors and the flood of natural light.

Daddy ended his call with Dev. He pocketed his cell and turned to me. "Keep the search warrant."

I glanced at him. "I intend to."

Stan shoved his hands into the front pockets of his baggy brown slacks. "My wife's not happy about the warrant, either. Said any family that cooks as well as yours would have too much respect for food to put poison in it."

I folded the warrant. "Maybe you should put *her* in charge of this investigation."

Bryce turned to me. "Do you have any questions about the warrant?"

"What kind of poison are you looking for?" I split my attention between Bryce and the shifting shadows against the blinds that indicated the crowd was still in front of our store.

"We don't know yet." His hazel eyes roamed the space as though expecting to find a bottle of poison in the bakery display case or on one of the dining tables. "We should get the lab results in a few days."

Stan turned to the police officers. "Blue, search the dining room and both restrooms. Be sure to check out the water tanks." Daddy followed the Rocky look-alike. "Del Rio, take this area. I think there are drawers behind the counter." Granny shadowed the young woman. "Easton, in the kitchen, and Zachary, you're on the office. They're both behind that door." Mommy marched after the two young officers. Her gait was stiff with tension.

I gritted my teeth. My temper grew as I watched them take over my store. I tracked Officer Del Rio as she moved behind our cash register and started opening the drawers beneath the customer counter. My lips tightened in displeasure. I needed a distraction before I blew a fuse.

Turning, I confronted Bryce. "We didn't have anything to do with Emily Smith's murder."

His eyes apologized. "Stan and I don't believe you're involved, but we have to do our job."

"Is your job wasting people's time?" My voice was gruff with disappointment.

In the month since his last homicide, when I'd been forced to do my own investigation to prove my innocence, Bryce had been coming to the bakery almost every morning. At first I'd been distant toward him. But his remorse for suspecting me of being a cold-blooded murderer had seemed sincere, so I'd forgiven him. I'd even let down my guard and admitted to myself that I still had a bit of a crush on him.

Stupid!

How could I have feelings for someone who was going to investigate members of my family for murder on a monthly basis?

"This is a bakery." Granny directed her scold toward Bryce. "We don't have anything poisonous here. It wouldn't be safe."

The tension rolling off of Granny battered against me like crashing waves. My family was innocent. Wasn't there anything I could say or do to convince him of that?

"Ms. Bain." Stan moved closer to the customer counter where Granny hovered beside the officer. "How'd you feel about Principal Smith?"

Warning sirens blared in my head. "Hold on, Detective Milner. Are you once again trying to fit a member of my family to a crime they didn't commit?" I looked at Bryce. "You remember how that turned out for you last time, don't you?"

"Of course I don't like anyone being rude to my family." Granny sounded offended. Her features wrinkled in disgust. "That doesn't mean I'd *kill* them."

I stared at Stan, disappointment warring with temper. "I can't believe you'd suspect my grandmother of killing someone. That's ridiculous."

"Lyndsay, we have to ask these questions." Bryce massaged his forehead with his right hand as though the conversation pained him. "We wouldn't be doing our job if we didn't."

I threw up my hands. "Do you have to check boxes off of a standard form or can you tailor your questions to the situation?"

"That's not fair." Bryce shook his head. "Your bakery's the last place the victim was seen alive. The prosecutor's office will ask how thoroughly we checked your business and the people connected with it. I'm sorry you're upset, but we have to do our due diligence—for all of our sakes."

Stan moved to the swinging door that led to the kitchen. "I'm going to chat with Ms. Murray."

Not without me he wasn't. Feeling harassed, I hurried after him. "What're you going to ask my mother?"

He ignored me. Fixing a winning smile to his thin lips, he approached Mommy. "Ms. Murray, how're you, ma'am?"

"Mind you put these back where you found them, please," Mommy instructed the full-figured officer who was unpacking the cupboard beneath the sink. With a sigh, she turned to Stan. "What do you think, Detective? How would you like it if I came to your job and just tossed all of your supplies, equipment, and belongings everywhere?"

Stan surveyed the kitchen with a quiet, thoughtful expression. "I'm sure I'd be unhappy, ma'am. I'd find it very disruptive."

"That's right, Detective. You!" Mommy pointed across the room at the heavyset officer pawing around the bakery's office. My mother was using her high school teacher voice. "I'm watching you, you know. Everything back exactly as you found it and where you found it, please. Thank you."

I watched the young officer's movements with a sour taste in my mouth. He was combing through the items on the desk and taking pictures. Each click of his black digital camera made me wince with discomfort and resentment. "What're you photographing?"

He looked at me and shrugged. "Everything."

I gritted my teeth. Such an invasion of privacy. Before I could form a response, Stan addressed my mother again. "What did you do when you worked for Kings County Early, ma'am?"

Mommy tilted her head, giving Stan a narrow-eyed look as though calculating an equation that would show her where his questioning would lead. "I was a maths teacher with Kings County Early for twenty-five years, ten of those while Emily was the school's principal."

Stan nodded as he wrote heaven-knew-what into his long, narrow notepad. "How would you describe your relationship with the deceased?"

Mommy looked at me. Using my eyes, I tried to signal her to answer carefully. She shifted her attention back to Stan. "I'd describe it as professional. Why? Has someone led you to believe something else?"

Good way to redirect the questioning! I shifted my attention to Stan, anxious for his response.

He glanced up from his notepad to look at my mother. "No, ma'am. It's just that the people we spoke with yesterday and this morning who worked with her at the school said no one liked her. That got me wondering about you and whether you liked her. Did you?"

Mommy leaned back against the pale gray countertop beside the silver sink. She tipped her head to study the ceiling. I sensed her gathering her thoughts. "Emily and I didn't have a *personal* connection." She met Stan's eyes. "I didn't like or dislike her. We didn't have to be friends. I was there to do a job, and I did it the very best I could."

"I'm sure you were a heckuva teacher." The twinkle had returned to Stan's cool gray eyes. "I bet your students loved you."

Still leaning against the counter, Mommy crossed her arms and her ankles. "I don't know about all that."

"But I do." I interrupted to do one of the things I enjoyed most: brag about my family. "During her thirty-one years in teaching, my mother earned numerous awards and commendations from the school board, the school, teacher associations, and her students."

Mommy closed her eyes, shaking her head in embarrassment. The praise made her uncomfortable. She didn't go into teaching for the accolades. But for me and our extended family, recounting Mommy's commendations never got old.

The recognition from her employers and peers was meaningful to us. But I knew her most cherished memories were of the tokens of appreciation from her students, the ones who loved math and the ones who struggled with it. My mother didn't just speak about doing your best and holding yourself to high standards. She lived it. She was my first and best role model. My heart swelled with pride.

And then Stan's next question yanked me back to our present, tense exchange. "Her employees who attended the principal's retirement dinner told me she was a difficult boss. Did you and Principal Smith ever argue?"

I stiffened, remembering evenings my mother would come home almost vibrating with stress because of some confrontation she'd had with Emily. Would Stan misinterpret her response, putting an unreasonable emphasis on their arguments the same way he and Bryce had overemphasized my conflict with Claudio Fabrizi?

Mommy paused again. "I'm sure they all told you she was stubborn. Emily was challenging, but who hasn't argued with their boss? You seem even-tempered, Detective, but I bet your boss has vexed you on occasion."

Stan chuckled, ducking his head. "Well, ma'am, you'd win that bet." He laughed again, turning to me. "What about you, Ms. Murray? What did you think of your mother's boss?"

The kitchen door swung open behind me. Daddy stood in the threshold. I sensed his restrained anger. A line of people continued behind him. I caught a glimpse of the top of my grandmother's head behind Daddy. Had she gone to get him? I had no doubt she'd been listening to our exchange in the kitchen. Officer Blue stood behind Granny, along with Officer Del Rio and Bryce.

"Detective Milner, neither my wife nor my daughter poisoned anyone." Daddy spaced his words. "No one in my family has poisoned anyone."

Stan nodded. "I'd still like to know what you thought of Principal Smith, sir."

I responded, hoping to give Daddy a few minutes to compose himself. "Yesterday was the first time my father, grandmother, and I had met or even spoken with Principal Smith."

Granny stepped out from behind Daddy. "And as I told you, I wouldn't kill someone for being rude to my family. Someone like that doesn't deserve that much of my time or attention."

Daddy stepped farther into the kitchen. "I can tell you love your wife, Detective Milner. You talk about her all the time. Would you kill her boss over a disagreement between them?"

Stan made a few notes in his writing pad. "No, Mr. Murray, I would not, sir."

I gestured toward my father and grandmother. "Even if my mother didn't like Principal Smith, she didn't work for her anymore. She retired almost a year ago. She's her own boss now."

Granny's eyes widened with surprise. "But, eh. All this time, I thought you were the boss."

Daddy's tense features eased into a smile. "That's right, boss."

Mommy chuckled. "That's what I thought, too."

I sighed, hooking my hands on my hips. "You know what I mean. We own this bakery together."

Mommy, Daddy, Granny, Dev, and I were partners in our bakery venture. I had the majority ownership at 40 percent. Mommy and Daddy each had 20 percent. Dev and Granny held 10 percent each.

"Well, that's all I have, Murray family." Stan pocketed his notepad as he looked around the room. He raised his voice. "Are you officers done with your searches?" A chorus of various affirmative responses echoed around us. "Do you have any further questions, Jackson?"

Bryce glanced at me. "I'm good. Thanks."

"Thank you for your time." Stan looked at each of us in turn. "Again, we're sorry for the inconvenience. We'll be in touch. Enjoy the rest of your day."

Stan led his team out through the rear of the bakery. With any luck, leaving the back way would allow them to avoid those nosy neighbors still mingling in front of the store. Others were probably already busy, spreading the news about the police search. I closed my eyes and rubbed my brow, trying to ease the tension stitching permanent wrinkles across my forehead.

Despite my pleas to the Almighty, it seemed history was determined to repeat itself. Why did I have the sense the damage from this case would be so much worse than the last?

I turned to my parents and grandmother gathered around me. "This time, we're not going to wait to do our own investigation. We're going on damage control today."

CHAPTER 7

The bakery's kitchen felt heavy early Wednesday morning. The smell of fear fought with the scents of cinnamon, nutmeg, sugar, baked fruits, and flour. A chill overpowered the warmth from the commercial oven. Tension stilled the banter and drowned the joy that usually brightened the room. The brittle silence was broken by Bob Marley's greatest hits and Daddy's low, sporadic singing.

"*Woi.* José's article in today's paper was rough, boy. Even worse than the one they put in yesterday's paper." Granny removed another loaf of coconut bread from the oven. Twin strokes of anger reddened her high cheekbones.

Anxiety rippled across the bakery's kitchen and rolled down my spine. The muscles in my neck and shoulders tightened.

"It makes me look bad, *oui.*" Mommy's fingers trembled as she worked the dough for the currant roll. "He wrote that I'd taken early retirement after Emily was named principal as though her coming to the school was the reason I left."

I heard the pain in her voice and my heart broke. Those few gratuitous sentences had seemed more sensational than newsworthy. "It makes us all look bad."

Mommy continued, her voice becoming more strident

with each thought. "He didn't write anything about anyone else."

I'd noticed that, too. José hadn't mentioned Guy, Daniel, Miguel, Meera, or June. The spotlight had been solely on Mommy. How would the community react to the news report? How would it affect our business, our family? The two were one and the same. If I didn't find a way to save one, they could both be destroyed.

A shadow swept across Daddy's sharp features as he glanced toward the kitchen door. "I wonder how many people will be coming in today." He returned his attention to us. "And whether they'll be here to eat or to gossip."

I looked around the center island. "We're all wondering the same thing."

The alarm on Granny's cell phone sounded, causing everyone to jump. She turned it off.

"It's time to open the doors." Her somber tone was a depressing contrast to her excitement and energy when she usually welcomed our guests. "All you come, nuh? Let's say a prayer."

As we did every morning before opening the shop, Mommy, Daddy, Granny, and I gathered in a circle. We made the sign of the cross, joined hands, and lowered our heads as Granny led us in a brief prayer: "Dear God, grant us the strength and the wisdom to get through this troubled time. And help us remember with everything that happens, we're not going through it alone. You are with us. In Jesus's name we pray. Amen."

I sensed Mommy and Daddy behind me as Granny led us through the kitchen's swinging blond wood door into the customer service area. Despite the calming words, dread wrapped around me like a cold, wet towel. Through the large display window to the right of the entrance we could see patrons waiting to get in. Every morning people on their way to work or school would gather in front of the bakery, stopping by to get a pastry and bush tea, hot or cold. The line typically extended far beyond the window. This morning, there were only a handful of patrons waiting. Our collective gasps of dismay swept across the bakery. We had our answer as to how news of Emily's poisoning in our shop would affect our business: Disastrously.

Granny opened the door to let in the customers. There must have been half as many guests as usual on a weekday. My stomach lurched. I swallowed the mass of nerves that collected at the base of my throat.

Customers tiptoed across the threshold, their wide eyes bright with curiosity—and fear. They scanned the walls, flooring, tables, and chairs as though expecting Emily's ghost to greet them. Daddy had wondered whether hunger or nosiness would draw them in. Apparently, for some it was the latter. But at least they'd come. Now we needed to make the sales and hope they—and others—would come back.

Most of the patrons were friends and other familiar faces, including Joymarie. Tanya was back with her beau, Benny. The young man I thought of as the Knicks Fan looked smart in a soft gray suit. The Bubble-Gum-Chewing College Student's knapsack seemed heavier today.

Standing with Mommy and Daddy, I lowered my voice. "I'd hoped more people would believe in us." I should've known I was being unrealistic, considering José's two *Brooklyn Daily Beacon* articles, yesterday's police search, and the rapid-response neighborhood grapevine.

Daddy rested a large hand on the small of my back. "The day's still young, darling."

I forced my lips into a welcoming smile, squared my

shoulders, and settled in behind the checkout counter. Granny joined me. Mommy and Daddy drifted back into the kitchen.

"Good morning, Ms. Nevis and Mr. Parsons." My smile felt more natural as I greeted Tanya and her gentleman friend. "What can I get for you this morning?"

Tanya's dark eyes warmed with concern and twinkled with inquisitiveness. The notes of her Grenadian accent swept across her words. "Good morning, Lyndsay, Genevieve. How're all you holding up?"

Silence slammed into the bakery, making the swinging beats of Bob Marley's "Jammin'" seem louder. The weight of all those sets of eyes focused on me brought a scalding blush to my cheeks. In desperation, I turned to Granny. She shrugged.

Oh, brother.

Swallowing to ease my dust-dry throat, I made an effort to project confidence despite the detectives' interrogation, the police search, the gossip, and the negative media coverage. "We're fine. Thank you for asking, Ms. Nevis. The situation's upsetting, but we're cooperating with the police to help find out what happened to Emily Smith. Hopefully, they'll identify the person responsible for poisoning her soon."

As Tanya placed her order for two coconut breads and a loaf of hard dough bread, I replayed my response in my head. *Not bad.* All those years of developing crisis talking points for the marketing agency's clients had paid off. As I handed Benny his change, Granny patted my arm. Pride and approval brightened her dark brown eyes and helped reinforce my spine.

A customer I didn't recognize stepped to the counter. He was a few inches taller than me and dressed as though he'd stepped out of a photo circa 1970s: chocolate slacks and a white collared shirt with narrow blue and brown stripes. "Since the woman died in your bakery, I'd think the bo-bo would be looking at all you hard." His nasal voice resonated with a Trinidadian accent.

"Eh, if that's what you think, what're you doing here then?" Granny's tone should've drawn blood.

He shrugged stocky shoulders as he surveyed the shop. "I wanted to see where the murder happened."

My body went cold. *Was he kidding me right now?* "Sir, there's no loitering in our shop. Please place an order or leave."

He shared a dubious look between Granny and me. "What's safe to eat?"

Granny narrowed her eyes. "For you—"

I stopped her with a firm hand on her shoulder. I raised my voice for the people in the back. "The food's *safe*, sir. *Everyone* is safe. There's nothing to worry about. What can I get for you?"

"I'll have a coconut bread." He handed me cash. After giving him his change and his order, we watched him leave.

A young woman in a pencil-slim lemon yellow skirt suit came to the counter. She looked curiously at the jar of paper butterflies before requesting four currant rolls and a mauby tea to go. "I went to Kings County Early." Her Brooklyn accent was embedded in every syllable. "Principal Smith was a mean, evil witch. God rest her soul. She'd get right up in your face and scream at you if you were found in the hallway after the bell rang or were late getting back from lunch. Just shriek like a witch or something."

I was at a loss. "Really?"

Granny bagged her order as I gave her her change.

Conversation speculating about the principal's death continued in front of us.

"I read those articles in the *Beacon*." Toward the middle of the customer line, the Bubble-Gum-Chewing College Student snapped her gum. "Sounds like Five-O's looking at your bakery for another murder. This morning's story makes it sound like your mother's a suspect."

My body went cold. Our fears had come true. Because of José's article, some people—hopefully not everyone—thought the police were investigating Mommy for the murder. He hadn't come right out and stated she was under suspicion or even a person of interest, but his article had come that close.

I started to defend my mother, but Joymarie spoke first. Her tone was sharp and her Trini accent had deepened with outrage. "No one in the Murray family would hurt a fly."

"I don't know 'bout that." The Knicks Fan was next in line. He raised his Brooklyn-accented voice as several customers tried to shout him down. "Hold up. This is what I'm saying, right. Anyone could be pushed to the edge depending on motive and what have you. That's not the issue. Leave that to the side. Think about the *method* of the murder, right. Poisoning's premeditated. And who'd do that in their own place? Think about it. I mean, that's just bad for business. Am I right?"

Their murmurs of agreement were a salve to my sagging spirits. Maybe they didn't believe my family was a secret society of ruthless killers. I raised both hands palms out. "May I have your attention for just a moment, please? Your patronage means a lot to my family and me. We're grateful for your concern and your support. Because of that, I'd like to make a brief statement before we take any more orders. No one in my family had anything to do with

Emily Smith's tragic murder. We were hired to cater her retirement dinner. That's all. And there's nothing to connect anyone in my family to her death. And that's all my family and I have to say about it. All right?"

"Can I quote you?" José let the entrance door close behind him. His clean-shaven, tanned face creased into what was supposed to be a winning smile. It was lost on me.

"You." I squinted at him. "No, you can't. But I want to speak with you."

I circled the counter, leaving Granny to handle the customer order line on her own. Leading José into the empty dining area, I felt the patrons tracking our movements. They weren't even pretending to give us privacy.

My fists clenched at my sides. "You could've at least included a quote from me or someone in my family in one of your multiple articles about Principal Smith's murder. Instead, you added sly sentences that made it seem like we were under suspicion."

José smoothed the sapphire linen shirt he wore with a thin white tie and black khaki pants. His thick ebony curls shone beneath the bakery's fluorescent lights. "I was on deadline. I had to turn my story in."

I stared at him. "Are you serious right now? Making your deadline's more important than *fair* and *balanced* reporting of *facts*?"

He rocked back on his heels as though I'd struck him. "Do you want to make a statement now?"

"What do you think?" My face burned with anger. I was very aware of our audience. Thankfully, Granny was urging them to place their orders to keep the line moving.

José crossed his arms over his chest. "Spice Isle's been connected to two murders, Claudio Fabrizi's and now

Emily Smith's. What do you think is the reason for these back-to-back homicides involving your bakery?"

"First, neither of those people actually died *in* the bakery. God rest their souls. Let's start there." Was I splitting hairs? Yes! But I needed to put as much space as possible between our shop and those deaths. "Second, do *not* quote me. This conversation had better not reappear in your paper. Third, there's no loitering in our bakery. Order something or leave." The reminder had worked on the Trinidadian tourist.

The bell above the door chimed. Bryce and Stan entered the bakery. Bryce turned to me as though he'd sensed my eyes on him. His expression froze when he noticed José. He nodded once, then continued across the customer service area to the front of the line. In their matching dark suits and ties with crisp white shirts, the detectives looked like secret agent extras from the Men in Black movies.

Fear hit me in the face like a cold ocean wave. I forced my legs forward, speed walking around the five guests still in the line. I sensed José behind me. In the back of my mind, I knew the remaining customers were focused on the events happening around them, taking mental notes to distribute through the neighborhood grapevine. No time to worry about that now.

"What're you doing here?" I threw myself between the detectives and Granny, who stood behind the counter.

"We need to speak with your mother." Bryce's voice was somber. His eyes expressed his regrets.

I wasn't having it. "What do you want with her?"

José whipped out his reporter's notepad. "Detectives, José Perez with the *Beacon*—"

Stan interrupted. "We know who you are, Mr. Perez."

José continued. "Is Cedella Murray a suspect or person of interest in your investigation?"

Stan raised his hand, palm out. "No comment, sir."

Granny turned to the pass-through window behind her. Her voice was thin. It wavered around the edges. "Della, the bo-bo want to speak with you, love."

My patience strained as I repeated my question. "What do you want with my mother?"

"Detectives, how can I help you?" Mommy's voice came from behind me. I turned to see Daddy follow her from the kitchen.

"Ms. Murray. Mr. Murray." Stan inclined his head. "Ms. Murray, could you accompany us to the precinct, please, ma'am?" His request sounded like an invitation to Martha's Vineyard. Having seen it, I knew the precinct's interrogation room was a far cry from that.

Mommy's lips parted. The blood drained from her face. "Why, Detectives?"

Bryce glanced at the nearby patrons doing their best to eavesdrop. He kept his voice low. "We just have a few questions, ma'am."

Outrage overcame my fear. "I'm coming, too."

Stan nodded. "We thought you might want to, ma'am. That's fine."

Daddy took off his chef's cap. "So am I."

I turned to him with a heavy heart. "I'm sorry, Daddy, but I need you to handle the kitchen while Mommy's with me. Granny can take over the cash register."

His conflict—his tension and desperation—was like an entity between us. I didn't have to read his mind to know he didn't want to be separated from my mother, not now, no way. Holding his eyes, Mommy rested her hand on his forearm, and his emotions came under control.

"All right." He forced the word through clenched teeth. "But call me right away."

"I will. I promise." I pulled off my chef's cap. "And call Dev, please. We need him at the precinct."

"Stop pacing, lady. You're making me dizzy." The sharp command came from a barely sober, poorly dressed elderly white man seated on a bench just inside the police department.

I turned on him. Anger and impatience roughened my voice. "Stop staring at me."

He reared back as his bloodshot brown eyes widened. Pulling his tattered brown sweater more tightly around him, he looked away, grumbling to himself about emotional women. I turned my back to him. Pacing to the edge of the closet that doubled as the department's waiting area, I checked my pink cell phone again. Another minute had crept by. I did a visual scan of the hallway to make sure Mommy and Dev weren't back yet, then turned away.

Bryce and Stan had insisted on Mommy riding in the backseat of their cop car like a criminal. That made me so angry, but I was also scared spitless. I'd stayed on their bumper all the way to the precinct just as my brother had when I'd been hauled in for questioning last month.

Mommy and I had insisted on waiting for Dev before speaking with the detectives. It seemed we both needed the comfort of his confidence and solid presence. He'd joined us in record time from his law firm's office in downtown Brooklyn. His brown eyes had been dark with concern and his jaw tight with anger.

Now waiting for the interrogation to wrap up, I struggled to keep from charging down the hall and pushing my way into the room. Two things stopped me. First, I didn't want to be arrested. Second, I didn't know into which room they'd taken my mother and Dev. Fortunately, moments before I threw caution to the wind and barged into every room in the precinct Bryce and Stan escorted Mommy and Dev back to me. Watching them walk down the hall made me weak with relief. I braced a hand against the wall to steady myself. They looked fine, although I couldn't read their expressions. I couldn't read Bryce's or Stan's, either.

The four of them stopped in front of me. My eyes were drawn to Bryce. I sensed him trying to read my mind. Knowing he couldn't handle that much vitriol right now, I looked away before his feelings could get hurt.

Stan inclined his head toward us. "Thank you all for coming in this morning." His courtly nod was in keeping with his chivalrous tone. "We appreciate your time and apologize for disrupting your day."

I didn't know whether to take the older detective seriously. Was he genuine or was he trying to lull us into a false sense of security, hoping we'd slip up and say something incriminating? If he was trying to play us, he was wasting time and energy. We were innocent. I sent Bryce one last look of disappointment before following Mommy and Dev.

Bryce extended his arm toward me. "Lyndsay—"

Avoiding his touch, I cut him off. "What could you possibly have to say, Bryce? We both know considering my mother a person of interest in Principal Smith's murder is stupid."

He spread his arms. "I have to follow all the leads no matter how farfetched they seem."

I thought my head would explode. "Just tell me this: Are you going to drag every member of my family into your interrogation room every time someone in Little Caribbean dies?"

Without waiting for an answer, I hurried to catch up with Mommy and Dev as they made their way down the narrow gray hall toward the precinct's gray exit.

Dev put his arm around Mommy's shoulders. "Are you OK?" His voice was low, but I caught the care and concern in his tone.

"I'm worried." She leaned into him. "That room was a nightmare, and you know prison would be worse."

My heart almost stopped. "You're not going to prison, Mommy." My voice was harsher than I'd meant it to be.

"Lynds's right, Mom." Dev glanced over his shoulder at me. He looked me over as though reassuring himself I was OK. "The food wasn't poisoned. The detectives won't find any evidence connecting you to the murder."

Mommy kissed her teeth. "Then why bring me in and put me through all that?"

Dev sighed. "They need to do their due diligence by questioning everyone at the scene so they can eliminate you from their suspect list."

Bryce had said pretty much the same thing. I wasn't buying it from Dev, either. He was trying to reassure Mommy, but it seemed more likely the detectives questioned us because they think we're guilty. Behind Dev's back, I started to roll my eyes when I noticed José speaking with a uniformed officer.

I froze. The crime beat reporter's back was to me, but I'd recognize that thick head of wavy ebony hair anywhere. I also recognized his black khakis and sapphire shirt. What was he doing here? Was he working on more articles about Emily Smith's murder? My family didn't need another José Perez hit job. I could already see the headline: "Spice Isle Bakery Owners Dragged into Precinct for Questioning by Detectives in Connection with Yet Another Homicide." How many more customers were we going to lose because of that story? Weren't there any other crimes he could write about?

Shaking my head, I followed my mother and brother out of the police precinct. The warmth of the sun on my face and shoulders boosted my spirits. "Dev, let us drop you by the subway."

He glanced at his silver quartz watch and grimaced. "You're right. I'm sorry, but I have to get back to the office."

Mommy took his arm as we walked to my car in the parking lot beside the precinct. "There's no need to apologize, Son. Of course you have to get back to work. Thank you for coming to help me."

He helped Mommy onto the backseat before folding his long, slender frame onto the passenger seat of my compact car. "I hate to leave you after that police interview. Will you be OK?"

"Yes, we will." Mommy gave him a brave smile.

At least until we read José's article tomorrow, I added silently.

I started the engine and, after checking the traffic, eased onto the street. "Thank you so much for riding to our rescue. We appreciate your being here with us for the interrogation. Now tell me everything they said."

Dev shifted on the passenger seat so he could look at me and Mommy. "The police believe Mom has a motive for killing Principal Smith because of the poor employee evaluations Principal Smith gave Mom and her undermining Mom's position at the school."

What the heck? "Who told them Mommy was holding a grudge against Emily? Was it one of the dinner guests? Did their source also tell them Mommy hadn't had any contact with Emily *for almost a year*?" I pulled to the right to allow the police car with sirens blaring to pass me.

"Apparently not, but Dev did." Mommy's tone was

dry. "Why would I wait up to now to hurt her? Besides, I wasn't special. Emily undermined everyone and gave us all low marks."

"How did the detectives respond when you told them that?" I tightened my grip on the steering wheel as my frustration at being kept out of the interrogation room returned. I wouldn't need this summary if they'd let me into the interrogation room as I'd asked. All right, demanded.

Dev responded. "Stan thinks the dinner presented Mom with an opportunity for revenge."

"Almost a *year* later?" That was one of the most ridiculous things I'd ever heard, right up there with my mother being a killer. I braked in time to avoid colliding with a car pulling away from the curb.

"That would be one heck of a grudge, eh?" Mommy sighed as though she couldn't believe this was happening. Neither could I. "What is she supposed to have done to make me so angry?"

Dev continued. "I reminded the detectives that Mom couldn't have known which plate would go to Emily. She and Dad had been in the kitchen, cooking. You and Gran had served the meals."

I glanced at the rearview mirror, checking on the traffic and Mommy seated behind me. I was almost afraid to ask the most important question. "Did they actually find poison in the food?"

Dev's voice was taut. "The toxicology report hasn't come in yet. The labs could take another two days."

"That long?" *Urgh.* I hated that my family had to wait so long for our vindication. The food hadn't been poisoned. Emily had died, but no one else had even gotten sick.

And now I was depressed all over again that after all our hard work on the meal and dessert, we'd only gotten through the salad course. Our guests had barely started the main entrée before Emily had collapsed. After the incident, no one had wanted to take their meal or the spice cake with rum-marinated pineapple dessert home. Everything had gone to waste. Well, it had gone to the crime lab and then to waste.

We arrived safely at the Newkirk Avenue–Little Haiti subway station despite the traffic. I double-parked beside a car at the curb of the station entrance off of Nostrand Avenue.

Dev shared a look between Mommy and me. "Be careful getting back to the bakery."

Mommy got out of the car to take Dev's place on the front passenger seat. He kissed her cheek. Then with a final wave for both of us, he was gone. I merged back into traffic.

"Does Dev seem more troubled than usual?" It was as though Mommy had pulled the question from my mind.

"He's worried about you. We all are."

"It started before Emily's death." Mommy shook her head. "That one has been a worrier since the day he was born, but lately he's seemed even more anxious."

I had to agree with her. *What was on your mind, Dev, besides the possibility of your mother being unjustly charged with murder?*

CHAPTER 8

"Good afternoon, beautiful people!" My cousin and best friend, Serena Bain, was physically incapable of entering a room quietly. Even if she could, she'd still draw attention. She had the kind of energy that drew people to her.

Wednesday afternoon, she blew into the bakery in a whirl of plantain green and banana yellow. Her dress's linen material hugged her slim, hourglass figure. Its hem ended just below her knees, baring long, shapely calves. Her thick dark brown braids were similar to mine, except hers featured green highlights and cupped her chin. Mine grew just past my shoulders in a more conservative style. Reena had accessorized her look with matching chunky sterling silver earrings, a necklace, and bracelets. A large, neutral faux leather purse was draped over her right shoulder.

I dropped the antibacterial wipes I was using to clean the counter and pastry display case, then rushed across the customer service area to greet her. Granny rose from her table where she'd been working on her latest crochet project and followed me. Mommy and Daddy came in from the kitchen. They must have heard Reena's greeting above Bob Marley's "Three Little Birds," playing softly through our sound system.

"Ree, it's so good to see you." I could hear my heart in those words. Reena's presence radiated joy, and I really needed that now. We all did.

"It's so good to be seen." My cousin topped me by several inches. She pulled me into a tight hug and rocked us side to side.

I stepped away so Granny could embrace her oldest granddaughter. I adjusted my chef's cap as I watched the two fashionistas holding on to each other. Mommy and Daddy welcomed her next.

Reena took my mother's hands as she gazed around the bakery. Her heart-shaped face was shadowed with concern. "This doesn't look good, Aunty. It's lunchtime and the shop's so empty. Usually, it's packed up in here."

Today's lunch crowd—if you could call it that—consisted of five people in our dining room. We had a few carryout orders, but the count wasn't anywhere close to the numbers we'd previously reached.

Mommy shook her head. "This poisoning business hit us hard. People think they're not safe here."

"We don't know what people are thinking." Daddy put his arm around Mommy's shoulders in a comforting gesture. "But once this whole thing is over, people will come back. It'll be like it was before. You'll see."

"When will that be?" Granny gestured toward our handful of customers. "I'm not poor me one, but I know we can't go on like this much longer."

Granny was right. We couldn't sit around feeling sorry for ourselves. We had to take action.

Reena's purse buzzed. She pulled her cell phone from one of its many compartments and read the screen. "It's Mommy. She says hi and wants to know what happened at the precinct this morning."

Reena's mother was my aunt Inez Minnis Bain. Aunt

Inez and Uncle Al had two sons in addition to Reena, who was their middle child.

"Tell her hi." Mommy turned and wandered back toward the order counter. We followed. "The detectives think my past disagreements with Emily when we worked together give me a motive to kill her."

Reena gasped. "What? That's ridiculous." She typed the information into her cell, but it chimed again before she could send the text. Her device was getting a workout. That was life in a big, close-knit family. Everyone wanted to know what was going on with you. It wasn't nosiness. It was love.

Reena read her phone screen. "Daddy said to tell you hello and that he'd stop by later."

Granny glowed with pleasure from her son's message. "It's past time he shows himself. It's been too long."

I frowned my confusion. "Granny, it's been less than a week."

She rolled her eyes.

"OK." Reena sent her response. "Lynds, Daddy wants to know if you went to the precinct with Aunty Della."

My eyebrows knitted. Why would Uncle Al ask that? What difference would my being there make? "Yes, I went. Dev met us there."

"OK. Good." Reena's phone sounded again. She sighed, shaking her head. "Let me just text that I'll call them later."

Once she'd sent her final text, Mommy and Daddy made their farewells. Mommy kissed her cheek. "Thank you for coming, Reena. Your uncle Jake and I should get back to work."

Daddy gave her a hug. "Yes, the lunchtime crowd might still pick up, you know. And there's still the after work and after school customers to prepare for."

We hoped.

I gave my parents an encouraging smile. Business was slow today, but it was only the first day after the devastating event and the negative news coverage. We may bounce back later in the week. We had to. As Granny had said, we couldn't go on like this for much longer.

Mommy and Daddy disappeared into the kitchen. Granny returned to her crochet project at her nearby table. I wasn't under any illusions she wasn't listening in on my conversation with Reena. I didn't mind, though. I didn't keep secrets from Granny. I couldn't even if I wanted to.

Reena turned her back to the dining room and lowered her voice. "What are you going to do?"

What was she asking me? I studied her face close to mine: wide dark brown eyes in a heart-shaped face, bowed lips, and a short, tip-tilted nose. People often mistook us for sisters. We favored Granny, although Reena was several inches taller than me and our grandmother.

Keeping an eye on the bakery entrance in case more customers came through the door—*please, God*—I leaned closer to her and lowered my voice. "If business is this slow again, tomorrow, I'm going to take some free pastries to the nearby businesses. If that doesn't work, then Friday we'll run a lunch special: buy one meal, get half off another. Something like that." I was still trying to balance the budget for the discount.

"No, no." Impatient, Reena shook her head. "I mean about the murder investigation. We can't let the bo-bo railroad Aunty Della the way they tried to railroad you."

A bucketful of ice shifted around in my gut. "Absolutely not!" I startled myself with my vehement tone. Glancing to my left, I noticed three of our customers looking at us in surprise. I took a breath. Turning back to Reena, I lowered my voice. "Sorry."

Reena reached across the counter and squeezed my hand. "I understand."

Granny grunted, proving she'd been listening. "So do I. She's been my daughter a lot longer than she's been your mother or even your aunt. The next time those detectives come around here, I have half a mind to lock them out."

That wasn't a bad idea. I gave myself a mental shake and refocused on Reena's question. "Dev had to get back to work, so we weren't able to discuss what we're going to do about this latest investigation and the police's interest in us. I'll call him tonight."

Reena shook her head again. "Lynds, I'm not asking what *Dev* thinks we should do. I'm asking what *you* think we should do."

I blinked. "Me?"

Granny gave up her pretense of crocheting and joined us at the customer counter. "Dev's a lawyer and he's exceptional. No one's denying that. I'm glad he was there at the precinct. But *you're* the one who caught the killer last time. Tell us what *you* think we should do, nuh?"

I tilted back my head and studied the ceiling. I'd been thinking about this a lot since we learned Emily passed Monday night, and even more since the police had searched the bakery Tuesday. I had a few ideas, but I hadn't considered anyone would ask about them. I thought I'd have more of a struggle to get them to listen. Usually, the family wanted to know what Dev thought and what he was going to do about something. I understood. Dev was brilliant. I hadn't expected to now be the one the family turned to for answers.

I leaned closer to Reena and Granny, lowering my voice in the hope that our small audience wouldn't be able to hear us over the sound of Bob Marley's "One Love." "Mommy and Daddy are counting on the lab results proving the food wasn't poisoned. They think that will exonerate us. I don't think it will."

"Why not?" Granny's whisper was so low, I had to strain to hear her.

I held her eyes. "The detectives have given Mommy a motive and an opportunity. Now they're looking for means. When the food comes back clean, it won't matter. They'll look for another way Mommy could've poisoned Emily."

Granny's eyes grew wide with fear. "So what are you going to do?"

I exhaled, hoping to ease my growing fear and anger. "I'm going to figure out who killed Emily Smith and how."

Keep busy. Just keep busy.

The mantra was helping me cope with the anxiety of an all-but-empty bakery late Wednesday afternoon. This was the worst day the shop's ever had. Chores gave me a distraction, but I'd wiped every surface, swept every floor, cleaned the bathroom, and refilled supplies that didn't need to be refilled. Setting my hands on the hips of my tan slacks, I scanned the dining room and customer service areas. I needed *something* to do or panic would take over and I wouldn't be able to move at all.

I'd scrubbed the pots and pans, and tidied the kitchen while Mommy and Daddy took the cash receipts to the bank. Now I was back to drumming my fingers on the sand-toned counter beside the cash register. I slid a sour look at the jar of paper butterflies. It was supposed to bring us luck. Fat lot of good it was doing lately. Were the butterflies on vacation? If it weren't for Granny, I'd pitch it into the rubbish.

The bell chimed above the front door like the answer

to a prayer. Tildie Robinson, my grandmother's decades-long nemesis, entered. Granny's expression went from relieved anticipation to sour disappointment.

"Good afternoon, Genevieve and Lyndsay." Tildie's voice reminded me of a chirping bird. Her Grenadian accent was very formal. She stopped in the middle of the floor, adjusting her sky-blue purse on her right shoulder. Short silver curls framed her round face. Her gold, pink, and violet flower-patterned dress was simple but classy.

The older woman had inherited Lester's novelty goods from her deceased husband. The store was well-known in the Little Caribbean community for West Indian–themed novelty items like jerseys that read: "Someone in Grenada Loves Me." And nightshirts with the Grenadian flag and a caption that stated: "I left my heart in St. George's." She had a large collection of classic and current reggae, soca, and calypso CDs, as well as paintings and sculptures.

"Tildie." Granny barely spared the other woman a glance.

Granny'd told me they'd been best friends during their school days back in Grenada. Now they could barely speak to each other. Granny believed Tildie had always been jealous of her and never missed an opportunity to show off. Was that the reason Tildie often stopped by the bakery? Or was she perhaps hoping for a way to mend the decades-old rift between them?

I turned up the wattage on my smile to compensate for Granny's coolness. "Good afternoon, Ms. Robinson. May I offer you a hot cup of mauby tea and coconut bread on the house?"

Granny sent me a sharp look. I ignored her.

Tildie's dark features brightened with a pleased smile. "Thank you, Lyndsay. That would be very nice."

She settled onto the empty chair at Granny's table. My

grandmother's jaw tightened as though she was struggling not to ask her nemesis to leave. She packed away her crochet materials and pattern. "What brings you by today, Tildie? You looking for gossip?"

My back was to the older ladies as I prepared Tildie's tea. I stiffened when I heard Granny's question. I wished my grandmother would try to give the other woman a chance. I had the feeling Tildie was making an effort.

"I don't need to come looking for gossip, Genevieve." Tildie's words were smug and amused. "All of your family's business is in the paper. There was a story in the paper Tuesday and another one today."

"We read them, thank you, Tildie." Granny sounded like she was speaking through her teeth.

Tildie continued. "Your customers must have seen them, too. The news about the principal's poisoning must have upset them. That's why your shop's so empty, you know."

"Our food is exceptional. It didn't kill anyone." Granny's voice was cold.

Tildie sighed. "I know there isn't anything wrong with your food. That's not what I'm saying, Genevieve."

"Well, what are you saying, then?" Granny sounded suspicious.

I packed two cups of tea, two plates of coconut bread, teaspoons, napkins, and a bowl of sugar onto a tray and hurried to my grandmother's table. Hopefully, the treat would distract them from their impending argument.

Tildie looked up as I approached. "Thank you, darling."

"You're very welcome, Ms. Robinson." I served her order. "Granny, I thought you might like a snack, too. You didn't eat much for lunch."

Granny squeezed my hand. "Thank you, love."

Tildie pinched some of the coconut bread and popped

it into her mouth. Her eyes closed briefly as though in ecstasy. "I was trying to tell your grandmother that you and your family are very talented cooks and bakers."

Granny grunted. "We're exceptional."

Tildie waved a dismissive hand. "We all know there was nothing wrong with the food all you served for the principal's dinner, but people are still concerned. That's why your shop is so empty, you know."

Panic stirred again at her words. "You're right, Ms. Robinson."

"I know I'm right." She nodded. "So what are you doing to reassure your customers? They want to know they're safe. How will you make them feel so?"

Our elders—or old heads—interrogated people as though they had a right to ask anything and everything under the sun. Funny that we all felt obligated to answer. "My family and I are going to offer free pastry samples to nearby businesses and a lunch discount."

Tildie looked at me expectantly. "That's it?"

What more did Tildie want me to say? Granny seemed just as puzzled.

I took back the empty tray. "That's what we have so far. I'd appreciate any suggestions you may have. You've been in business a lot longer and you're very successful. What would *you* do if you were in our situation?"

"Go to the media!" Tildie threw up her arms. "The damage to your reputation is being done in the media. Fight fire with fire, nuh? Go to the media to tell them your food's exceptional."

Granny kissed her teeth. "Why would the reporter covering the murder write a story about our food? He's not interested in that."

I put my hand on my grandmother's shoulder. "We wouldn't take this story to José, Granny. He's a crime beat reporter. We'd take this story to the *Beacon*'s food reporter or one of the features reporters."

"That could help." Granny looked thoughtful. "It's a good idea, Tildie."

Tildie chuckled. "I've had some now and again, Genevieve."

Granny was right; it could work. I wish I'd thought of it myself. But that's one of the reasons I was always open to asking for advice. You learn more by asking questions than by talking.

I exchanged a smile with both women. "Thank you for the suggestion, Ms. Robinson. I'll call the paper."

Tildie finished her tea. Wrapping what was left of her coconut bread in a napkin, she stood. "And thank you, darling, for the snack. It was delicious. If the newspaper wants to speak with one of your loyal customers, give them my number." Tildie met Granny's eyes. "Good afternoon, Genevieve."

Granny inclined her head. "Tildie." She frowned, watching Tildie walk out the door. "You know the only reason she comes back is that you keep feeding her."

I tilted my head, searching my grandmother's expression. "You never told me why you and Tildie stopped being friends."

Granny grumbled as she went back to her crocheting.

I returned to the counter. "And I guess you never will."

CHAPTER 9

"There are mermaids in Grenada, you know." Granny spoke matter-of-factly to the brother and sister who'd stopped at her table to hear her stories while waiting for their takeout order. "There are mermaids all over the Caribbean. It's true."

Both siblings looked at my grandmother with a mixture of fascination and disbelief. The young man, Reggie, lived a few blocks from my family. Granny had gotten to know him during his frequent visits to his high school classmates who resided on our street. Granny took pride in knowing everyone in our neighborhood and the people who often came to see them. Mommy believed that trait came from Granny's years of working for the Grenville post office in Grenada before retiring and coming to live with us in the United States about ten years ago.

Today, Reggie had brought his younger sister, Rita, to our bakery. Their family resemblance was strong, especially when they smiled, which happened often when they spoke with Granny. They were both thin with dark brown skin and wide ebony eyes. They were well-groomed and nicely dressed. Granny would say that was a testament to excellent parenting. Reggie wore a chocolate long-sleeved jersey with straight-legged navy slacks. Rita's dark purple denim skirt hung to her mid-calf. Her hot pink blouse had a touch of lace ringing her curved collar.

The duo had stopped in on their way home from school late Wednesday afternoon. Rita looked to be between eight and ten years old. They reminded me of Dev and me when we were coming up. We enjoyed each other's company. We still did. Like Rita, I looked up to my big brother and not just because he's taller than me. It was obvious Reggie was very protective of his younger sibling, just as Dev watched over me.

"Have you seen one?" Rita's question came out on an excited breath.

"Of course." Granny straightened on her chair. "More than one. Once when I was a child like you." She pointed at Rita. "And once when I was about your brother's age." She looked up at Reggie, standing beside his sister's chair.

Rita's big brown eyes widened. Her lips made a perfect circle in her round face. "Tell us!"

Granny settled back on her chair with a smile. She tilted her head and her eyes grew dreamy as she settled back into her childhood memories. "There's a river in Sauteurs, Saint Patrick River. The mermaid, we called her La Chanteuse, lived there."

I'd heard this story so many times, when we visited my grandmother in Grenada and later when she'd come to live with us in New York. I wasn't certain I believed it. But I still loved to hear her tell it. I shared a smile with Mommy and Daddy as we stood around the checkout counter, preparing to enjoy one of Granny's many mermaid tales again.

She leaned into the table, sharing a look between Reggie and Rita. "Mermaids love shiny objects, especially jewelry. That's why you're not supposed to enter the sea with jewelry. They'll think you've brought an offering for them and take it from you whether or not you're willing to part with it."

Rita exchanged a wide-eyed look with her brother.

Reggie put a hand on her right shoulder. "Are you OK? Are you scared?"

Rita shook her head confidently. "No, I'm not scared."

"Are you sure?" His Brooklyn accent was laced with skepticism. "I don't want you to have nightmares and then Ma gets made at me."

"I'm sure." Rita turned back to Granny. "And then what happened?"

"Let me know if you're scared and I'll stop, eh?" Granny gave her a kind smile. "Winnie and I were ten and nine when we decided to try to see La Chanteuse."

Great-aunt Winnifred had been my grandmother's older sister. She'd immigrated to Toronto, Ontario, Canada, a decade before to be with her children around the same time Granny had come to live with us. Great-aunt Winnie had passed of ovarian cancer a few years ago. Granny's tone was still wistful when she spoke of her.

"The night before, we took a few pieces of our mother's jewelry and packed it up to lure La Chanteuse from the lake. It was a few miles or so from our house in Sauteurs to Saint Patrick River. We traveled up hills and down hills, and across fields and dirt roads."

Based on our trips back to Grenada, I knew Saint Patrick River wasn't far from where Granny had grown up. It had taken us five minutes to drive the distance. It must have taken Granny and Great-aunt Winnie close to half-an-hour to walk there. They'd been two very determined little girls. I exchanged a puzzled look with Mommy and

Daddy. They shrugged and returned their attention to the story.

Unaware of our silent exchange, Granny continued. "And it was dark, you know. We had to leave when the sun was still asleep." She paused when Rita giggled.

"Why'd you have to get up so early?" Reggie asked.

Granny spread her arms. "We had to get to the lake by dawn. It's in the early part of the day, when everything is still and quiet, that La Chanteuse comes out of the lake. We chose a cloudless night, and packed water and bread in case we were hungry."

"That's smart." Rita nodded her approval. "And then what happened?"

"We reached the lake." Granny's dark eyes became more distant as though she was settling further into her memories. She set the scene so we could join her. "It was pitch black. The only light came from the moon, the stars, and the fireflies. And it was quiet. Just the crickets singing and the owls hooting to one another. But I swear I could hear my own heart beating, you know. *Babum! Babum! Babum!*"

Rita covered her mouth with her small hand as though trying to smother her gasp. I didn't think her eyes could grow any wider.

"And then what happened?" Her hand muffled her words.

Reggie put his hand on her shoulder again. "Rita, if you're scared, we should go. I don't want you to have nightmares." His words were heavy with reluctance. Even if he took Rita home, I suspected Reggie would return to hear the rest of the story.

Rita dropped her hand and looked up at her older brother. She shook her head so vigorously that her hair, parted in the center and neatly brushed into two thick braids, swung above her tiny shoulders. "We can't leave now. I have to know what happens."

"Winnie and I crept toward the lake, looking all around to make sure we were alone." Granny matched her actions to her words, looking over both of her slender shoulders before turning back to Rita. "We walked right up to the water's edge and laid our mother's jewelry in the short grass. Then we hurried to lie down behind some nearby bushes and weeds. We waited and waited and waited. Then, just before the sun started to rise, we heard a splash in the water. We must have fallen asleep, because it woke us."

"What did you see?" Reggie sounded as wondrous as his little sister.

"Was it La Chanteuse?" Rita demanded to know.

"Yes, it was." Granny nodded. "As certain as I'm looking at you and your brother right now, I saw La Chanteuse that morning."

"What did she look like?" Reggie leaned forward as though anxious to hear every word.

"From her torso up, she was a beautiful woman." Granny sat back against her chair. "Her skin was black and she had long, long black braids. But from her hips down, she was a fish. Her tail was green and gold and red. And she used it to lift herself from the water onto the grass."

Rita gasped. "Were you scared?"

Granny smiled. "No, sweetheart, we were amazed."

"Did she see your mother's jewelry?" Reggie asked.

"Yes, she did." Granny nodded. "She seemed so pleased and happy to see it. She looked around as though trying to see who'd left the offering for her. But she didn't spot

Winnie and me behind the bushes. We were too well hidden. So she took my mother's bracelets, earrings, and the necklace. And in return, she left us her brush."

"A brush? A mermaid's brush?" Rita's jaw dropped. "Do you still have it?"

Granny chuckled. "No, when my mother realized her jewelry was missing, Winnie and I told her about our going to see La Chanteuse. She didn't believe us. Since we didn't have her jewelry, we gave her the brush. I don't know what became of it over the years."

"She lost the mermaid's brush?" Rita dropped her eyes to the table. Her lips turned down. She looked crestfallen.

"Never mind that now." Granny offered the little girl a smile. "I still have the memory to share with you."

Rita looked at Granny, then her brother. "I wish I could have an adventure like that."

Reggie took her hand to help her from the chair. "Just as long as you take me with you."

Yes, that young man definitely reminded me of Dev. That was something my brother would say even today.

With waves and a round of goodbyes, the duo left the bakery. I was grateful for the break from thinking about Emily Smith's murder and how it was keeping customers from our store. But now that story time was over, the strain of our situation hit me again.

I sighed, straightening from the counter. "This has got to be the longest day ever. First, we have only a third of the usual number of customers when we open. Then the police question Mommy about Emily Smith's murder. And now, we have hardly any customers from our usual after-work-after-school crowd."

Daddy crossed his arms over his chest. He'd removed his chef's cap. "The question is how long will it stay like this?"

I fisted my hands on the laminate checkout counter. "Until the toxicology report comes back, the poisoning and police investigation are hanging over our heads."

From her table set against the nearby wall, Granny caught my eyes. "Then you know what you need to do, don't you?"

I nodded, looking from Granny to Mommy and Daddy. "I need to do my own investigation. I need to clear Mommy's name."

My parents' horrified looks morphed into granite expressions of disapproval.

"No, Lynds!" Mommy clamped her hands onto her slim hips.

"Absolutely not." Daddy's verdict merged with Mommy's command.

Tuesday, I backed down when faced with their disapproval. But not today. Today, I didn't even blink. I wasn't in high school, deciding whether to stay out late with Reena or come home before curfew. I was an adult, and the choice I was facing was to either prove my mother's innocence or sit on my butt, waiting for her to be charged for a murder she didn't commit. I couldn't believe we were debating this.

I shook my head even as they spoke. "I'm not going to sit on my hands while the police build a case against Mommy for first-degree murder."

Blood drained from Mommy's elegant sienna features, but her protective instincts for me were still working overtime. "That's the trouble, Lynds. This is a *murder* investigation. You'll be putting your life in danger, chasing after a stone-cold killer."

I swallowed to ease my dry throat. I wasn't saying I wasn't scared. I was. "I'm not taking this lightly—and neither should you. What choice do we have?" I paused, looking into their eyes. "I promise to be careful, but we all know what's at stake."

"Last time, you were almost killed." Daddy's words were anguished. He turned away, dragging his right hand over his tight, still-dark curls. "Every time I think about that, my blood runs cold, *oui*."

So did mine. "Daddy, the way people drive in Little Caribbean, I could be killed crossing the street."

Mommy narrowed her eyes. "This is not a joke, Lyndsay Catherine."

Uh-oh. Both names. Not a good sign.

Granny stood from her table and crossed to us. She rested her hand on Mommy's shoulder. "Della, you *want* to go on trial for murder?"

"Of course not!" Mommy shifted to look at Granny over her shoulder. Her voice was tight, reflecting her struggle between protecting herself and protecting me. "But I'd rather go to prison than have anything happen to my family."

"But let Lynds try, nuh?" Granny dropped her hand. "If it gets to be too dangerous, we'll stop. She won't be alone. I'll help like I did last time."

"I'll help, too." Mommy angled her chin as though expecting me to object.

"We all will." Daddy's tone was grim.

A small smile curved my lips as I looked at my parents and grandmother. "I wouldn't expect anything else."

Jab! Cross! Hook! Uppercut! Body blow! Front right kick! Squat! Front left kick! Squat! Repeat!

I called out the moves in my head with each execution as I attacked the six-foot freestanding foam-filled body bag at my neighborhood fitness center. The black vinyl bag stood toward the center of the fitness room, surrounded by free weights, benches, and other toning machines. Similar bags were stationed at other spots around the space.

The gym was old. It had opened decades before my family had moved into the neighborhood. The stench of sweat had soaked into its walls. New paint and flooring would be a good investment. Otherwise, the facility suited my needs. It was clean, and the owners took pride in the exercise equipment. The machines were cutting-edge and well maintained. The rooms were spacious enough so patrons weren't exercising on top of one another. It was open 24/7/365 with round-the-clock security. For me, its best feature was its location. It was walking distance from home and the bakery.

In preparation for the center's annual fall kickboxing exhibition, I was gradually intensifying my training. I'd added timed sprints to my three-mile run on the gym's elevated track to improve my cardio and increased the weights for my upper- and lower-body strength building. I'd even enrolled in the intermediate advanced kickboxing class. It was scheduled to start in two weeks. Hopefully, I'd be able to keep up.

My parents had enrolled me in kickboxing classes when I was thirteen, after finding out about the school bullies who were constantly badgering me. Mommy and Daddy hadn't wanted me to get into fights, but they'd wanted me to be able to defend myself if the fights came to me. I'd resisted the idea at first, but I'd soon learned to love the training. It taught me discipline and gave me confidence. I felt stronger. The bullies must have noticed the change in my attitude. The harassment had continued even in college, but it wasn't anywhere near the levels it had been in elementary school.

It was about a quarter till six Thursday morning.

Through the gym's front windows, I could see the sun rising as I lashed out again with my thick yellow vinyl boxing gloves. With each punch, the six-foot bag, anchored by a round sand-filled base, snapped back, then rocked forward. *Jab! Cross! Hook! Uppercut! Body blow!* The physical exertion eased my tension as I tried and failed to find answers to my questions.

Who would kill Emily Smith? Many people may have wanted to, but who would go through with it? Why did they wait until she was about to retire?

And the big question: How had they administered the poison? If we figured that out, we could identify the killer and clear Mommy's name.

"I saw your bakery's in the news again."

I turned at the sound of Roxanne "Rocky" Stewart's voice. She was the one who'd convinced me to enter the gym's fall kickboxing exhibition.

Rocky, as she preferred to be called, was a tall, attractive woman, perhaps six or seven inches above my five-foot, three-inch height. Her deep auburn close-cropped hair—compliments of a professional dye job—set off her warm brown skin. Her black unitard covered her from shoulders to knees, leaving her sculpted arms bare while hugging her long dancer's figure.

I pulled off my yellow boxing gloves. "I was prepared for our first year in business to be challenging. I didn't know it would involve so many tragedies."

Rocky studied my face as though looking for answers. "I didn't realize Cedella Murray was your mother. She was my eleventh-grade math teacher."

"That's a small world." I paused in surprise. She knew my mother.

"It was seventeen years ago, but some teachers you

never forget." Rocky's chuckle sounded self-conscious. "I didn't learn to love math until I took Ms. Murray's class. She was great at explaining the formulas and how to apply them to everyday life."

I blushed as though Rocky was complimenting me instead of Mommy. "Seventeen years ago; then you weren't there when Principal Smith arrived."

Shaking her head, Rocky pulled her fluorescent pink boxing gloves from her crimson gym bag before dropping the bag to the floor. "No, I wasn't, but my cousins' children were. I heard all about her from them. None of them liked her."

Hmmm. So far, the feeling was unanimous. "Why not?"

"She was always screaming at someone—students, teachers, secretaries, janitors, security guards. Her rage was universal and nondiscriminatory." Rocky shook her head as she tugged on her gloves. "You know the type."

Yes, I did. I'd hated it when teachers and administrators would scream at us. They weren't all like that. But a few treated it like a disciplinary tool for inner-city students. Instead, it made some of us nervous wrecks, unable to concentrate on learning. Others would rebel even more. In short, their scream fests were epic fails.

"It sounds like no one liked her." I dropped my gloves into my green nylon gym bag. "I wonder what made her so angry. She must have known her behavior was making her unpopular."

"She obviously didn't care." Rocky did some gentle stretches, raising her right arm across her chest and pressing it back with her left arm to limber the muscles in her right triceps. "She couldn't have been a witch with everyone, though. I heard she was dating someone."

I blinked. "Did your cousins' kids tell you this? How did they know?"

"You know how kids gossip about teachers and what have you." Rocky changed position to stretch her left triceps. "You think they're going to school to learn, but for them, it's like live-action soap operas. The rumor was Principal Smith was dating the father of one of the teachers." She paused, scrunching her face as though she'd gotten a whiff of someone's dirty gym socks. "Could you imagine how awful it would be if a member of your family was dating your boss, especially if you couldn't stand your boss?"

Yuck! My boss had been a tool. The idea of his marrying into my family would've kept me up at night. "I don't even want to think about that."

"Exactly." Rocky nodded decisively. "My boss's a jerk. I'd have to find a way to put an end to that relationship with a swiftness."

Yeah, I completely sympathized. But would it drive me to murder? That seemed farfetched to me, but perhaps not to everyone. "Are you sure it was a *teacher's* father?"

"No-o-o." She dragged out the word, making it three syllables. She got a faraway look in her dark brown eyes as though she was trying to recall a past conversation. "Come to think of it, it might not have been a *teacher's* father. It may have been a member of her staff. I could ask. Are you thinking of investigating this murder, too?"

"I might." West Indians tended to be a cautious group. We didn't like having people all up in our business. I know this seems like a contradiction since we also enjoyed good gossip. We're a complex culture.

She touched my shoulder. "Just be careful." She let her hand drop and forced a smile that was shadowed with concern. "I don't want to be the only woman in the kickboxing exhibition again."

"I promise that won't happen." I hooked my gym bag onto my shoulder. "Please let me know if you find out anything else about the principal."

"I will." She flashed a smile and raised her hand.

I returned her wave then hustled out of the gym. I wanted to share this new information—and possible new motive—with my family.

CHAPTER 10

"Has José completely lost his mind?" Struggling to control my voice, I wanted to slam my copy of the *Brooklyn Daily Beacon* onto the white laminate counter in our bakery's kitchen. I managed not to.

It was minutes before the bakery was scheduled to open Thursday morning. I'd just finished reading José's article to Granny, Daddy, and Mommy. It was supposed to update readers on the investigation into Emily Smith's murder. However, the story read more like he was trolling for a libel lawsuit. It actually listed my mother as a "person of interest" in a murder investigation.

Urgh!

Granny settled her hands on her hips. Her brow was furrowed with anger and disgust. She turned to Mommy. "You still think he's just doing his job?"

"He's not doing it very well." Daddy's voice was rough with anger. "There goes our hope of getting more customers back today."

Breathe in; breathe out. My family needs me to stay calm.

"Daddy, we'll get our customers back. It'll just take some work." I gestured toward the trays of currant rolls, coconut bread, and banana bread. "I told you I'm going to take some of these pastries to the local businesses along with the coupons I made, promoting our buy-one-get-one-free lunch offer."

"What if it doesn't work, uh?" Mommy sounded on the edge of panic.

I steeled myself not to let her nervousness affect me. "What are you and Daddy always telling me?" I gestured for them to join Granny and me near the kitchen door. "Don't borrow trouble. Now, let's pray before opening for the day."

Granny led us in a brief prayer; then I grabbed one of the trays of pastries and followed her into the customer service area.

Minutes later, panic threatened to settle in as I studied the queue of guests waiting to place their orders. There were even fewer today than there'd been yesterday. The line used to be out the door. People would gather on the sidewalk. Today, everyone fit comfortably in our small customer service area. They were all familiar faces, including Joymarie, Tanya and Benny, Grace Parke, the Knicks Fan, and the Bubble-Gum-Chewing College Student. I was thankful for their continued support, but we'd need more than these few patrons to keep our doors open.

The cold knot in the pit of my stomach was growing bigger.

"I don't care what that foolish newspaper says. No one believes Cedella's a murderer, you know." Tanya's small, round face was a wreath of angry wrinkles.

"You're right, Ms. Nevis." I raised my voice. "My mother's *not* a murderer."

Tanya and Benny requested their usual currant rolls and bush teas with hard dough bread. I often wondered how much bread the couple ate in a day. Without blinking, I rang their order while Granny bagged their items and poured the teas.

"Then where is everybody, eh?" The Grumbler stood toward the middle of the line and gestured around the sparse crowd. She was one customer I wished would stay home, but we needed the money. "It must be everyone's worried about the food."

Joymarie crossed her arms over her chest and sent a stern look behind her toward the Grumbler. "There's not a single thing wrong with the food. I eat here every day."

Her fierce defense of my family and our food made me breathe a sigh of relief. Everyone in marketing knows that if you want to get out of a tough situation with your reputation intact, it's better to have others defend you than to defend yourself. Customers will trust their peers before they believe in you.

"What did the police ask, Ms. Murray?" The question came from the Knicks Fan. He was in another smart suit today.

I wasn't comfortable discussing the investigation, but I wanted to reassure our loyal customers. "The detectives asked the same kinds of questions you see on TV. They wanted to know about my mother's relationship with Principal Smith."

"What, nuh?" Tanya interrupted. "But Cedella hasn't worked for the school in almost a year."

"I know." I gave Tanya her credit card and the slip to sign, then turned to the next customer in line, Joymarie.

"So what'd she tell them?" The Bubble-Gum-Chewing College Student called from the middle of the line.

Granny answered, "My daughter spoke the truth. When they worked together, their relationship was professional, as it should be. Remember, *they* came to *us* to host the retirement dinner. We didn't go to them."

"Mmm-hmm." Tanya nodded. Her voice was gentle. "And how is Cedella holding up, eh?"

Granny handed her friend her order in a green Spice Isle Bakery paper bag. "She'll be fine. Thank you for asking. The truth is on our side."

"Please tell her we're thinking of her, Ms. Bain." Joymarie turned to Granny after placing her usual order of coconut bread and corailee tea.

Granny smiled her pleasure. "I will, sweetheart. Thank you."

"Who else are the police talking to?" the Knicks Fan wanted to know.

A new voice entered the discussion. "As far as I can tell, no one."

Recognizing the speaker, I looked up. José. A surge of outrage raced through me. I gripped the countertop in front of the cash register to keep myself from snatching him.

"But, eh." Granny planted her hands on her hips. "You have some cheek, coming here after that story you wrote."

His attempt at an innocent expression had the same effect on my temper as a lit match on a full tank of gas. "My article's accurate. Detectives Milner and Jackson did take your daughter in for questioning in connection with the investigation into Emily Smith's murder. I didn't misrepresent the facts."

Anger made me want to stomp around the counter to face him. Reasoning—and my granny's hand on my back—kept me in place. "It was unfair of you to not include a quote from my mother."

The customers around us voiced their agreement.

"You shoulda talked with the family."

"You doin' the bo-bo's job for them, harassing an innocent woman."

"How would you like to wake up and find your mother in a murder article?"

"OK. OK." José raised his arms in surrender as he surveyed the crowd. A winning smile brightened his handsome face. The man really had no shame. "One of our neighbors was murdered. You have a right to know how the police investigation is progressing."

"Ha!" Granny scoffed. "Shows what you know. Emily Smith didn't live around here. How you didn't know that?"

José spread his hands. "All right. She wasn't a close neighbor." He turned to me. "But, Lynds—may I call you Lynds?"

Unbelievable. "No, you may not."

"We're still not there yet?" He tried his winning smile on me and lost.

"And we never will be." I scowled at him.

"Lyndsay, I don't think you're angry with me." He gave me a wounded look. "I think you're upset with yourself."

"What's this?" Granny pitched her voice above our audience's laughter.

I couldn't believe my ears, either. "What could possibly give you that idea?"

José shrugged. "Every time I've asked you for a quote, you've refused to give me one. I bet you're wishing you'd been more cooperative with me now."

"So this is payback?" I narrowed my eyes, trying to impress upon him that I wasn't someone he should taunt. "That's very unprofessional."

José inclined his head. "You're right. I apologize." He gestured between me and Granny. "So, do either of you want to give me a quote for tomorrow's article? Or perhaps your parents?" He craned his neck as though trying to see Mommy and Daddy from the pass-through window.

I leaned sideways to block his view. "I have a quote for you. My mother, Cedella Murray, is innocent. If the police won't get to the bottom of this, our family will."

The stunned silence in the bakery was loud.

José whipped out his reporter's notebook. "And I can quote you on this?"

"Yes, you can." I watched him hurry out of the shop, presumably to work on his follow-up article.

Granny's voice interrupted my thoughts. "The bo-bo won't like this, you know."

"The killer won't like it, either." I turned to her. "I've put all of them on notice."

Maybe today wasn't the best day to go door-to-door, delivering pastries to the nearby businesses. Late Thursday morning, I packed several Spice Isle Bakery white cardboard boxes of fresh assorted pastries: currant rolls, coconut bread, banana bread, as well as sugar cookies for the less adventurous. But I was still stressed from our disappointing breakfast turnout and the tense encounter with José. With that in mind, I made Tildie Robinson's store my first stop. A friendly face and relaxed conversation would help settle my nerves and boost my confidence for this promotional effort. Besides, good customers should also be rewarded. We'd never charged Tildie, but that was neither here nor there.

A loud bell sounded as I pushed open the door to Lester's. Tildie looked up from her position near the checkout counter as I crossed the threshold. She'd been chatting with one of her clerks. The mid-sized store was packed with a variety of customers: young, old, singles, couples, white, Black, Asian, and Latino. Several store assistants were fanned out across the floor, engaging with customers. It was a shop owner's dream. I so desperately wanted Spice Isle Bakery to go back to being crazy busy again. And one day, I wanted us to be successful enough to hire servers who could engage with our customers.

I fixed a cheerful smile to my lips as I crossed farther into the novelty shop. On my way to Tildie, I passed a display of handcrafted bags with embroidered images of coconut trees, mangoes, seashells, and fish.

I lifted one of the boxes from my oversized brown canvas tote bag. "Good morning, Ms. Robinson. I hope you'll accept these complimentary baked goods from Spice Isle Bakery. We made them fresh for you."

Tildie's face lit up as she took the box with the Spice Isle Bakery logo sticker from me. "Oh, how nice. Thank you." She lowered her voice. "I saw the article in the *Beacon* today. How's your family?"

I felt a wave of sadness but did my best to rise above it. "We're managing. We'll get through this. Thank you for asking."

Tildie set the pastry box on the counter. She gave me a brief, hard hug before stepping back. "I know you will. We're all rooting for you. Thank you for the treats."

The hug was just what I needed. With a final wave to Tildie and her staff, I left the store to continue my mission.

There was a bounce in my step as I swept into a travel agency a few doors down from Lester's. "Good morning. I'm Lyndsay from Spice Isle Bakery. We're a couple of blocks—"

"I know about your bakery." The office manager's words were clipped in her Brooklyn accent.

She adjusted the side of her black-rimmed glasses with a well-manicured hand. Her warm brown features were burdened with expensive-looking makeup. Her micro braids were swept up and away from her face into a bun on the crown of her head, and her pinstriped black pantsuit seemed a little snug.

On the other side of the dark wood half wall, two aging white male travel agents watched our exchange as though they were at a theater.

"Yes, well, we'd like to offer you these complimentary pastries." As I spoke, I pulled a box from the tote bag. I stepped forward and offered it to her.

She held up that same well-manicured hand with its daggerlike red-tipped nails to stop me. "No, thanks. As I said, I know about your bakery. I read about it in the paper." She arched an eyebrow, then turned her attention to her computer screen.

I'd been dismissed. I sensed the trio couldn't be persuaded. I struggled to keep my shoulders squared. "Have a good day."

Head high, back straight, I strode out. But after similar reactions from the next two businesses, it was hard to keep going. Frustrated and dejected, I needed a break—or a warmer welcome. I looked up and down the street for a storefront that might offer a more hospitable reception.

A familiar figure strode down the block across the street. My eyebrows knitted. Wasn't that Meera Singh, the nurse at Kings County Early College High School? Shouldn't she be at work? Based on her outfit, it didn't seem like she'd taken the day off. Her cream skirt, matching jacket, and blue blouse looked very businesslike. Then what was she doing in Little Caribbean so late in the morning? It would probably take an hour to get from the high school to this neighborhood. What was she up to? There was only one way to find out.

I trailed the nurse to see which business she was going to. She weaved around and through slower-moving pedestrians. Her movements were quick and stiff. She seemed agitated. She sped past a shoe store, a jewelry shop, a couple of eateries, and a clothing store. Where was she going? She finally stopped at the Bronze Mixer Pharmacy. Meera looked up and down the block as though making sure she hadn't been followed. Only then did she push open the door and disappear inside. Odd.

Why was the school's nurse going to a pharmacy in Little Caribbean in the middle of the morning on a workday? I needed to find out.

Hurrying to the crosswalk, I had to wait for the light to change. I rocked from leg to leg as tension took over my body.

Come on. Come on. Come on.

Green light!

Finally!

I jogged across the street, rushed into the pharmacy, and went in search of Meera and answers.

Bronze Mixer smelled like chewing gum and cough syrup. It took my eyes a moment to adjust to the change from the bright sunlight to the pharmacy's almost cavernous interior. I strode across the front of the store, peeking down narrow aisles of beauty aids, greeting cards, candies, paperback novels, and health care products.

No Meera.

How was that possible? It hadn't taken me that long to follow her into the store. And my eyes had been glued to the entrance. She hadn't left. I walked down the last aisle and turned at the pharmacy counter that extended almost the length of the back of the building. I maneuvered around a handful of customers making product selections: elderly neighbors, women with infants, men with toddlers. I didn't come across Meera. I searched the aisles again, in reverse: health care products, paperback novels, candies, greeting cards, beauty aids. Still no Meera.

Where could she be?

My attention was drawn to the pharmacy counter. Could she have an appointment at the clinic behind the counter? Part of me wanted to hang around to find out, but I didn't have time. According to my cell phone screen, I needed to get back to the bakery to help prepare for the lunch customers. Hopefully, we'd have some.

CHAPTER 11

Granny's soft, warm hand covered mine on the kitchen island. In her hot mustard jumper, she looked like a genie. "Mind you add the liquids slowly. You don't want the dough to be lumpy."

"Yes, Granny." I nodded as she took her hand away.

I looked longingly at the bread maker. Granny insisted I learn to make hard dough bread by hand. She believed it would give me a better feel for the consistency of the dough. Ha! I think she didn't want me using the bread maker because that's not the way she'd learned to bake bread.

It was Thursday afternoon, but the bakery was slow. So far, we'd only had about a dozen takeout orders. On a normal day, we had double that amount by now. The few patrons who'd come in had presented the two-for-one coupons I'd promoted on social media and distributed to nearby businesses. Granny suggested we take advantage of the downtime for a baking lesson. I sensed her primary goal was to distract me from our dwindling sales.

We joined Mommy and Daddy in the kitchen. The space was fragrant with the aromas of spicy jerk meats, savory curry dishes, sweet fried plantains, rich macaroni and cheese, and seasoned rice and peas. These scents floated through our vents in search of hungry pedestrians. Yet and still, we weren't getting the foot traffic we were used to attracting before this investigation. I needed to concentrate harder on Granny's effort to distract me.

I took the first container, which held a mixture of yeast and one cup of room temperature water. I poured a slow but steady stream into the large mixing bowl of flour, salt, sugar, and butter. I repeated the process with the half cup of almond milk. I then added the milk with the same slow, steady method. I combined the wet and dry ingredients with a wooden spoon, making sure everything was thoroughly mixed.

"Brave." Granny rubbed my shoulder. "You're coming along well, Lynds. Isn't she, Della?"

"What? Oh, yes. Yes, she is." Mommy turned her head to smile at me from her position in front of the sterling silver stovetop where she was frying sweet plantains. The look in her eyes was unfocused. I sensed she'd been lost in thoughts about the case.

Her anxiety was my fault. It felt like a fist slammed into my heart. My throat was dry with guilt and shame. I'd never meant to put my mother in such a horrible position.

How do I fix this?

I released the spoon. "Mommy, I'm sorry I pressured you into catering Emily Smith's retirement dinner. If I hadn't pushed you, none of this would've happened. You wouldn't be a person of interest in a murder investigation, and we'd still have a good amount of customers coming in."

Granny nudged my upper arm with her fingertips. "Don't let the dough stand so."

"Sorry, Granny." I continued stirring the mixture.

Mommy's eyes were wide with surprise. Her dark arched eyebrows had all but disappeared beneath the band of her black chef's hat. "Is that what you think, Lynds? That you *pressured* me? That this is *your* fault?"

"You hadn't wanted to do the event, remember?" I certainly did. Cupping my palm, I filled it with olive oil. As I rubbed the liquid over the dough, I molded the mass into a medium-sized ball and returned it to the mixing bowl.

Granny huffed. "*You* didn't want to take on the booking, either. Emily's assistant—what's his name? Guy?—pestered you into it."

"And I persuaded Mommy." Now she was suspected of killing someone. My heart jumped into my throat at the thought of my mother being on trial for murder.

After covering the bowl with a clean kitchen towel, I set it on the counter behind me. I programmed the alarm on my cell phone for thirty minutes. The dough needed to be left alone to rise.

Granny barked a laugh. "Don't you know your own mother? Since when can anyone convince Della to do something she doesn't want to do? Only God has that kind of power. Listen, if Della hadn't wanted to cater the dinner, it wouldn't've been here."

"That's true, you know." Daddy arranged place settings on the kitchen island behind Mommy. Usually, we ate after the lunch rush, but with so few customers coming through our door, my parents were preparing our meal in advance. "She was born stubborn and the years haven't changed her."

Mommy looked at Daddy from over her shoulder. "Are you any different?"

A reluctant smile curved my lips. It was true. My parents—and my grandmother—were some hardheaded people. Once they made up their minds about a thing, only God could change it.

"But you know, whether you'd convinced to me do the

event or not, none of this is your fault, Lynds." Mommy's tone was firm. "Don't ever think that. It's the killer's fault."

"This isn't the first time our family's been in this situation." Granny gave me a pointed look. "We managed to prove *your* innocence. We'll do the same with Della."

I had to believe she was right. Considering the alternative would make me throw up. "The toxicology report will clear us. The food wasn't poisoned."

"Della, mind the plantains." Granny pointed toward the stove and the extra smoke wafting up from the frying pan before turning back to me. "But what's holding up the report? I may not live long enough to see it."

"Granny, you're going to outlive us all." I shut down that topic with a swiftness. "Mommy, tell us about Principal Smith. Teachers, staff, and students didn't like her. Do you have any idea why she was so miserable?"

Mommy flipped the fried plantains onto four plates. "Emily held people to high, high standards, ones she'd fall short of herself. When things went well, she'd preen like a peacock, even if she didn't have anything to do with it. But when things didn't work out, she was the first to cast blame on others. She never accepted any responsibility herself."

I'd worked for bosses like that, too. They leaped to take credit for your hard work and were equally eager to throw you under the bus at the first sniff of something being wrong. They couldn't be trusted.

I poured four tall glasses of cold mauby tea. "Can you think of something she may have done to the people who came to her dinner that would give them a motive to kill her?"

Granny helped Mommy carry the plates to the table.

I took the place setting closest to the kitchen door, listening for the bell above the bakery's entrance. I didn't want to miss any customers. Granny led us in saying the grace over our meals.

Mommy sliced into a succulent plantain. Its sweet aroma slipped free, kissing me from across the table. "Emily often blamed her admin if she'd neglected to do something that was her responsibility. If she'd missed a meeting that was on her calendar, she'd say her admin still should've reminded her. Or if she'd missed a deadline, she'd say it was because of her admin when they weren't even aware of the project."

Daddy swallowed a forkful of rice and peas. "Guy started working for Emily *after* you left. How do you know she did those things to him?"

Mommy swallowed another slice of plantain. "In the seven years I worked with Emily, she had ten admins and treated them all the same. What would make him different?"

Granny paused with her fork halfway to her mouth. "Ten assistants in seven years? *Woi.*"

Mommy nodded. "She complained and fussed, but she never fired them, you know. They always quit."

I considered the possibilities. "But Emily was retiring. Even if Guy felt she'd created a hostile work environment, would her behavior still be a reason to kill her?"

Seated beside me, Granny nudged me with her elbow. "Maybe he didn't think it was right that she should be able to retire and live her life after she'd made him so miserable."

I wasn't sure I agreed with that theory, but it was worth consideration.

Mommy took a deep drink of her tea. "She also was miserable to Daniel."

"He seemed very sure of himself." Granny sliced into her jerk chicken. "What'd she do to him?"

Mommy looked around the table at us. "When parents and teachers complained about the policies *she'd* created, she'd blame *him* for them."

Granny kissed her teeth.

"Wow." Daddy shook his head.

"I hate to speak ill of the dead, but Emily was a piece of work: mean, egotistical, manipulative. She also sounds like a coward." I would've hated working for her. I ate a bite of jerk chicken. Its full, spicy seasoning popped against my taste buds while I mulled over this image of Emily. "How'd she get along with Meera Singh? I told you about that argument they had in the restroom."

Mommy chewed thoughtfully. "Meera started working there a few months before I retired. But I remember she could never get to work on time. And she couldn't manage her inventory of medicines, either. She was always running out. Now maybe that's changed. It's been almost a year, you know."

I pictured again the middle-aged nurse slipping into the pharmacy, then disappearing. I didn't think much had changed in the year since my mother'd been away from the school. But that left the question what did Meera want at the pharmacy and why was she having so much trouble with her inventory?

Minutes later, we were clearing away the last of our lunch Thursday afternoon when the bell alerted us to additional lunch customers. *Hallelujah!* I quickly washed my hands before hustling back to the customer counter. My welcoming smile collapsed when I saw who'd walked through the doors, Bryce and Stan.

"Good afternoon, Detectives. How can I help you?" My tone was cool.

As usual, Stan looked like he'd climbed out of a shipping

box that had traveled from the opposite coast. His comfortable dark gray suit may have been in fashion fifteen years ago. His black loafers looked like they'd logged a lot of miles.

In contrast, Bryce looked ready for a photoshoot for a men's clothing catalog. He'd shoved his hands into his front pant pockets like he was striking a pose. "We have an update on the case."

So they came to the bakery rather than calling? I swallowed. Hard. Whatever he had to say, it couldn't be good.

I leaned toward the pass-through window. "Mommy, Daddy, Granny, could you come, please? The detectives have some information for us."

They gave me wide-eyed, worried looks. Dragging footsteps carried them to the customer service area.

Granny folded her hands in front of her. "What's this information you have for us?"

Bryce looked from me to my grandmother. "We have confirmation that Emily Smith was poisoned with strychnine."

"Oh, boy." My eyes stretched wide with dismay. "That's supposed to be really painful."

Strychnine was a pesticide. It was toxic. If ingested, death would come after painful convulsions and asphyxiation.

Stan furrowed his brow. "You're familiar with it?"

That was a loaded question. Should I pretend not to have heard of it and risk being caught in the lie? Or should I admit I'd heard of it and have them look at me with suspicion the way Stan was staring at me now?

"I've heard of it." I shrugged uncomfortably. "It's mentioned in a lot of mystery novels and crime shows."

Bryce took my attention from Stan. "The toxicology report didn't find any traces of poison in the food. We even tested the plates, silverware, glassware, and napkins. Everything came back clean."

"And this surprises you?" Granny arched an eyebrow. "Of course everything was clean. Our food is exceptional."

Stan smiled. "We know that, Ms. Bain."

Daddy nodded. "Good. So this means you've removed my wife from your suspect list."

Bryce exchanged a look with Stan. "Well, our investigation will continue to look at everyone who was present and had a motive, Mr. Murray. So although Ms. Murray's no longer at the top of the list, she still remains a person of interest."

Blood drained from my mother's face. Tears welled in her eyes. She blinked rapidly to hold them back. Daddy wrapped an arm around her waist to steady her.

A burning anger shot through me. "You've already interrogated my mother. You know she hadn't worked with, spoken to, or seen Emily Smith in almost a year. So what motive would she have to kill her *former* boss?"

Stan raised both of his hands. "Ms. Murray, I'm very sorry, but until we can prove your mother didn't handle the poison, our brass says she has to remain a person of interest."

My heart pounded so hard and fast in my chest, it made me sound breathless. "Do you know how Principal Smith was poisoned since we've already confirmed the poison wasn't in the food?"

"We haven't determined that yet." Stan massaged the back of his neck.

Daddy scowled. "You still have a lot of work then, Detectives." I heard the pain in his voice and it shattered me.

Bryce spread his arms. "Lyndsay—"

"Nope." I held up my hand, palm out. "Not one word from you."

"Unless it's to order something to eat." Granny gestured toward the menu on the wall behind the customer counter. She caught me staring at her. "Whaddayou? This is business. They've chased away our customers with their foolish talk about testing our food for poisons when there was *nothing wrong with it*. The least they can do is order something so the neighbors see them eating our food."

Stan's cheerful smile seemed inappropriate in the moment. "Actually, I did want to get some banana bread, two slices for me and one each for my partner here and my wife, please."

Granny circled the counter to cut the fresh slices of banana bread and package his order. The scents of bananas, sugar, butter, and vanilla were sweet distractions. With an effort, I held on to my mad as I processed Stan's payment. Bryce gave me another look before leaving. He wanted to speak, but I didn't want to hear him. Good looks could only get him so far. The fact was, we were once again on different sides of a conflict. I was standing with my family, and he was set against us.

Mommy's voice trembled. "I really believed once we proved the food wasn't poisoned, I'd be cleared. I never thought they'd still keep my name on their list."

"Neither did I." Daddy fisted his hands at his sides. "This isn't right. What can we do?"

"We'll have a family meeting tonight." I heard the anger in my voice and tried to tone it down for Mommy's sake. "I'll also call José to tell him about the toxicology report. Hopefully, he'll run an article reassuring people it's safe to return to the bakery. Bryce and Stan act like they have the whole summer to find Emily's killer, but every day they waste is another day for people to think you're a suspect and that our bakery's dangerous."

Mommy hugged her arms around her slim waist. "I'm still not comfortable with you investigating another murder."

Granny put her arm around my shoulders. "Don't worry. I'm not going to let her investigate alone."

My heart lodged in my throat. Having Granny along would guarantee *I* didn't take any risks. I couldn't say the same about her.

CHAPTER 12

We'd hung the Closed sign in the door and shut the blinds in preparation for our family meeting Thursday night. The bakery was a convenient place to gather. It was located halfway between all our homes and close to the subway for relatives getting off work like Dev, Uncle Al, Aunt Inez, and Manson, Reena's older brother. Reena telecommuted and Uncle Roman worked an early shift with the post office.

Granny, Mommy, Daddy, and I'd cooked dinner: stew chicken, callaloo, and dumplings, which we washed down with sorrel. The herbal drink looks like grape juice but tastes more like lemons. We'd pushed several tables together so the ten of us could sit as a group. During dinner, the conversation was light and filled with laughter. It continued as we worked together to clean up afterward. Many hands make light work. After the kitchen was once again spotless, we got down to business.

"It makes sense that the killer was one of Emily's guests." I wrote their names across the top of the whiteboard we used to highlight the bakery's daily specials.

"Which means the killer can't be too bright." Uncle Roman was my father's older brother. He must've gone home after his shift at the post office, where he worked as a mail carrier, to change into a bright orange jersey, baggy denim jeans, and nearly immaculate white sneakers. "Who's goin' to kill someone and make themselves a suspect? Not I. Why'd the killer decide to do the deed like that anyway? There're only six people there. And the principal, she didna kill she self. So that leaves only five people. You're not goin' to hide like that. Nah, man."

"Those are good points, Uncle Roman." Dev had taken a seat on the same side of the table as our uncle. He'd hung his emerald green tie and silver suit jacket on the back of his dark wood chair and unfastened the first button of his still-crisp white shirt. My chair stood empty between them. "I've been wondering the same thing. And why was the principal so adamant about having her dinner at the bakery? Lynds had turned them down several times before agreeing."

Uncle Roman warmed to his own speculations. "Listen, it would've been better to have poisoned her on the job, right? Put the poison in her coffee or something. Then you could blame the whole school. More people to give you cover and we wouldna be having all this mess, right?"

Granny scowled at him from her seat diagonally across the table. "But that's not what they did, eh? So what good does it do to talk about what they *should've* done, when it's not what they *did*?"

I jumped in to prevent an argument that would've wasted more time. "Uncle Roman, that's a good point. Thank you." Turning back to the whiteboard, I wrote: *Method: Strychnine.*

"We know the killer used strychnine. I've done some research on that poison. It's very toxic. It's mainly used as a pesticide. If someone ingests a lot of strychnine, it could cause them to go into convulsions. They would die from asphyxiation in fifteen to thirty minutes."

Aunt Inez sat at the front of the table. She looked very professional in her navy blue skirt suit. "But the food was fine. So how did she get the poison?"

Self-doubt slapped me like a cold wind.

I stood in front of my relatives, leading the meeting, writing on the whiteboard as though I knew what I was doing. I didn't. I felt like a fraud.

My eyes swept the tables we'd pushed together. Nine sets of eyes stared back at me, waiting for me to give them answers, a plan, hope. I locked my knees, praying they didn't start to shake. Yes, I'd been able to solve Claudio Fabrizi's murder when Bryce and Stan had me on the top of their suspect list. But could I do it again?

There was so much at stake this time, my mother's reputation, her freedom, the bakery. Did I have a choice?

I coughed to clear my throat. "That's a good question, Aunt Inez. Figuring that out will help us identify the killer. I'm sure of it. Someone must have given her the strychnine after she arrived at the bakery but before we served the food. We know we're dealing with at most a thirty-minute window for the drug to take effect. If we could estimate a timeline from when Emily entered the bakery until the convulsions started, we might be able to determine who'd been with her during that window of time to administer the poison."

"That's a good idea." Granny clapped her hands together. "From the time she arrived to the time she fell from her chair was about an hour, eh?"

Mommy pressed her right index finger against her lips. She lowered her eyes as she tried to remember that evening. "Emily was the next to last to arrive at the bakery. Meera reached after her, so it must have been minutes after six. We served the salad a good fifteen minutes after that."

Daddy took up the timeline. "Then we served the main course after twenty minutes passed."

"And minutes later, she was convulsing." Granny's voice was somber.

Uncle Al was beside Aunt Inez at the front of the table. Like Dev, he'd hung his red tie and dark suit jacket on the back of his chair. He'd rolled the sleeves of his snow-white shirt up to his elbows. "Had she been with everybody the whole time?"

"No, she hadn't." My answer drew all eyes to me. "When she arrived, she chatted with us and her staff." I looked to Mommy, Daddy, and Granny. They'd all been there with me. "Remember? She'd said things that upset every one of her guests."

Granny harrumphed. "How could I forget? She made everyone so vex no one wanted to smile for the photos."

I remembered the pictures. "Granny, could you email the photos to me? I want to send them to Bryce."

Granny wrote on her notepad. "I'll make myself a reminder to do that."

Before the meeting, Granny, Mommy, Daddy, and I had looked at the electronic files on Granny's camera. Each photo of Emily standing with one or more of her guests showed the principal unsmiling as she looked into the camera. The other people in the pictures had what seemed to be huge fake smiles.

"But after she spoke with us, Emily went to the restroom." I turned back to the board to make a note. "The nurse, Meera Singh, joined her. I heard them arguing." I could still hear the angry words. "Meera said, 'Why are you always so cold and callous?' Then Emily said, 'He'll get over it.' And Meera responded, 'You don't know that.'"

Everyone's eyes were wide with surprise and interest.

Reena broke the silence. "Who's 'he'? Who were they talking about?"

Manson was seated beside Reena. "That's what I want to know."

"I'm not sure." I rolled the marker between my hands. "But I was speaking with someone at the gym. Her young cousins attend Kings County Early. They told her about a rumor that Emily was dating the father of one of her staff."

"Eew." Reena's reaction made me smile. "Could it have been Meera's father? Do you think they were talking about him?"

"We should ask Meera." I added that to our notes.

"Wait, nuh." Uncle Roman sat up straighter on his chair. "By 'we,' d'you mean 'you'? Because I'm willing to contribute my brain to the investigation, but me, I don't think I have the time to question all these people and so."

Granny turned to Daddy. "Are you *sure* you're related?" It wasn't the first time she'd asked him this. She looked at Uncle Roman. "Don't worry, Roman; I'll help Lynds with the questioning."

"So will I," Reena chimed in. Manson and Aunt Inez echoed her words.

"I will, too." Uncle Al's voice was tight with concern. "I won't let my baby sis go on trial for a murder she didn't commit."

"Thank you." I smiled at everyone, including Uncle Roman. He could be a dark cloud on an otherwise bright day, but he was still family and we loved him. "The *Beacon* reported that there's a wake for Principal Smith tomorrow night. Our suspects may be there."

"That's a great idea." Uncle Al looked at Aunt Inez, Reena, and Manson. "We can make it."

"I can, too." Dev nodded. So did Mommy, Granny, and Daddy.

"I can try." Uncle Roman looked sheepish. "I'll check to see if I'm free."

"That's fine, Uncle Roman." I smiled to help ease his mind. "If you can make it, we'd love for you to come. Either way, we start questioning our suspects tomorrow night."

"'Investigating detectives confirmed toxicology tests came back negative for poisons in the food served during Smith's retirement dinner Monday evening at Spice Isle Bakery.'" By popular demand, I reread José's article in Friday's *Brooklyn Daily Beacon* as my family and I prepared to open the shop. Having the truth reported in black-and-white the same way Emily's death had been announced eased some of our anxiety.

Granny grunted from her spot in the doorway between the kitchen and the customer service area. "Hard to believe all this happened in only the last five days."

"It feels like a fortnight." Daddy mixed the ingredients for the hard dough bread.

"Or a month," Mommy added as she flipped the fish bakes in the frying pan.

I continued reading the news story. "'The community can be reassured that the food at Spice Isle Bakery is safe,' said Detective Bryce Jackson, one of the lead homicide investigators assigned to this case. Police believe Smith was the sole target for the poisoning. They're still looking into when and how the poison had been ingested, and the motive for the murder."

Granny jerked her chin toward the front of the store. "I

can see them so lining up now, and the line is long, *oui*. It looks like things are going back to the way they were."

"I'm glad Bryce made a point of emphasizing that our food is safe." Mommy gave me a deliberate look from over her shoulder. "It makes it sound more official coming from the police. Hopefully, it will bring the customers back sooner."

I heard the hidden message in my mother's words, *Bryce Jackson's not a bad guy.* Oh, yes, he is. "That quote is the least Bryce could do. Just because he can bring himself to say a few nice words about our cooking doesn't mean we're going to forget that he keeps trying to put members of our family in prison. At least I'm not going to."

Daddy shaped the fresh dough in preparation for placing it on the commercial baking tray. "Lynds, to be fair, he was doing his job. The community needed to know about the murder in the neighborhood. That's why he gave José that interview."

I wasn't willing to give Bryce any leeway in this case. "People need to be informed, especially about events happening right outside their doors. But Bryce—and José— implicated us before they had all the facts. That was irresponsible. It meant the only information our neighbors had was that someone died after eating at our bakery. Of course they worried that our food was tainted."

"Yes, it could've been handled better." Granny patted the bun at the nape of her neck, and smoothed her turquoise cotton blouse, which she'd paired with slim ruby polyester pants, in preparation for opening the bakery.

"All that's in the past, right? We have to move forward." Mommy removed the fish bakes from the frying pan, setting them on a colander to drain. "I think the young man likes you, you know, Lynds."

My face burned with embarrassment. Fortunately, it

was time to open the bakery. Avoiding eye contact with my parents, I crossed the kitchen to join Granny. "Investigating my mother for murder isn't the way to get my affection."

Daddy's laughter followed me as we gathered for the prayer before opening the bakery.

Later, I took my position behind the customer service counter, checking to make sure my chef's hat still completely covered my hair. Granny opened the front door and stepped back to greet our early-morning customers. Tanya and Benny were first in line again. Granny gave Tanya a strong hug before greeting Benny.

Tanya stepped to the side. "It was good to see the story in the paper. I didn't need it, but I know it was vindication for all you."

"Thank you." Granny squeezed her friend's hand.

Tanya hurried to join Benny at the front of the line to place their orders together.

I smiled at them. "Good morning, Ms. Nevis, Mr. Parsons. It's good to see you. How can I help you today?"

Seeing the bakery crowded again with familiar faces and even more unfamiliar ones felt like coming home. My heart was full. There was joy in my movements as I hurried to fill our guests' orders. It didn't even bother me that some people were looking around as though still expecting to find Emily's ghost.

"The bakery's back!" a youngish woman announced from the middle of the floor. She struck a pose, causing everyone behind her to retreat a step or two.

Startled, I turned to watch her. She'd been to the bakery a few times since we'd opened almost two months ago. She usually ordered hot items: beef patties, fish bakes, callaloo, and dumplings.

From her seat at her table, Granny arched an eyebrow

at her. "Oh-ho? And I thought we'd been here the whole time."

The woman's grin fell away. "I mean that, you know, we never believed anything was really wrong with you-all's food in the first place."

"Really?" Tanya stopped on her way out the door. "Then where were all you?"

Several guests looked away in discomfort. An embarrassed silence lay over the store.

I cleared my throat. "Thank you, Ms. Nevis. You're a good friend." I turned my attention to the rest of the room. "We understand that, out of an abundance of caution, many of you were waiting to get an official announcement that it's safe to return to our bakery. I'm glad you're giving us this opportunity to reassure you. We take your safety very seriously, which is the reason we use only the highest-quality ingredients and serve our food fresh."

Granny interrupted. "That's one of the reasons our food is exceptional."

I continued. "You're back now. Welcome. We're so glad to see you again."

Their applause was unexpected. It started as a trickle and built to a crescendo. Granny joined, her dark eyes gleaming with pride. The commotion drew my parents from the kitchen. They wrapped me in a hug between them.

"We heard what you said," Daddy whispered. "We're so proud of you, Lynds."

Mommy kissed my cheek. "This bakery will be a success and it will be because of you."

"But why did someone poison the principal in your bakery?" the Knicks Fan asked. "Were they trying to target your business?"

My muscles stiffened in reaction to his question. I'd

wondered the same thing. Was someone trying to shut down our bakery? "I don't think so. There are ways to hurt our shop without killing someone."

No, the more I thought about it, the more it seemed the harm to our business and to Mommy's reputation wasn't intentional, but that didn't make the need to solve the case any less urgent.

CHAPTER 13

"Where is everyone?" I scanned the room assigned for Emily Smith's wake in disbelief. Attendance was dismal at the Tailor Avenue Funeral Parlor Friday evening.

The school had thousands of students with thousands of parents, scores of teachers, and dozens of staff. That wasn't counting members of the school board, their support staff, and representatives of other schools in the system. Yet fewer than fifty people had shown up in a room that could easily seat two hundred. Such a shame. It was a reminder of how poorly Emily must have treated the people she'd worked with and those she'd worked for.

The room was well lit and at least twice the size of the bakery's customer service and dining areas combined. It smelled old and dusty. Cushioned dark metal folding chairs were assembled in three sections across the worn red, blue, and gold paisley-patterned carpeting. Faded blue-and-silver-striped paper covered the walls.

Emily's casket was a simple, unfinished wood structure placed in the front of the room. The funeral home had done a wonderful job preparing her for the service. She looked as though she was finally at peace. A beautiful, large wreath of white roses and carnations was arranged beside the casket. Its note was signed by the school board members. The modest arrangement of white lilies next to it was sent anonymously.

My family and I had paid our respects to Emily before taking seats on the right side of the room near the doors. Granny, Mommy, Daddy, Dev, and I had arrived minutes before eight. Uncle Al, Aunt Inez, Manson, and Reena had joined us shortly after.

"Maybe not everyone saw the announcement about the wake in the paper." Seated on my left, Granny looked around the room as though searching for spaces where people could be hiding.

I could believe her theory, but a better reason for the poor attendance was that Emily was universally disliked. "At least most of the people we want to speak with are here. Meera's the only one I haven't seen yet."

When we'd first arrived, I'd given everyone their assignments. Mommy and Daddy would speak with Guy Law, Emily's administrative assistant. I knew Daddy wouldn't want to speak with Daniel Rawson since he was convinced the assistant principal had a crush on Mommy. Instead, Uncle Al and Aunt Inez would question Daniel.

Reena and her older brother, Manson, would try to get information from Miguel Morales, the guidance counselor. I'd asked Dev and Granny to talk with June Min-ho. I'd paired them because I needed someone assertive enough to keep Granny from doing her best police procedural impersonation. Also, since the librarian and Mommy were friends, if Mommy spoke with her, her report could be biased. That left me to question Meera Singh, the school nurse. I needed to find a subtle way of asking whether her father had been in a relationship with Emily and why she'd gone to our neighborhood pharmacy during school hours.

The front rows, usually reserved for the deceased's family and close friends, were empty. Either Emily didn't have living relatives or for some reason they couldn't make the trip. That would explain the inexpensive casket.

I reached around Granny's back to tap Mommy's shoulder. "Do you see any of Emily's family?"

Mommy shrugged. "I wouldn't know them. As I said, Emily didn't discuss her family, at least not with me. And she didn't have pictures of them."

That was weird. I talked about my family with everyone who'd listen. But people were different. Maybe Emily had a strict code about keeping her personal and professional lives separate. But then what about the rumor that she was dating the father of a member of her staff? Talk about breaking the rules.

Guy and Daniel stood toward the front of the room, conversing with a tall woman whose professionally styled chestnut hair gleamed under the fluorescent lights. She was the school board president. I recognized her smooth white features from newspaper photos. Guy was doing most of the talking. Daniel kept checking his watch. The school board president had zoned out.

Across the room, June sat alone in the second-to-last row. Behind her, Miguel stood speaking with José. I'd had a feeling the crime beat reporter would be here. After all, the event was connected to the homicide he was covering. What was the guidance counselor telling him? And what were the chances either of them would share their information before José's article appeared in tomorrow's paper?

I glanced at the door behind us in time to see Bryce

and Stan stride across the threshold. Stan looked his usual rumpled self in a brown suit with matching tie. Bryce looked like a fashion model in a slate gray suit and cobalt blue tie. As though sensing my attention, he turned his head. His hazel eyes locked onto mine. I felt warm. Did we stay like that for a few seconds or a few minutes?

I broke eye contact and turned away. "Detectives Jackson and Milner are here." Granny frowned and started to turn. I put my hand on her shoulder to stop her. "Don't look. It would make it obvious we're talking about them."

Reena must not have heard me. Seated on my right, she shifted toward the door and waved. I closed my eyes in misery. For my next investigation, I'd need people who knew how to stay under the radar.

She spoke without looking away from the detectives. "It's too bad Detective Fine keeps trying to put our family in prison. He's not hard on the eyes."

I know, right? "Focus on the mission, Reena."

She shifted on her seat again. "I wish they'd get started already. This place smells. It's after eight. These seats are uncomfortable. And did I mention this place smells?"

Daniel was the first speaker to approach the podium "Good evening, everyone, and thank you for coming." He spoke slowly as though trying to fill time. "We're here to remember our late principal, Emily Smith, who died just days before her retirement. I only worked with Emily for a few years. She was a very private person, so we didn't know each other well. But I did learn that she was tireless and relentless. I'll now welcome School Board President Alice Duran to say a few words."

The school board president seemed startled to have been called on so abruptly.

Reena gave a surprised laugh. "That's it? No comments

about how he'll miss working with her or what she meant to the school?"

Granny leaned forward to catch our attention. "Maybe guilt held his tongue."

Reena narrowed her eyes. "Yeah, we have to talk to that guy."

Meera arrived as the school board president was walking to the podium. She entered through the far doors behind June. Her arm was around an older man who was sobbing inconsolably into a handkerchief.

I tipped my head in their direction. "Meera Singh's arrived. Do you think the man with her is her father? He must've been the one dating Principal Smith."

"What can I say about Emily Smith?" Alice Duran's question made me think she either hadn't prepared anything or she didn't know Emily well. "She was a tough administrator who'd dedicated twenty-seven years of her life to education. She'd spent almost half of that time here at Kings County Early College High School. She understood the importance of a good education. And for that, we will always be grateful. Thank you."

Granny leaned against me. "Her speech was real short, too. Maybe we should put her on the list."

I chuckled. "Granny, if that was the criteria, everyone in this room would be a suspect."

Daniel returned to the podium. "Thank you, President Alice Duran, for your remarks. And with that, we'd like to open up the floor for anyone else who'd like to share a remembrance of Principal Smith." He paused. "Anyone?" This time, he waited a little longer. "Well, feel free to spend a few more moments mingling and talking among yourselves. If anyone changes their mind and would like to say a few words, we'll be happy to listen."

I waited for Daniel to step away from the podium before standing. "We have our assignments. Let's get our answers, then meet back here in half an hour."

"Excuse me, Meera." I rested a gentle hand on the school nurse's shoulder, drawing her attention from the older gentleman beside her. Her brown cotton blouse was soft beneath my palm. "I wanted to express my sympathy to both of you on Emily's passing. She must have been very important to you."

"Thank you." Meera sounded distracted. She continued rubbing her right hand in comforting circles against the older man's back. Her warm brown eyes were dark with pain.

My attention shifted to her companion. Was this Meera's father—and Emily's ex?

Drawing the scraps of my self-confidence around me like a cloak, I stepped in front of him. His grief hit me like a blast of hot air. "I'm Lyndsay Murray, sir."

He cleared his throat and dried his cheeks with his wilted handkerchief before meeting my eyes. "Raza Singh."

Ah. My suspicions were confirmed. Here was Meera's father. "I'm so sorry for your loss, Mr. Singh. I can tell you're in a lot of pain. Did you know Principal Smith well?"

Meera ran interference. Her voice was hard. "My father's not up to speaking just now."

"I understand." I'd anticipated her objection. I'd have been the same way if my parent was in so much grief and a stranger tried to question them. "Sometimes when you're grieving, it helps to talk with someone you may not know well. Someone who can just listen rather than trying to fix a situation for you."

Raza cleared his throat again. "We'd been dating for a

while. I cared for her. I'd hoped to marry her." The admission brought another round of sobs.

Meera resumed rubbing his back. I caught snatches of the words she murmured to him. "I'm so sorry, Dad. I'm here. I'm so sorry."

Emily's thoughtless words whispered in my ear, *He'll get over it.* She must have thought it would be a lot easier for Raza to "get over" their breakup. After meeting Emily, so did I. She must've been very different around Meera's father.

My heart was breaking for him. I didn't know if I had it in me to cause this man more pain by questioning him, at least not this evening. But time wasn't on my side. Even as I stood there dithering, the detectives were circling the wake like sharks, looking for suspects in Emily's murder. My mother was near the top of their list. I needed to clear her name, the sooner the better for her, our family, and our business.

Noticing again Raza's well-used handkerchief, I fished a packet of tissues from my purse and offered it to him.

"No, thank you, Lyndsay." Raza struggled to his feet. "I'm going to get some water from the fountain in the hall-way."

Meera stood, too. "I'll come with you."

"No, stay and talk with your friend." He gestured toward me. "I won't be long."

Meera looked like she wanted to argue, but instead she watched him leave, her face creased with concern.

I returned the tissues to my purse. "Your father was the reason you and Emily were arguing at the bakery Monday evening, wasn't he? When did she break up with him?"

Meera's eyes shot daggers at me. That's when I remembered how much I disliked confrontations. I wasn't good at them. Why, for heaven's sake, had I chosen to question a suspect on my own? I'd paired everyone else. Why hadn't I chosen a partner for myself?

My reflexes urged me to take a step back, away from the conflict. But my need to protect my mother kept me rooted in place.

Meera fisted her hands at her sides. "How is that any of your business?" Her voice trembled with fury.

"I understand your anger. She'd hurt your father. I would've been angry, too."

Her frown darkened. "What's your point?"

I gathered my courage. "How angry were you at Emily, Meera? Were you angry enough to hurt her?"

"How dare you?"

I'd dare a lot to make sure my family was safe. Thanks for asking. "You're the one who'd predicted one day her cruelty would come back to haunt her."

She glanced over her shoulder before looking back at me. "I'd warned my father not to get involved with Emily. He's a kind and sensitive man. She was a witch. I was glad when she'd ended things with him, but I hated the way she did it. She didn't have to hurt him, but she did because she enjoyed it. And she knew how much it would hurt me."

Before I could respond, the other woman turned and marched out of the room. Her three-inch heels were silent against the worn carpet. *Darn!* I didn't get a chance to ask why she'd been in Little Caribbean Thursday morning when she should've been at work.

"Tell me you're not investigating another murder, Lyndsay." Bryce's voice came from behind me.

I cringed. How much of my exchange with Meera had he overheard? And why should I care? I had every right to speak with her. Since Bryce was focused on my mother, I wasn't getting in the way of his investigation. That was sarcasm, by the way.

Turning, I was startled to find him so close. I stepped back. "My family and I are here, paying our respects. What're *you* doing here?" I was buying myself time to gather my wits for this latest confrontation with one of New York's finest—literally and figuratively.

His eyes swept back and forth across my face. Was he searching for signs of subterfuge? "Stan and I are working. Usually, the killer attends the wake or funeral of their victim. They like to see the effects of their actions on the community and the victim's loved ones." I heard a hint of disgust in his voice.

It took a special kind of evil to inflict so much pain on people, then sit back and gloat about it. As I scanned the room, I felt his eyes on my profile. "Have you learned anything to help your investigation?"

"You know I can't discuss an open case, especially with—" He stopped himself, but it was too late.

I arched an eyebrow at him. "Especially with . . . the daughter of your prime suspect?"

"Your mother's not my prime suspect."

"But she *is* a suspect."

"I'm sorry, Lyndsay." Bryce moved forward, shrinking the distance between us again. "I promise I'm doing everything I can to rule her out. But I hope you're not investigating. This is a *murder*. It's too dangerous for you to get involved. I almost lost you last time."

I blinked, backing up again. Was that a blush staining his sharp cheekbones? "You almost lost me?"

"You know what I mean." He looked around uncomfortably.

"Do *you* know what you mean?" Irritation bubbled in my veins. This time, *I* stepped forward. "Let's be clear. You can't *lose* me because you don't *have* me. I don't get involved with people who're trying to put members of my family in jail."

Without giving him a chance to respond, I turned on my heel and went in search of my relatives.

Bryce Jackson had been my high school crush. I'd be lying if I said I wasn't still attracted to him. But Detective Fine wasn't going to talk me out of proving my mother's innocence.

CHAPTER 14

The shop had been crazy busy Saturday and Sunday. As I dragged myself into the office Monday morning, I was almost glad the bakery was closed. Don't get me wrong. I was grateful business had picked up again. We needed to do even more to increase foot traffic. But it was as though after staying away for two days—Wednesday and Thursday—customers were making up for lost time.

Crossing to the cherrywood desk, I turned on the laptop. As I waited for the system to boot up, I put away my purse and settled in. There were a lot of maintenance tasks to do on our down days, including updating the bookkeeping, checking produce and non-produce inventories, scheduling marketing and promotion, and cleaning. But the first item on my task list was reviewing our notes on the suspects for Emily Smith's murder. As important as the bakery was, my family meant more.

We'd had a debriefing after the wake Friday evening. We hadn't gotten as much information as I'd thought we would. It's not like I'd expected one of our main suspects to make a spontaneous confession, but I'd hoped someone would say too much—or just enough. Today, I planned to supplement our debriefing notes with additional research on our suspects. The past few days, I hadn't been able to focus on anything other than the bakery. It had been that busy, and Dev had spent all weekend at the firm, so he hadn't been able to help. I made a mental note to check on him before the end of the day. We hadn't had much of a chance to talk Thursday or Friday. I wanted to make sure he was all right.

The phone rang, scattering my thoughts. The caller ID displayed a Kings County Early College High School phone number.

"Spice Isle Bakery. May I help you?"

"Hello, Lyndsay? This is Guy Law, administrative assistant to the principal of Kings County Early College High School." He sounded like he was representing the President of the United States. He could've introduced himself as "Guy." I'd've known who he was.

"Good morning, Guy. How can I help you?"

He cleared his throat. "Lyndsay, Kings County Early has decided against paying the remainder of the bill for Principal Smith's retirement dinner last Monday evening."

What? Oh, no, no, no. This is not the time and I am not the one.

Fisting my hands, I called on the ancestors to keep me from acting a *foofool*. I unclenched my teeth. "How did the school come to make that decision?"

Through the line, I heard a series of staccato taps as though Guy was nervously hitting his fingertips against his desk. This wasn't an easy call to make. It wasn't easy to receive, either.

Guy's deep breath sounded through the receiver. "The school board feels that it would be unfair to make us pay for food we didn't eat."

I closed my eyes. This was ridiculous. "It doesn't work

that way, Guy. The food was purchased and prepared specifically for your event. The plates were individually served to each of you during the dinner—"

He interrupted me. "But we didn't eat it."

"That doesn't matter. It was purchased, prepared, and served for your event. According to health department guidelines, we can't serve it to anyone else once it was served to you. And, you'll remember, we offered to make takeaway bags for each of you before you left the bakery."

Guy stammered, "B-b-but we turned it down."

"That doesn't matter. None of that matters." I took another calming breath to control my rising voice.

Guy paused. "The board's made its decision, Lyndsay."

And that decision put me in an unacceptable position. Not only were we owed money for our time and services, but there were other factors to consider, like our reputation once again. On the one hand, arguing against their position would be distasteful in light of Emily's death. On the other hand, accepting the school's verdict could make us seem guilty of her murder. No, I couldn't let this judgement stand.

I made an effort to sound calm and reasonable. "We have a contract, Guy. The bakery acted in good faith. We expect to get paid what we're owed."

The tapping returned. "It's out of my hands."

That wasn't going to fly with me. "Then tell me whose hands it's in, because someone's going to pay us."

Guy cleared his throat again. "You could speak with Assistant Principal Daniel Rawson. He's the interim principal until the board officially names Principal Smith's replacement. Do you want me to transfer you?"

I thought quickly. "No, I'll call him back."

After saying goodbye to Guy, I called my parents and

grandmother to update them on the billing situation. They were part owners of the bakery, along with Dev. As I expected, they were outraged. During our conference call, they spoke over one another.

"They need to write the check." Granny raised her voice.

"But how do they think we're not supposed to be paid?" Mommy's voice went up several octaves.

Daddy's voice deepened. "Do you want Dev to call them as our lawyer?"

"Let me speak with Mr. Rawson first." The idea made me uncomfortable. Remember, I was confrontation averse. But as the majority business owner with 40 percent of the bakery, I felt I had to try to resolve the issue on my own.

"Good for you." Granny sounded surprised.

"That's a good idea." I heard the pride in Daddy's voice.

"Are you going to call him?" Mommy asked.

I shook my head, though they couldn't see me. "I'm going to the school. I don't want to give him the chance to duck my calls."

Kings County Early College High School was a public school, but they weren't above private industry tactics and I was well aware of those games. I could fill their voicemail with message after message, which they'd just keep ignoring in the hopes I'd go away. Well, surprise, surprise, I wasn't going away without a check for payment in full. We needed this money. We were entitled to this money.

We were getting our money.

I ended our discussion with a promise to call them after meeting with Daniel. As I drove to the high school, I realized I was surprising myself. I didn't like confrontations. I especially didn't like face-to-face ones, but growing this bakery was taking me into experiences way out of my comfort zone.

Like murder investigations.

The dimmed hallways were empty when I arrived at Kings County Early College High School. That made sense. It was minutes after nine o'clock Monday morning. Classes were in session. The two-inch heels of my brown shoes tapped against the gray cement flooring. The sound echoed against the dull walls. The air was stale and stuffy, and as muggy as a midsummer day in New York. The HVAC system must be on the fritz. That had happened often when I'd attended the rival Flatbush Early College High School.

The walls were lined with aged metal combination lockers that were a deeper gray than the scuffed flooring. Interspersed among the lockers were dark wood class-room doors. I walked through the smells of adolescent sweat, hair gel, cheap perfume, and bargain disinfectant on my way to the administrative offices. The surroundings brought back memories of my high school years. They weren't pleasant. I'd been small, shy, and bookish. Those qualities had labeled me a nerd and made me a target of the "in" crowd and those who'd aspired to be popular. Being back in this high school setting reawakened the tension from those experiences. I shrugged my shoulders, trying to dislodge the strain. The administrative office was waiting at the end of the hall. I'd speak with Daniel Rawson, make him understand the school's contractual obligation to pay our bakery, then get out.

"Lyndsay, it's good to see you again." Miguel Morales paused in the hallway outside the administrative office.

The guidance counselor was average height, perhaps

five feet ten, and fit. He looked smart in a slim navy suit, snow-white cotton shirt, and wide cool gray tie.

"Good morning, Miguel." I came to a stop in front of him. "I didn't get a chance to express my condolences to you yesterday during Principal Smith's wake."

Instead, Reena and Manson had spoken with him. They'd thought Miguel had seemed solemn enough for the occasion. He'd told them he'd started working for the high school after the Christmas break, so he hadn't known Emily well. She'd been a tough boss, but he'd had other tough bosses, something Miguel and I had in common.

"Thank you. And to learn she'd been murdered." He shook his head as though speechless. "The police were at the wake Friday night."

"Yes, I saw them."

"It was unsettling." He seemed to shake off this disquiet. "Is there anything I can help you with?"

I inclined my head toward the double glass doors leading to the administrative suite. "I'm meeting with Daniel Rawson."

Miguel's expression shifted as though he was masking his feelings. "You'll find him in the principal's office."

I raised my eyebrows. "That didn't take long." I hoped my response would encourage more confidences from him.

"It's been barely a week. Emily's name's still on the door. And there's no reason for him to move to her office. I would've thought he'd have waited until the summer, especially since the police are investigating her murder." Miguel reached around me to open the door and hold it as I preceded him into the suite.

During the family debriefing Friday night, Uncle Al and Aunt Inez had said they'd asked Daniel who the interim principal would be since Emily had been murdered before the school board had identified her replacement. He'd said he'd fill the position and that he was going to make a lot of changes, but he didn't give specifics. Daniel had been impatient to ascend to the throne.

Impatient enough to kill the queen?

Miguel pointed me toward the principal's office before disappearing in the opposite direction, presumably to his own work space.

As he was the principal's administrative assistant, Guy's desk was outside Emily's—now Daniel's—door. My steps slowed as I had a mental flashback of him hanging Emily's coat on the back of her chair. Had he done something with the strychnine then?

I pushed the thought to the back of my mind. For now. "Good morning, Guy. I'd like to speak with Daniel, please."

He looked up in surprise. His eyes widened and his lips formed a perfect O. He must not have expected me to make the trip to the school. That made two of us. Mommy and Daddy had spoken with him during Friday's wake. He'd been friendly and polite, but they'd said he'd seemed uncomfortable. He'd avoided eye contact with them. What had he been hiding? Was it information about Emily's murder—or had he known Friday night that the school was going to break our contract and not pay its final bill?

"Oh, hello, Lyndsay." His eyes drifted away from mine. "I'm sorry. I don't know if Interim Principal Rawson is available."

I nodded toward his phone. "Why don't you check?"

"Sure." He swallowed. Picking up his receiver, he tapped a few buttons with visibly shaking fingers. "Mr. Rawson, Ms. Murray's here to speak with you." A pause. "No, not Cedella Murray. Her daughter, Lyndsay." Another pause. "Yes, sir." He cradled the receiver. "Please go in."

"Thank you." I walked past him and into the principal's office.

All traces of Emily Smith were gone. Any photos she may have hung, knickknacks she'd displayed, or mementoes she'd kept had been removed. The room was stuffy and carried the faint smell of old carpeting and strong coffee. Desks, walls, and bookcases exhibited awards, certificates, and photos of Daniel with various high-profile officials, including the school board president, borough president, and mayor. It looked as though the space had been his for years.

"Good morning, Lyndsay." Daniel's voice was deep and calm. He set his black porcelain mug on his desk beside his phone and sat back against his chair. "I understand you're upset about the retirement dinner, but the board has made its decision."

I stepped forward and positioned myself behind one of his two navy-cushioned guest seats. I locked my knees and dug my fingertips into the chair's cushioned back. "The board didn't sign the contract, Daniel. You did. And your signature is your commitment to pay for the services my family provided."

Daniel leaned into the table. "As you know, Emily collapsed before the dinner ended."

My grip on the chair tightened as my anger stirred again. "Do you read the news? The police's toxicology report confirmed our food wasn't tampered with. Wherever she got that poison, it wasn't from us." *Which means it had to have been from one of you.* "You have to pay us the money we're due."

"But no one ate the food." Frustration bled from Daniel's words.

Welcome to my world. "That was *your* choice. We were hired to provide the venue, cook the food, and take the photos. You'll remember we offered to fix to-go boxes. No one took us up on our offer."

Daniel threw up his arms. "Can you blame us? Emily had just been poisoned. We didn't know whether the food was safe or not." He paused, narrowing his eyes at me. "Why're you looking at me like that?"

"How could you have known Emily had been poisoned *before* she'd been taken to the hospital?"

Daniel's expression went blank. He stared at me, frozen for a heartbeat. "We'll pay you what you're owed, the full amount. I'll have the check cut by the end of the week."

"How had you known about the poison, Daniel?" A pulse fluttered in my throat. Was I once again alone in a room with a killer? Luckily, there were other people in the office suite.

Daniel sighed, running a hand over his hair. "I didn't. It's just . . . the way she convulsed . . . I assumed. And then the newspaper confirmed it. But I didn't know. That's the truth." He sat back on his chair. "I'll have the check for you by Friday, before noon."

"I'll pick it up then. Thank you." I tossed the words over my shoulder as I hurried from his office.

Had Daniel been telling the truth about *assuming* Emily had been poisoned before the newspaper had confirmed it? That had been a significant slip of the tongue. And he'd already moved into her office. My steps slowed as I remembered Emily stumbling against Daniel as she'd left the restroom with Meera. Had he planned that somehow so he could inject her with the strychnine?

He had motive and opportunity. Daniel Rawson had just moved to the top of my suspect list.

CHAPTER 15

I stopped at Guy's desk again before leaving the high school's administrative office suite Monday morning. "The check for the remaining balance of Emily's dinner will be ready Friday afternoon. I've told Daniel I'll pick it up."

Guy's thick red eyebrows leaped up his wide forehead. "You got Daniel to change his mind?"

"Why does that surprise you?"

His brown eyes widened. "Daniel's really stubborn. He used to make Emily crazy. Once he made up his mind, he wouldn't budge no matter what. I don't like speaking ill of the dead, but Emily was bullheaded, too. Anyway, I'm glad you're getting paid."

"So am I." My mind was spinning.

Why had Daniel changed his mind? Was it guilt? Was he trying to buy my silence about Emily's poisoning?

Guy glared over his shoulder toward Daniel's office. "I can't believe he had me make that call. And then to tell you it was the board's decision when it was really his. He said he was going to be different from Emily, but they're both the same. Egomaniacs who're too chicken to do their own dirty work. So they get other people to do it."

I shifted my stance, leaning my right hip against the front of Guy's dark wood desk. This let me keep one eye on Daniel's doorway. I didn't want the interim principal sneaking up on us. "How did you come to choose our bakery for Principal Smith's retirement dinner?"

"I didn't." Guy shrugged. "She did. She really liked Caribbean food. So do I. I'm sorry I didn't get to try yours. It smelled great. I'll be back."

"Thank you." The compliments on our food always made me feel great, but I had to stay focused on my investigation. "There are a lot of other bakeries and restaurants in the area, though. Why had she been so insistent to have the dinner at ours?"

"I just thought she'd picked your bakery because she knew your mother. She always spoke highly of her. Then after you caught that other baker's killer, she became obsessed with having her retirement dinner at your restaurant."

Obsessed? That was strange. "But why?"

Guy shrugged. "I don't know. Maybe she wanted to be associated with your family because you were seen as community heroes."

Strange. "From what people have told me, Emily was an abusive boss."

Guy held my eyes. Sparks of fury shimmered in his. "They're right. She was impossible to please. Nothing was ever good enough for her. She was always *looking* for things to criticize. But, as I said, I don't like speaking ill of the dead."

"Why did you stay?"

"I want to work in education. And I do like my job. It's not all ordering office supplies or answering the phone. I get to organize events like retirement dinners, school concerts, fund-raisers, open houses, stuff like that."

Was Granny right? Could Guy have decided to poison Emily because she was a horrible boss and he didn't want her to be happy in retirement?

Guy's expression cleared as though he'd realized he was being too free with his responses. "I already spoke with the police. Did I think Emily was a nightmare to work for? Yes. We all did. She was a witch. May she rest in peace. She treated us like chess pieces, lining us up to fight each other. It was ridiculous. Your mother was smart to leave. I'm looking for another job, too."

"Even though you have a new boss?"

Guy laughed without humor. "I told you. They're both the same. Besides, this job was never supposed to be permanent. It's a first step in my education career."

Education was a noble field and very important in our society. How far did he want to go? I looked around the office. "Did Emily know about your ambitions?"

He frowned. "Why're you asking?"

"You didn't want to be here permanently, but you've lasted longer than your predecessors. Why do you think that is?"

"I've been looking for other employment. I just haven't found anything suitable yet." Guy looked at me as though it was my fault he couldn't find a new job.

Sensing Guy wasn't willing to answer any more questions, I straightened to leave. "I wish you luck with your search."

Wanting your boss's job, like Daniel, and being sick of her abuse, like Guy, didn't seem like strong enough motives for murder, especially days before your victim retired. But the police were pinning a similar motive on Mommy. There was one big difference in applying that motive to my mother versus Guy or Daniel, though. Emily hadn't been my mother's boss in almost a year. At the time of her murder, Guy and Daniel had still been working for her.

"Lyndsay!"

I turned at the sound of someone shouting my name down the school hallway as I left the administrative office suite Monday morning. June Min-ho, the school's librarian, was hurrying toward me. A big smile brightened her delicate features and drew a smile from me.

"Good morning, Ms. Min-ho."

"Please call me June." She stopped less than an arm's length from me. "What're you doing here?"

I nodded toward the suite to our right. "There was a little confusion with the retirement dinner invoice. I came to clear it up."

"Confusion?" June's dark eyes twinkled. "Did Daniel try to stiff you on the bill? What a tightwad. He's always trying to cheat our vendors. He's giving the school a bad reputation."

I matched my steps to June's as we walked toward the exit. "We'd signed a contract. Fortunately, I was able to get him to change his mind."

"Good." June nodded. "You'd think the money was coming out of his wallet. He thinks saving money makes him look good to the board." She lowered her voice. "Actually, it made *Emily* look good. I don't think Daniel realized she took the credit when he cheated vendors."

I shook my head. "Daniel made the decision to cheat the vendors. Guy made the call to them, and Emily took the credit? Poor Guy."

"No doubt." June slipped her hands into the front pockets of her chocolate jumper. The color warmed her eyes. "How's Cedella? I'm so glad the toxicology report cleared the bakery."

"She's doing well." It was a small fib. "Thank you. I'll tell her you asked."

"Thank you. Although I knew there wasn't anything wrong with the food. I think I ate more of my entrée than Emily had and I was fine. It was *so* delicious. I'll definitely be back."

Her promise to return to the bakery took the sting out of the memory of June declining our offer of a to-go box. The period change bell sounded as we were within steps of the exit. I'd timed that well. I didn't want to be caught in the hall during classroom changes. The environment already was giving me post-traumatic stress. Period change would send me over the edge. June followed me through the door.

I turned to her. "How are *you*? Emily's murder must be very upsetting."

She nodded. "Emily wasn't well-liked, but I can't believe someone would kill her. It's scary to think I'm working with a murderer."

I glanced back at the school, then lowered my voice. "You think one of your coworkers poisoned Emily?"

"It's the only thing that makes sense, isn't it?" June also was whispering. "I mean, since that night a week ago today, we've all been looking at each other differently."

"Do you have any idea who would've done it?"

"That's just it." She looked over her shoulder as though checking to make sure no one heard us. "We didn't *like* her, but I can't believe any of us would *kill* her. We've worked together for years." She hesitated. Her gaze wandered back behind her shoulder. "Although I was wondering about Daniel."

Mr.-Skip-Out-on-My-Bills? "What about him?"

"Well . . . I really shouldn't gossip."

Was she serious? "Emily was murdered, June. You said

you were afraid. The only way you can feel safe again is if the killer's caught."

She wrung her hands. "But this probably doesn't have any bearing on anything. I mean, I probably shouldn't've said anything. Pretend I didn't say anything."

"I can't. Someone was attacked in my bakery. The police are looking at my mother—"

"Cedella!" June gaped. *"That's crazy."*

"I know." I clenched and unclenched my fists at my sides. "June, if you have any information that could clear my mother's name and help identify the killer, you've got to tell me."

June hesitated. I sensed her struggle between helping to prove her friend's innocence and implicating a potentially innocent person. I understood the dilemma. I didn't like digging into other people's private lives, trying to find proof of their guilt. But it was the only way to get to the truth.

She sighed. "Daniel and Emily had worked together for years. It wasn't a secret that they didn't like each other. Emily was always blaming Daniel for mistakes she'd made, whether it was missed deadlines for projects she was supposed to complete or unpopular school policies she'd decided unilaterally to implement."

"I'd heard that." I hoped admitting that would make June feel better about sharing this information with me.

She smiled as though relieved. "Well, his performance evaluations had always been OK. Nothing to brag about, but they didn't cause him any problems. Until last year."

"What happened last year?"

"Emily decided to retire. Everyone knew Daniel wanted her job. It wasn't a secret. He'd wanted it for years. But out of the blue, Emily decided she didn't want him to have it. So she gave him a bad evaluation. A really, really bad one. He's contesting it."

"Good for him." That kind of petty meanness was inexcusable. But was it enough to push Daniel to kill Emily out of revenge? "If the board rules in his favor, he could still become principal, right?"

"That's right."

I started to leave but turned back. "June, how did you know about Daniel's evaluation and that he's contesting it?"

She hesitated. "I have a friend on the board. They told me in confidence." A faint blush highlighted her cheekbones.

I'd read enough romcoms to recognize the signs. "Are the two of you also keeping your relationship a secret?"

She gaped at me. "I . . . We're not . . ." A deep breath. "Yes, so please don't say anything."

"I'll keep your secret. My family will, too." I waved goodbye as I jogged to my car.

I told my family everything, but I'd only tell them about June's informant if it was necessary. I was more excited to tell them—and the detectives —all the reasons Daniel should now be their prime suspect.

CHAPTER 16

"Have you looked into Daniel Rawson, the high school's assistant principal?" I asked Bryce over the phone at the Spice Isle Bakery office later Monday morning. I took a breath to compose myself. My words were coming too fast, tripping over one another in excitement.

Before calling Bryce at the precinct, I'd called Granny, Mommy, and Daddy to reassure them Daniel had agreed to authorize payment for the outstanding balance we were owed for Emily's retirement dinner. I told them I'd pick up the check from the school Friday, please God. I blushed again, remembering the praise they'd poured over me for handling the situation successfully on my own. It felt good to have faced my fears. It was even better when the results turned out in my favor.

I also told them why I thought Daniel should be the police's prime suspect in Emily's murder. I didn't want to get their hopes up, but it was important for everyone to know we were making progress in our investigation.

"Lyndsay, we spoke with everyone who was at the restaurant that night. You know that." His warm baritone flowing straight into my ear made it hard for me to think.

I set the receiver on the table and put him on speaker.

Better. "I'm not asking if you spoke with him. I want to know whether you dug into *his* background the same way you dug into my mother's." I sensed him thinking, trying to figure out where my question would lead him. I didn't have time for that. My mother's freedom and reputation were on the line. My family was worried and my business was suffering. "Well? Did you?"

"We've collected some information on his employment history." His delivery was cautious. "And we know that, like your mother, Rawson didn't get along with the victim. But you know I can't discuss open cases. Why're you asking?"

"*Not* 'like my mother.'" My tone was sharp. His response had tweaked my temper. Although he couldn't see me, I tapped a finger with each comparison. "*Unlike* my mother, Daniel still worked for Emily at the time of her death. And, *unlike* my mother, Daniel had applied for Emily's job and hoped to be promoted after she retired. And, *unlike* my mother, Emily had given Daniel a scathing review on his last performance evaluation, which could jeopardize his chances for said promotion. Did you know any of that?"

"We didn't know about the performance review."

Sigh. That wasn't comforting. I pictured Bryce seated behind his dark hardwood desk. I'd caught a glimpse of both Stan's and Bryce's desks when they'd dragged my mother into the precinct for questioning. Bryce's work surface seemed tidier than Stan's. Since Stan's desk was a disaster area, that wasn't saying much. But did their lack of organization explain why they didn't have such critical information as Daniel's poor employee evaluation?

I took a calming breath. The scent of the mauby tea I'd set to brew soothed me. "Now that you know, you should speak with him. Emily's bad review jeopardizes Daniel's chances of being promoted. He's contesting it, but it still gives him a strong motive."

I heard someone address Bryce in the background. His voice became muffled as though he'd cupped his hand over the receiver and turned his face away. I strained to listen. "It's Lyndsay Murray. She has some information about Daniel Rawson, the assistant principal."

The voice sounded again. I couldn't make out the person's words. Who was he talking to?

"Stan says hi." Bryce's voice was clear as he returned to our discussion.

I blinked at the phone. Did the detectives understand this wasn't a social call? Where was their sense of urgency?

"Um, are you going to follow up with Daniel Rawson?"

"Isn't Rawson the interim principal? Doesn't that put him on the fast track to become principal?"

"'Interim' means 'temporary.'" My tone was dry. "He's basically a placeholder until they find a suitable replacement—which may not be him."

"But the board's giving him a chance to prove himself." His tone was growing more impatient by the minute. "Besides, Emily was retiring. Why would Rawson need to kill her to get her out of the way?"

I stared at the black plastic phone on my well-organized cherrywood desk. "Why are you defending him, Bryce?"

"I'm not." He spoke quickly. "I'm just pointing out Rawson's motive isn't any stronger—or weaker—than your mother's."

"Of course it's stronger." I longed to climb through the phone line and shake him until he got some sense. "First, he still worked for Emily while my mother hadn't seen or spoken with her for almost a year."

"But, Lyndsay—"

I spoke over him since he'd interrupted me. "Second, his motive could be revenge. Emily's poor evaluation of his job performance threatens his future. Look, he really wanted that job. It's more money, more prestige, more power. He's already moved into Emily's office. I'm not the only one who thinks that's fishy."

"You're still questioning people about this case?" Bryce's sigh was angry and exasperated. "Lyndsay, I've told you it's too dangerous. Do I have to spell it out for you? We're going after a *killer.* The last time you involved yourself in a murder investigation, someone shot at you. Do you want a repeat of that?"

Not especially. "*I* didn't involve myself. *You* did by going after my mother. So are you at least going to talk with Daniel?"

Bryce sighed again. He was doing that a lot. Perhaps his obstinacy was too heavy a burden. "How would Rawson have delivered the poison? He wasn't sitting near Emily during the dinner."

"Neither was my mother. But, hey, you can ask him that when you question him about his motive. How 'bout that?"

His exhale was the sweet sound of defeat. "All right, Lyndsay. I'll ask Rawson to come back in for more questioning." He paused, lowering his voice. "Look, it's Monday and the bakery's closed today. Why don't I take you to lunch? We can talk about what else you think Stan and I should ask Rawson."

Seriously? He was so transparent. "Is my mother still a person of interest in your investigation?"

He hesitated. "Lyndsay, the lieutenant still believes she had motive and opportunity."

"So that's a yes?"

"You've gotta eat, Lyndsay."

"But I don't have to eat with you. As long as my mother remains a person of interest or a suspect in your investigation, I will not be hungry for the foreseeable future." I disconnected the call.

My sixteen-year-old self would've passed out from over-excitement to know that, eleven years into the future, her secret crush, Bryce Jackson, would ask her to lunch. But that was my sixteen-year-old-self. Today, twenty-seven-year-old me was angry. How could I still be attracted to someone who thinks my family's a bunch of serrated-bread-knife-wielding, poison-pushing murderers?

The office phone rang about an hour later Monday morning. I was relieved to have finished updating the books, but with so much to do and all of these unexpected interruptions, I could see it becoming a very long day.

My hand stilled over the receiver. Caller identification read: "Brooklyn Daily Beacon." I sat back on my seat in resignation. "Spice Isle Bakery. May I help you?"

"Lynds, it's José. I'm standing outside your bakery. Lemme in!" He was shouting to hear himself above the traffic behind him.

Did the fast-talking crime reporter think I'd run to the door? Think again, José. "First, it's 'Lyndsay.' Don't call me Lynds."

"I thought we were friends."

"We're not. Second, the bakery's *closed* Mondays and Tuesdays. Come back Wednesday." I saved the book-keeping file with the updated information on our accounts, then grabbed a pad and pencil to check on our inventory. I couldn't let José monopolize my attention if I was going to get through my task list.

His tone went from insistent to wheedling. "I know you're closed, but this will only take a few minutes."

"I'm working, José. You should've called before making the trip over here."

"Come on, Lyndsay. Lemme in. Please?"

Oh, brother. "Fine." I hung up the phone and walked out of the office.

I pushed my way through the kitchen's swinging door and into the customer service area. The space was in shadow since I'd left the window blinds and curtains closed. I didn't bother with the fluorescent overhead lights, though. At ten o'clock on this late-spring morning, there was enough sunlight for me to make my way across the room and deactivate the alarm. Besides, I wasn't letting José into the bakery. Slipping through the entrance, I pulled the door behind me.

José stood on the sidewalk right in front of the door, wearing slim navy slacks and a crisp white stiff-collared shirt under a navy sports jacket.

I showed him my cell phone. "You're on the clock."

He gestured toward the door. "You're not going to let me in?"

"Nope." I tapped my cell. "Clock's ticking."

He opened his notepad to a blank page. "You're breaking my heart, Lyndsay. I'm just trying to get a quote for my follow-up on the investigation into Principal Smith's murder."

I frowned at his weapons of choice, a pen and reporter's notepad. "What do you mean? The bakery's been cleared. You wrote about that just a couple of days ago in Friday's paper. Why're you still focusing on us?"

"The toxicology report proved the food wasn't poisoned." José held my eyes. "But the cops still consider your mother a person of interest. How do you feel about that?"

I should've known Friday's article about the toxicology

report clearing the bakery wouldn't be the end of José's dogged coverage of the case and my family's connection to it.

I gave him a stern look. "No comment."

He dropped his shoulders. "Lyndsay. Lyndsay. Lyndsay. I thought we'd gotten past this during our last collaboration."

My eyes were drawn again to his notepad as he stood with pen poised to transcribe my words. "Speaking off the record." I offered this in self-preservation. "My mother isn't the only person of interest in this investigation. Why haven't you spoken with the guests, Assistant Principal Daniel Rawson, Administrative Assistant Guy Law, Guidance Counselor Miguel Morales, Nurse Meera Singh, and Librarian June Min-ho?"

I hated giving José June's name, but she'd been a dinner guest. Besides, there was no way she could be the killer. She didn't have motive or opportunity to kill the principal.

"I've spoken with them." He nodded and that lock of thick, wavy hair fell across his forehead again. "And I want to speak with your mother. But I also wanted to include a quote from you as the bakery's owner and daughter of one of the suspects."

I held up my hand, palm out. "She's a person of interest, not a suspect. And neither my mother nor I have anything more to say to the press. The bakery's just starting to get back to normal. I don't want to keep feeding this story. It's bad for business."

I was tired of playing defense under the negative spotlight directed on my family. None of this would've happened if I'd followed my initial instincts and refused to cater Emily's retirement dinner. Why had I caved?

Because the school offered good money, which would

help us get out from under our crushing business debt that much sooner.

José was still speaking. "Didn't my article on the toxicology report help you and your family? This would be the same thing. Share your side of the story with the public. Speak your truth. That's the way to win in the court of public opinion and what have you." His words were almost poetic.

They didn't sway me. "Or the article will open us to more questions and second-guessing. I don't want to prolong that spotlight on my family."

"Forget about it, Lyndsay. The spotlight's going to be on you until the killer's caught. But I can help you change the type of spotlight. We worked well together last time when you were investigating Claudio Fabrizi's murder. Let me help you again."

I shook my head. "I'm not ready to have that kind of help." I gestured toward his notepad. "I'm not comfortable having my family's name repeatedly appear in a newspaper article about a murder investigation."

"OK." He put his notepad back into his satchel. "But your mother's on the cops' radar. Do you really want her in that situation?" Without waiting for my response, José turned and walked away.

Of course I didn't want Mommy to be suspected of murder or, even worse, charged with it. A deep sigh raised my shoulders. Time for another family meeting.

CHAPTER 17

"We need more information about Emily. I think that could help us determine who'd have the strongest motive to kill her." I looked around the bakery's dining area Monday night where once again my extended family had gathered to help with the investigation.

Arriving straight from work, Dev, Reena, Uncle Al, and Aunt Inez were dressed in formal business wear. Manson was in business casual, coming from the recording studio where he worked as a sound engineer. His loose wine red long-sleeved jersey hinted at his broad shoulders. His jet-black hair was styled in a fade on the sides, thick tight curls on top, and a straight part on the right.

Uncle Roman's shift at the post office finished early enough for him to go home, shower, and change into baggy canvas pants and an oversized button-down shirt with a pattern of mangoes, coconuts, and palm trees. I wondered if he'd purchased it from Tildie's shop.

Granny, Mommy, Daddy, and I had fixed a dinner of stew chicken, macaroni-and-cheese pie, and callaloo. Everyone had helped clear the dining area and clean the kitchen before reconvening for our meeting. But the cheesy, spicy aromas lingered.

Reena waved her arms, part stretch and part frustration. "I don't think Emily had any social media accounts. At least, I couldn't find any."

Reena and her older brother, Manny, had been tasked with researching our victim's and suspects' social media footprints.

"That makes sense." Mommy entwined her fingers with Daddy's as they sat together at the head of the table. "Emily didn't talk about her personal life a'tall. We didn't know if she had family or friends or even pets. All she ever talked about was the job."

I flexed my shoulders to ease the tension building there. It had been a long week since Emily's murder. "Why was she so private? It's as though she was hiding something."

Manny's tone was dry. "Like a criminal past?" He was only a few months older than Dev. Like Dev, Reena, and me, his accent was barely discernible.

Mommy took his suggestion seriously. "To work in the school system, you have to go through a thorough background check. If she had a criminal record, it would've been found out."

Reena continued her report. "I couldn't find anything on any of the platforms for June Min-ho, either."

Mommy shook her head. "I didn't think so. She never mentioned being on social media to me."

Reena shrugged. "She's your friend. She would've told you if she had a particular account. But we still had to check, Aunty." She looked back at the sheet in front of her. "The only one I found who had any social media was Emily's admin, Guy. He posted about having hard days at work, but he never went into any details. His communities on both platforms were very sympathetic."

"It sounds like he was careful with his posts." I don't

know what I expected to find on their social media, perhaps questions about where people could get quantities of strychnine or how to administer it without getting caught.

I studied the whiteboard I was using for our meeting notes. So far, I'd only written Emily's name and our primary suspects: Daniel, Guy, Miguel, Meera, and June. "I found two online news stories about Emily. The first was on her promotion to principal. The other announced her retirement. Before that, she'd been the assistant principal at St. Hermione Academy High School on Staten Island. I checked, but I'm pretty sure none of our suspects worked with her before Kings County Early."

"Good thinking to check. Brave." Uncle Al's praise brought a smile to my lips.

I was still unsure of whether I was the right person to lead our team of family sleuths. The nearly blank whiteboard mocked me. "Manny, did you find anything on social media about our other suspects?"

He looked up at me. "Nothing on the guidance counselor, Miguel Morales."

I swallowed a sigh. We didn't have clear motives for June or Miguel, and neither of them had any social media presence to help us learn more about them. Frustrating.

Manny continued. "The nurse, Meera Singh, complained constantly about Emily. She didn't use her name, though. She referred to her as 'my boss.' So, if you knew where she worked, you knew who she was talking about."

Dev shook his head. "People shouldn't do that. Posts like that could hurt your career if your boss or colleagues saw them. They could hurt future opportunities, too, if prospective employees found them."

Manny continued, referring to the notes he'd brought with him. "Daniel, the assistant principal, never mentioned Emily in any way. When he posted about work, which wasn't often, he'd brag about the students: how well they performed on standardized tests, the graduation rates, their community service, stuff like that."

That caught my attention. "It sounds like he loves the students and the school."

"Yes, it does." Manny sounded as impressed as I felt.

"Is it possible his dedication to the school and the students would be a motive for him to poison Emily?" I asked.

Granny's brow furrowed in confusion. "What d'you mean, love?"

I turned to my mother. "Emily was mean to everyone. Maybe Daniel wanted to poison her to save the school."

Daddy spread his hands above the table. "But why kill her when she was already leaving?"

"Jake's right, eh." Uncle Roman gestured toward my father. "Why he goin' waste *ten years* only to kill she weeks before she retire? Better to get she coming than going."

Uncle Roman had a point.

"When I worked at the school, her retirement was what we'd all been waiting for, even the students," Mommy's eyes were distant as though she was remembering her days at Kings County Early College High School. "Everyone was anxious for her to leave and take her meanness with her."

Aunt Inez looked around the table. "It seems to me, you know, that Roman's point can speak to everyone's motive. Right? If Guy doesn't like the way she treats him, why kill her if she's leaving?"

Dev picked up the thread. "And she gave Daniel a poor evaluation, why kill her? She's leaving."

Reena gestured toward the whiteboard. "She was dating Meera's father, but they broke up, so why kill her?"

Granny crossed her arms as she considered the board. "I don't want to make this look hopeless, but all of you have a point. None of this makes any sense, because Emily was leaving."

I reached to play with my charm bracelet. I'd stopped wearing it when the bakery was open, but we were closed Mondays. "Along with figuring out why someone would kill Emily when she was getting ready to retire, we also need to ask why poison her at the retirement dinner? Why not poison her at the school?"

Manny rubbed the back of his neck. "Maybe they couldn't get to her at work."

Mommy shook her head. "That wouldn't be a problem. Guy, Daniel, and Miguel worked in the same office suite with her. Meera had her own office and June's in the library, but they were free to go in and out of the administrative office suite."

I was desperate to put something on the board, but everything kept getting knocked down. "I feel the key to everything is solving the mystery of how the poison was delivered. If we figure that out, we'll have our killer."

"Then we need to get on it." Granny nodded decisively.

"We're trying, Granny." I turned back to my bare board.

But it was easier said than done and I was tired of our efforts leading us in circles. We needed a lucky break—or to create one of our own.

I squared my shoulders, raised my chin, and strode into Kings County Early College High School Tuesday morning as though I belonged there. I'd timed my arrival for minutes after the start of its eight o'clock classes. The hallways were empty.

As I made my way to the administrative office suite,

I rehearsed what I'd say to Daniel. I'd been giving myself a pep talk since I'd rolled out of bed and had continued it during my morning workout. This confrontation I was walking toward was necessary. It would take us one step closer toward clearing Mommy of suspicion. For my family, I could do anything. I would do anything.

"Lyndsay?" Guy looked up from his desk as I approached, interrupting my mental rehearsal. His brown eyes were dark with confusion. "Were we expecting you?"

"I don't know. Were you?" Nerves. I took a calming breath. "I'd like to speak with Daniel, please."

Guy's pale brow furrowed. "Is he expecting you?"

"This won't take long." I struggled to sound adamant instead of anxious. It didn't seem to be working.

"Principal Rawson's very busy, Lyndsay." Guy continued his obstruction. "May I ask what this is about?"

Did he have to? "Daniel's not the only one who has a busy schedule." I pulled my cell phone from my purse and checked the time. I straightened my shoulders even more and strode toward the interim principal's office. "The sooner I get this over with, the sooner we can all move on to other tasks."

"Wait, Lyndsay. Wait." Guy's voice was too close behind me.

I sped up, pushing Daniel's office door open. "Good morning—"

Guy interrupted, "Principal Rawson, she walked right past me."

That wasn't completely true, but I wasn't going to become distracted. I locked my trembling knees and fisted my sweating palms. "We need to talk, Daniel."

"Principal Rawson—"

Daniel waved a dismissive hand. "It's all right, Guy. Please close the door on your way out."

I sank onto one of his two faded and aging visitor's chairs almost limp with relief. Glancing over my shoulder, I waited until Guy closed the door before speaking. "'Principal Rawson.' You must like the sound of that."

Even if the title was only interim, he seemed to be dressing the part, trying to make an impression. The gray pinstriped, three-piece suit looked new. So did the crisp white shirt and scarlet tie. Was he wearing cologne? The thought of this man having a crush on my mother made me uncomfortable. I didn't know why. Even if he did try to woo her away from Daddy, according to Granny my parents had been inseparable since childhood.

"Why are you here, Lyndsay?" Daniel pulled his dark gray executive chair farther under the table. "I told you your check wouldn't be ready until Friday. You can come back then."

I wished it was that easy, but I couldn't leave until I followed up on Daniel's motive to my satisfaction. I braced myself. "I wanted to ask about the poor performance evaluation Principal Smith gave you."

His arrogant expression shifted and hardened into annoyance. "How do you know about that?"

I couldn't reveal June as my source. I thought quickly. "I heard it through the school's grapevine. It's pretty long."

Anger sparked in his dark eyes. I wasn't sure he believed me. "And you think that would give me a motive to kill Emily?" He blew a short, dry breath. "All right. Emily did give me a poor review on my last performance evaluation. She was trying to get rid of me so her friend could get my job."

"How do you know that?" I couldn't imagine Emily telling him. I couldn't imagine Emily having friends, either.

Daniel arched a well-shaped eyebrow. "I heard it through the grapevine. Unfortunately for them, I wasn't leaving. But Emily was. So tell me, why would I kill her if in a few weeks she was leaving?"

"I've heard the review she gave you was so bad, it cost you the promotion. Perhaps you wanted revenge." I settled back against my chair. I felt the pulse at the base of my throat fluttering with anxiety. I struggled to manage my breathing so I wouldn't pass out.

Daniel laughed without humor. "You're mistaken. Emily did try to sabotage me, but she failed. Miserably."

I searched his features, wondering if he was telling the truth. Using the back of my hand, I dabbed at the beads of sweat I felt collecting on my upper lip. "Why didn't her plan work?"

His tense features once again settled into arrogance. "I contested the review with the board. They ruled in my favor. They overturned Emily's evaluation in light of the fact that every other review had been satisfactory and her complaints didn't have any merit."

"So are you going to be the new principal?"

He hesitated. "Yes. The board will make my promotion official with an announcement at the end of the school year. They don't want to announce it now because of Emily's death. They think it would look insensitive."

"Congratulations, Daniel. I'm happy for you." In a minute or two, my knees would be steady enough to stand.

Daniel's lips tightened. "Are you really?" His voice was thick with skepticism.

"Emily gave you an unfair review." I held his dark, doubting eyes. "I'm glad you were vindicated."

He remained stubbornly disbelieving. "Even if it means you can't clear your mother by accusing me of murder?"

Anger pushed me to my feet. "Now *you're* mistaken.

My mother's innocent. I don't need to falsely accuse someone else to prove it."

I turned on my heel and marched out of his office. My emotions were all over the place as I returned to the parking lot. Confrontations still unnerved me. You'd think I'd be used to them by now, but my muscles continued to tremble. I was irritated Daniel had implied I'd implicate an innocent person to protect my mother from a murder charge. My parents had taught me better than that. But I was also scared. Daniel no longer had a motive to poison Emily. But my mother remained on the list.

CHAPTER 18

As I waited for the traffic signal at the intersection of Tailor and Parish avenues, Meera walked past my car without noticing me. I watched her in disbelief.

Oh, Meera. Are you playing hooky again?

I quickly navigated my car into the bakery's rear lot late Tuesday morning after returning from Kings County Early College High School. Once I'd parked, I hopped out of my vehicle and hurried to the sidewalk. I waited impatiently for the traffic signal to give me permission to cross Parish Avenue's busy four-lane traffic. Even after the light turned green, I checked both ways before running across the asphalt. It was better to be safe than sorry with New York drivers.

"Meera!" I hailed the school nurse as I leaped onto the sidewalk in front of the neighborhood pharmacy. I was pretty sure that was her destination.

She froze for a second, then looked around. Her movements were jerky as though she was uncertain of her next move. Was she going to run from me? I would've followed, but I didn't think the crowds would part as easily for us as they did on TV. Luckily, I didn't have to make that decision. With heavy steps, Meera closed the gap between us.

I waited for her, taking a deep, calming breath as I gathered my thoughts. The air was heavy with the scent of salty jerk smoke, fresh fish, and ripe produce.

"I saw you here last Thursday morning, too." I hoped a friendly smile would put her at ease.

"What is it that you want?" Meera glowered at me. Her East Indian accent had sharpened.

My smile wasn't working, so I let it go. "I want to know why you're on Parish Avenue when my tax dollars are paying for you to be miles away from here."

She lifted her chin and stared me down. "How is that any of your business?"

Oh, it was on now. I was going to get my answers. "How is it not?"

A moment of uncertainty revealed itself in her eyes before she dropped them to check her watch. "Let me pass."

I stepped to my right, blocking her again. "Meera, this is ridiculous. I just want to know why you're in this neighborhood, visiting this pharmacy, when you're supposed to be at work. Does it have anything to do with Principal Smith?"

Meera's eyes widened. Her voice rose several octaves. "You think I killed Emily?" She seemed sincerely shocked by the suggestion. Could I believe her?

"You're acting very suspicious. What am I supposed to think?" I shifted farther to my left, trying to make myself as small as possible to keep from getting swept up by the teeming waves of Brooklynites moving over the sidewalk. "Put yourself in my position. What would *you* think?"

"I don't care what you think." Her glower returned. "I didn't kill Emily, and I won't let you implicate me to the police just to turn their attention away from your mother."

My temper stirred. "I wouldn't do that." Why did everyone think I would?

"Wouldn't you?" She gave me a narrow-eyed stare, then tried to go around me again.

I wouldn't let her. A warm breeze came up from behind me and ruffled my braids. I pushed my hair from my face. "Not if you're innocent. So convince me."

She gaped at me once more. This time she wasn't as shocked as she'd been the first time. Maybe I was growing on her. "I don't have time to play games with you. I have things to do. Now get out of my way."

I'd spoken too soon. Our exchange escalated to a game of chicken. Whoever blinked first would have to concede. With our investigation on the line, I was determined to stand strong.

"Meera, I'm not getting out of your way. I'm going to dog your steps until you tell me why you make multiple trips to this pharmacy each week in the middle of the morning when you're supposed to be at work. The sooner you tell me, the sooner you can get rid of me."

"I want to get rid of you now." Meera's voice was rising into the histrionic zone. People were openly looking at us. "Step aside."

I looked around at the curious pedestrians who didn't even make an effort to look away. "No. Either you tell me what I want to know—or I'll cause a scene that'll have everybody paying attention to us."

A muscle jumped in Meera's right cheek as she ground her teeth. "You wouldn't."

Of course I wouldn't. I'd die from the embarrassment. But Meera didn't know that. Would she be willing to call my bluff?

"Try me." I imagined I could see plumes of smoke coming from her ears. I drew a deep breath, filling my lungs with air as though I was going to emit a sustained and piercing scream.

"Wait!" Meera's shout made us the center of attention again. She extended her hand as though she was going to cover my mouth.

I stepped back out of reach and waited for her to continue.

"All right." She sighed. "It's my father. He has hypertension. He has to monitor his blood pressure, but he won't do it on his own. He needs supervision."

I frowned. "What does that have to do with your coming to this pharmacy in the middle of the morning?"

She made an impatient tsking sound. "This pharmacy is close to where he lives. I meet him here so we can use its sphygmomanometer."

"What's that?"

"The blood pressure cuff. It's free." She checked her watch again. "Now will you get out of my way? My father's probably wondering where I am."

I stepped aside, falling into step beside her. It's not that I didn't believe her explanation. I just wanted to see for myself. "Of course. Thank you for taking the time to explain that to me."

She pinned me with hot, angry eyes. "You've made me even later for work. I hope you're happy."

"Actually, I'm not. But I'm sure your father's happy to have a daughter as devoted as you."

Some of the steam in her expression evaporated. Without another word, Meera turned and continued to the pharmacy. I followed her at a distance. After witnessing her greet her father, I left to return to the bakery.

The pharmacy didn't seem to have a connection to Emily's murder. It had been a long shot, I suppose. Meera wouldn't have killed Emily just to be able to help her father monitor his blood pressure. But would she have killed the principal for breaking her father's heart?

"So what's the verdict?" Rocky's voice drew my attention to her at the gym Wednesday morning. "Is training for the kickboxing exhibition inspiring you to enroll in the adult advanced kickboxing class?"

I pressed my yellow boxing gloves into my green nylon gym bag, then straightened to face her. "You don't give up, do you? I've only been training for a couple of weeks."

She chuckled. Her dark brown eyes sparkled with mischief. "If I'd given up, I never would've convinced you to enter the exhibition."

The gym wasn't overly crowded at five in the morning. That was one of the reasons I enjoyed my early-morning workouts. We didn't typically have to wait in line to use the equipment. But there were a good number of people, mostly women, using the weight machines, punching bags, ellipticals, treadmills, and free weights. I was the only woman using the foam-filled body bag, though. The other kickboxers were men.

With my peripheral vision, I could see some of the other exercisers giving her second and third looks. This wasn't the first time I'd noticed people staring at her. As usual, Rocky seemed oblivious of the admiration. She was an attractive woman. With her slim, well-toned figure in her trademark black unitard, she'd make a great spokesperson for the gym.

"I'm actually looking forward to the event." I squatted beside my bag to zip it closed.

Rocky gave a startled laugh. "You sound surprised."

I glanced up at her. "I am a little. I didn't think I'd be so excited. And I can feel my form and execution getting better."

"Hey, that's great."

"I appreciate the tips you've given me."

"Forget about it." She waved a dismissive hand as she stood above me beside the black vinyl body bag. Today's unitard ended mid-calf and completely bared her arms. "You make it easy because you're willing to learn, you know. That's why you're ready to take your training to the next level and what have you."

Drawing a breath, I caught the scent of disinfectant cleansers, equipment oil, and sweat. I hoisted my gym bag onto my shoulder as I stood. "I've just started the intermediate advanced classes."

Rocky's eyebrows leaped in surprise. "Good for you." She pulled her gloves from her black nylon gym bag. "Truth. What's the real reason you never registered for the skilled classes before?"

I shrugged restlessly. The room was warm. I could feel the beads of perspiration in the air. "I've always seen the classes more as exercise than training. In the higher class, I'd have to concentrate more on my form and execution. I didn't feel ready for that before."

"Well, all I have to say about that, you know, is I'm a hair stylist and makeup artist." Rocky set her left hand on her hip. "My business may not be as demanding as running a bakery. But I get you with ordering supplies, scheduling promotions for new clients, and doing the accounting. On top of that, I have to do training on new treatments and keep up with fashion trends. If I can do all that and these kickboxing exhibitions and advanced classes, so can you."

"You do have a lot going on." I could totally see her as a hair stylist and makeup artist. She always looked so well put together, like Reena in gym clothes.

"And I'm in a relationship, so there's that to balance as

well." She smiled. "He's not a kickboxer, but he comes to my events."

"It's great that he supports your interests." I tossed her a grin. "How long have you been dating?"

"Two years." Her face lit up like the sun. "He's in computers. He's also a drummer in a reggae band. He plays at a club usually, Nutmeg's on Samuel Avenue."

"I know that place. My cousin and I have gone there. The band's really good."

Rocky blushed as though I'd complimented her. "How's your investigation into Principal Smith's murder going?"

"Pretty much like the first one, two steps forward and one step back. I feel sort of encouraged that we were able to identify Claudio Fabrizi's killer and clear my name. Hopefully, we can do it again."

"Well, you know what they say?" Rocky didn't wait for my response. "The top motives are usually the four Ls."

I frowned. "Four Ls? What're those?" This felt like something I should know.

Rocky counted off her fingers. "Lust, love, loathing, and loot. I'd heard that in a mystery movie."

Three of the four Ls could be applied to everyone at the dinner party. Meera's motive would be love since Emily broke her father's heart. Loot applied to Daniel's ambition to become principal once Emily was gone. And loathing fit everyone: Meera, Daniel, Guy, Miguel, and June. But whose motive was the strongest?

CHAPTER 19

I was hot, sweaty, and desperate for a shower. I'd talked with Rocky longer than usual after my workout. Our chat had been great, but I'd wrecked my schedule. My morning routine was timed to the minute. To help Granny, Mommy, and Daddy open the shop by seven, I had to get to the bakery no later than 6:30 AM. I'd have to hustle to get back on track.

I wiped the sweat from my eyes and upper lip, then swiped my keycard to access the locker room. Like the rest of the gym, this space was bright, clean, and smelled of honest sweat. Although it was well maintained, it was showing its age. The paint on the cream walls was fading. Masking tape kept the tears in the maroon padded benches from growing. But the lockers were secure, and the restrooms and showers were clean and smelled of citrus disinfectant.

There were four aisles of dark gray metal lockers, three long units with eight lockers on each side. Most people didn't use the facility. I only used it to secure my gym bag until I finished my three-mile run on the indoor track. Then I collected my bag and moved to the weight room. But today, it had been raining when I'd arrived after 4:00 AM, so I'd stored my jacket and umbrella there, too.

Rustling sounds and snippets of conversations let me know I wasn't alone in the room. I nodded a greeting to the young woman at the end of the aisle. She responded with a polite smile before disappearing behind one of the lockers. I turned into the second aisle, which held the unit I was using.

My steps slowed when I spotted a sheet of paper sticking out of my locker's door. What was that about? My annual membership wasn't due until January, more than six months from now. Yes, I'd signed up for the gym during its New-Year-New-You discount. Because of my West Indian upbringing, I was always looking for a bargain. So the paper couldn't be a late fee or renewal notice. I sped up and snatched it. It was a letter-sized, thin sheet of white paper, folded in half. I unfolded it. The typed message was curt, direct, and terrifying: *I can reach you anywhere. Stop investigating Principal Smith's murder or I'll add you to the body count.*

My muscles went lax. The paper dropped from my hands. It landed faceup at my feet. Minutes before, my body had been warm from my workout and dripping with sweat. Now I was chilled to the bone. Every muscle quaked. I'd stopped breathing.

Pull yourself together. Breathe. Think.

I crouched to pick up the threatening note. It took a couple of tries. My fingers were still numb and shaking. The paper was ordinary, no identifying marks, letterhead, logos, or watermarks. It was as though the author wanted to make sure they couldn't be traced. I looked over my shoulder. How had they gotten into this secure, members-only area? Did they belong to the gym? And how had they known which locker I was using? Had they followed me without my noticing? That was hard to believe. I would've been aware of someone following me into this room.

I surged to my feet, grabbing my jacket, umbrella, and gym bag. I searched the area, checking every row. A young man and young woman sat beside each other on a padded bench one aisle over.

"Excuse me. Did you notice anyone push this note into one of the lockers this morning?" I held up the paper. "It would've been around four."

They shook their heads. I moved on to the fourth aisle. "Excuse me." The woman who'd greeted me moments ago looked up. "Did you see anyone tuck this note into a locker this morning? It would've been very early."

"No. Sorry." She looked away, repacking her gym bag.

I needed help. Adjusting my bag on my right shoulder, I strode out of the locker room to the nearest security desk. An older woman who looked decades past retirement age sat at the station closest to the lockers. I groaned. Jordan, at least that was her last name, according to her silver name badge. Shrouded in negativity and anger, she was the grouchiest of all the guards. Beneath the dark brim of her cap, her blue eyes were chips of ice. Her button nose was wrinkled and her thin lips were curled as though the gym didn't agree with her. Her dark brown uniform was baggy on her full figure. Her short iron gray hair was bone straight.

"Excuse me." Stopping in front of the desk, I waited for her attention to shift from the front door to me. She took her time. "Has anyone asked for Lyndsay Murray?"

"Is that you?" She wasn't impressed.

"Yes."

"No." She went back to staring at the glass front doors.

I followed her gaze. What was so interesting? The rain had stopped. The night sky was easing into a silvery gray. The lights above the entrance cut through the shadows and seemed almost welcoming. Unlike Jordan. Over the years, I'd heard several members complaining about her to one another. Was that the reason she was assigned to the shift with the fewest guests? The older woman was my least favorite aspect of the facility, her and the smell. I could put up with the smell, though, since I was contributing to it.

I turned back to Jordan. "Have you noticed anything out of the ordinary at the gym today? Any disturbances? Or maybe guests you didn't recognize?"

"What do I look like, a concierge?" Jordan spread her arms, inviting me to take a closer look at her circumstances. "I don't know everyone who comes into this place."

I held on to my patience. Sniping back at Jordan would get me even fewer answers than what she was giving me now. "The reason I'm asking is that I'm trying to identify the person who left a threat at my locker. How am I supposed to feel safe in a place where anyone can get into the members-only areas, deliver a threat, and leave unnoticed?"

Interest flickered briefly in Jordan's ice-blue eyes, then died. "How'd you know a member didn't leave that threat for you? Maybe you've ticked someone off. Lemme see it." She extended her hand as though she expected me to just give it to her.

But I could tell by the look in her eyes that she wasn't asking to see it because she was concerned for my safety. She was nosy. I turned and walked away, ignoring her repeated requests for me to come back. I wasn't going to show the threat to just anyone. It was scary and unnerving—and further proof that my mother didn't kill Emily Smith.

"Someone stuck this note in the hinge of my locker." I tried to read Bryce's and Stan's reaction to this latest evidence that cleared my mother of suspicion in the murder of

Principal Emily Smith. I got nothing. They'd been turned to stone.

"What time was this?" Bryce's voice was as expressionless as his face.

We were standing around Granny's table in our fairly busy customer service area Wednesday morning. I wasn't comfortable having this discussion near so many curious ears, but there wasn't any other place to meet. I wouldn't let the detectives into the kitchen without hairnets and aprons. That would be an invitation to the Department of Health to join the NYPD's campaign to shut me down. Also, I wanted to be near the customer counter in case Granny needed me. These were a few of the challenges of investigating a murder while running a bakeshop.

I'd called Bryce as soon as I'd gotten to the bakery— right after I'd told Granny, Mommy, and Daddy about the note. By the time he and Stan arrived, the bakery was full, although not quite as crowded as those mornings before Emily's murder. Fortunately, as I'd stepped away from the counter, Tanya realized what was going on. She'd hurried to take my place to help fill the guests' orders as Granny handled the cash register. Mommy and Daddy were preparing the food in the kitchen. The older woman had donned a chef's cap, apron, and disposable gloves and was greeting customers and taking orders as though she'd been part of the staff from day one. I made a mental note to give her free fish bakes and fried plantains for a month.

I kept one eye on the counter. "I found the note in my locker about half past five."

Bryce checked his black wristwatch. "Why did you wait almost two hours before calling us?"

I sensed more than a dozen sets of ears straining to catch

our every word above the soca music bouncing from the sound system.

I gave him a look. "Why did it take you half an hour to get here? Your precinct's not that far. You can walk the distance." That was a stretch, but my point was made. A few stray chuckles punctuated my statement, proof that we had a live audience. "As I explained on the phone, after finding the note I asked some of the members and the guard on duty if they'd seen anyone or anything suspicious. No one had. I got dressed, came to work, then called you."

My parents and grandmother had been horrified about the threat. Mommy had been so distracted, she almost burned her hand on the stove. Daddy had called Uncle Roman. Mommy had called Dev, and Granny had called Uncle Al. They'd all be upset if we didn't let them know right away. We counted on them to share the update with the rest of the family.

Stan looked from the note to me and back. "Since you found it in the locker room, it must have been left there by a woman."

I shook my head. "Not necessarily. The locker room is gender-neutral. All members get access to the room. But if you want to take a shower or use those restrooms, you need to sign out a special card pass."

Bryce stuck his hands in his front pant pockets. He wasn't even pretending to take notes. "Do you know whether any of Principal Smith's dinner guests belong to your gym?"

"No, I don't." I'd wondered about that, too. I tapped the note. "This threat proves my mother didn't kill Emily Smith."

Bryce's eyes searched mine. "How do you get that?"

I was momentarily speechless. "How do you not? My mother wouldn't threaten to add me 'to the body count' if I didn't stop investigating Principal Smith's murder."

Gasps rose up from the customer service area as one voice. Startled, I looked around to find everyone in the order line staring at me in fear and concern. Frantic whispers floated around the room.

Mommy and Daddy came rushing from the kitchen.

"What's happening?" Mommy stripped off her disposable gloves.

Granny cut the detectives a look. "The cat's out of the bag about the letter."

Grace Parke, the negative older woman who was always looking for someone to blame and something to criticize, crossed her arms. "You couldn't see if someone followed you into the gym? You need to pay more attention to your surroundings."

"Do a handwriting comparison on the note." The suggestion came from the Bubble-Gum-Chewing College Student.

"Why don't you dust it for prints?" The Knicks Fan collected his order of coconut bread and crossed to the door.

I glared at Bryce and Stan. "If you'd worn the hairnet, this wouldn't have happened." I raised my hands in a motion of surrender as I waded into the gathering of concerned citizens. "Everyone! We appreciate your support, but my family and I are working with the detectives to get everything settled. Please let us handle it."

Stan spoke up to be heard above the crowd and the rhythm of the music. "Ms. Murray's right, folks. We have to investigate all possibilities."

I turned to him, outrage stirring in my gut. "You mean

like the possibility I may have faked the letter to clear my mother of suspicion? I wouldn't do that."

"You're darn right she wouldn't do that," Tanya snapped from beside Granny. "Lyndsay comes from a good family. The Murrays are good, God-fearing people. They don't have a dishonest bone in their bodies."

"Lyndsay." Bryce drew me farther away from the crowd and lowered his voice. "Stan and I don't believe your mother killed Principal Smith."

"Then why is she still a 'person of interest' in your investigation?" I pulled my arm free and made air quotes with my fingers. He'd had suspicions about me in the previous homicide investigation and now he was unfairly investigating my mother. So not cool.

Bryce ran a hand over his tight, dark curls. His voice was so low, I could barely hear him. "Because your mother has motive, means, and opportunity."

He expected me to believe he and his partner didn't think my mother was guilty, but they did believe she had means, motive, and opportunity. What was I missing? "Who else are you looking at?"

He threw up his arms. "Everyone."

Everyone? "Does that include me, my father, and my grandmother?" Silence. "Do you have any other questions for me, Detective Jackson?"

"Lyndsay—"

I cut him off. "No? In that case, I have to get back to work. Enjoy the rest of your day."

Turning, I almost bumped into Stan. I ignored the apologetic look he gave me. He couldn't be any sorrier than I was. As disappointing and painful as it may feel, I wasn't interested in sharing a personal relationship with someone who was so determined to put members of my family on America's Most Wanted list.

I glanced over my shoulder to make sure the detectives were leaving. Instead, I saw Stan get into the back of the line.

Bryce frowned. "What're you doing?"

Stan pulled out his wallet. "I want a currant roll for my wife. She really loves the stuff."

Sighing, I secured one of the fresh-from-the-oven rolls in a plastic wrap, put it in a Spice Isle Bakery bag, then marched down to Stan. "This one's on the house."

Anything to get them out of my bakery.

CHAPTER 20

"Welcome to Spice Isle Bakery. How may we help you?" Did my smile look natural enough? My fingers tightened on the customer counter beneath the cash register as I strained to appear pleasant and welcoming to the man and two women standing in front of me late Wednesday morning. They were dressed professionally in somber monochromatic suits.

Although it had been more than two hours since Bryce and Stan had left our bakery, I was still rattled. Bryce had practically accused me of creating the threatening letter to clear my mother of suspicion. If he was standing in front of me now, I'd sm—

"I'm Sheryl Cross, president of the Caribbean American Heritage Festival Association." The tall, full-figured woman in front of me introduced herself before sweeping her right hand to draw my attention to the man and the other woman beside her. "This is Sean Baptiste, vice president, and Gina Good, secretary."

My smile eased into a much more relaxed expression. "It's a pleasure to meet you in person. I'm Lyndsay Murray." I gestured toward Granny, crocheting at her table. "This is my grandmother, Genevieve Bain. We co-own this bakery with my parents and brother."

"Can we speak privately, Ms. Murray?" Sheryl Cross ignored my introduction.

Her humorless demeanor caught me off guard. My smile wavered, then disappeared. Why did I have the feeling they weren't here to walk me through the processes of being a festival vendor?

"Granny, could you watch the counter, please?" I escorted the trio to a table for four in the dining room.

"Of course." Granny's tone was confident, but I saw the concern in her eyes.

I hoped my small smile offered her ease and encouragement.

In this lull between our morning and lunch rushes, there were only four customers in the area. I was reluctant to have our conversation here, but I had the sense the association representatives would not agree to wear hairnets and aprons.

Next month, June, was Caribbean American Heritage Month. It was a time for the West Indian community—those who'd emigrated from the islands, were born to people from the islands, or had been accepted into the fold—to recognize and highlight our culture and contributions to our adopted home. West Indians had been serving important roles in the U.S. government and society at large since before the country had been born, from founding father Alexander Hamilton, who had been born on what is now Saint Kitts and Nevis, to Eric Holder, the eighty-second Attorney General of the United States, whose parents were from Barbados.

The celebration culminated in the festival, which was essentially a large West Indian family picnic, in Brooklyn's Prospect Park. People from all over the city attended. There was a parade with floats representing the more than thirty island nations and dependencies, live bands, events, and vendors.

My family had submitted our first application to be a festival vendor. Mommy and Daddy had been reluctant to apply because this was our bakery's first year in business. They weren't sure we could manage the bakery and preparations for the festival at the same time. But Granny, Dev, and I were confident we could. More importantly, we had to try. Our extended family had been thrilled beyond belief when our application had been approved last month. Everyone was looking forward to our participation.

So it was unsettling to have the top festival representatives make an in-person visit to speak with me in private.

"Good morning!" Mommy's greeting came from behind me.

I turned to find her and Daddy hurrying to catch up with me and the festival representatives. A smile curved my lips. Thank goodness for Granny. She must have told them to join me. I hadn't realized how much I needed them until they appeared.

I gestured toward the festival representatives. "Sheryl Cross, president, Sean Baptiste, vice president, and Gina Good, secretary, these are my parents, Cedella Bain Murray and Jacob Murray."

Sean and Gina looked to Sheryl as though waiting to follow her lead.

"Good morning." The association president glanced at my parents as she settled onto one of the chairs at the table for four. Gina joined her.

I added a nearby table for two so we could sit together. Mommy took the seat beside Gina. Daddy sat across from Mommy.

I sat between Daddy and Sean. "How can we help you, Ms. Cross?" I was proud of how steady and confident my voice sounded.

Sheryl's back was ramrod straight. She stacked her hands flat on the table before her, then pinned me with her no-nonsense gaze. "Ms. Murray, it's come to our attention at the Caribbean American Heritage Festival Association that Spice Isle Bakery is once again the site of a brutal murder."

Mommy gave a soft gasp of outrage and anger. Catching her eye, I gave a subtle shake of my head, urging her to remain calm.

Folding my trembling hands on my lap, I drew a deep, steadying breath and called on my public relations training to carefully word my response. "It's a mischaracterization to say our bakery has been the site of multiple brutal murders. We were just as shocked and saddened by the deaths of Claudio Fabrizi and Principal Emily Smith as the rest of our community, but neither of them was murdered in our bakery."

To be accurate, Claudio was killed in his home and Emily died at the hospital.

"You're splitting hairs." Sheryl waved a dismissive hand. "Principal Smith was poisoned here." The gleam in her eyes made me think she was enjoying the scandals stalking our business.

That vexed me. "As the newspapers have reported, the police lab's results confirmed our food was not poisoned."

"Be that as it may, we, the organizers of the festival, are concerned that the poisoning itself occurred in your bakery." Sheryl tapped her right index finger against the table. "All you have been involved in two scandals in two months."

Mommy's cheeks flushed an angry red. "You keep

saying our bakery is *involved* in these murders as though we *created* them. That's not true."

Sheryl leaned into the table to look at Mommy. "Take it up with the police. They're the ones linking your bakery to the murders."

"You're leaving out our positive contributions." I gestured toward the window behind our table to draw attention to the neighborhood. "In the two months we've been open, we've become a hub for the community. People come to the bakery to discuss the news, events in our neighborhood, and how those events affect our lives."

Sheryl raised her left hand, palm out. "I'm not here to argue, you know. We're here to tell you the festival *cannot* be affiliated with these scandals. Having you at the event would hurt its image."

Hearing her say those words to us was like feeling a knife twist in my heart. I was speechless. Luckily, Daddy wasn't.

"But how can you say our being at the festival would hurt its image?" His face was stiff with anger. "We're a family-owned shop and our customers support and trust us."

Sheryl looked around the dining area with its sparse attendance. Her smile was a taunt. "Really? They're supportive? They don't look that supportive to me, you know."

Gina and Sean giggled as though their boss had made a great joke. My temper stirred more. I took several seconds to control it.

Mommy leaned forward. "If you were familiar with bakery operations, you'd know that late mornings are slower business. You want to see a crowd? Stay for the lunch rush, nuh? The customers start arriving at half past eleven."

Sean gestured toward our four guests. "Whether you

have a handful of customers or a store full of them, it doesn't matter. President Cross and the festival administration have made their decision."

Gina nodded. "That's right. We can't have Spice Isle Bakery at the festival. It would be as though we were condoning violence, and we have a strict policy against violence at the event. It would be hypocritical to include a vendor associated with so many violent deaths."

Were they serious? Were they claiming my family was part of a violent enterprise? This couldn't be happening.

I shook my head. "Ms. Cross—"

Sheryl held up one hand, palm out. "*President* Cross."

Oh, brother. "President Cross, our bakery has had some bad luck with these investigations. However, the community *is* still supportive of us. They know we've had nothing to do with these tragedies."

Sheryl laughed her surprise. "How can you say you have nothing—"

It was my turn to interrupt her. "We've been cleared by the police. The community loves our food and our customer service. That's why more and more guests keep coming to our shop."

Sheryl stood. Gina and Sean followed her lead like puppets on strings. The association's president looked down at us. "We came here today because we want all you to know the festival committee will be holding a vote to officially decide whether your shop's application approval should be formally withdrawn."

My mouth went dry. I rose, pressing my hands against the table to steady myself. "When are you holding the vote?"

Sheryl sniffed. "Don't mind. We'll let you know the outcome."

I will mind. They were playing with my livelihood. We

were being punished, but we'd done nothing wrong. It was too unfair for words. "Has the festival ever revoked a vendor's application before?"

Sheryl cocked her head as she paused to think. "Not in my memory."

Sean and Gina murmured their agreements.

"This will be the first time we've done anything like this," Sean confirmed.

"In that case, and considering the gravity of this situation, it's only fair that my family and I have an opportunity to present our side of these events and to defend ourselves."

Sheryl was shaking her head even before I'd finished speaking. "There's no need for you to take up the committee's time with your testimony. We have all the information we'll need from the news reports of the police investigation."

Perhaps I should've given José more than one interview.

Daddy stood, cupping his hand over my shoulder. "My daughter's right. It wouldn't be fair to base your decision on the media coverage. It isn't complete. We need a chance to give our side of the story."

Mommy straightened from her chair. "We were proven innocent in Claudio Fabrizi's case. We'll be proven innocent in Emily Smith's as well."

I spoke up. "But we need your support. If you drop us from the festival, it will appear that you think we're guilty when we're not. *Do* you think we're guilty?"

The trio looked away from us. I caught my breath. They did. They thought we were murderers. It was as though a giant had socked me in the stomach. I exchanged looks with Mommy and Daddy.

Finally, Sheryl inclined her head. "All right. Your appearance at the committee meeting will give us a chance to ask you questions. We'll call you once we set a date for the meeting."

Without another word or glance, the association representatives left the bakery. I watched them push through our entrance. "It's time for me to give José another interview. We need to get our side of the story out."

CHAPTER 21

"I got a break in the case." Uncle Roman settled onto the folding dark wood chair on the other side of Granny's black laminate card table late Thursday afternoon. Having finished his mail delivery rounds for the day, he'd changed out of his postal uniform and into a more casual shirt with an orange-and-green print and baggy dark cream pants.

It was minutes after four o'clock. A trio of school friends were having an after-school snack in the dining area. Otherwise, business was slow between the lunch orders and guests coming in after work.

"A break? Really?" Daddy sounded as hopeful as I felt. He and Mommy had answered Uncle Roman's request to join him, Granny, and me in the bakery's customer service area.

"Yes, I!" Uncle Roman's grin lit up the room. He was so proud of himself.

"Then tell us, nuh?" Granny set aside her latest crochet project. The item was still in the early stages, but she was using a lot of bright red yarn. The shade was just a little brighter than the cherry red blouse she'd matched with turquoise wide-legged pants.

Uncle Roman settled back against his chair. He took

a deep drink of his hot mauby tea, drawing out the moment. "I finished my shift at the post office and I thought, 'Before I leave, let me just say hello to my good friend Bertie.' He's getting up there in age and thing, but we've been friends for a lot of years, you know. I like to make sure he's OK."

I could feel my uncle milking the limelight and building the suspense. I was used to it. We all were. I turned to the beverage station behind the customer counter and filled four dark gold porcelain mugs with ginger tea, one each for Mommy, Daddy, Granny, and me.

Daddy's brow furrowed. He exchanged a look with Mommy, who stood with us behind the counter. "But, Roman, isn't Bertie the same age as you?"

Uncle Roman jerked forward on his chair. His response made several false starts. "But, eh, I'm young in spirit."

Granny kissed her teeth. "Young in spirit and long in tooth."

I hid a smile behind my mug of tea.

Uncle Roman ignored Granny's comment. "Kings County Early's on Bertie's route. He's been delivering there for years. So I ask him, 'Man, what you know about what's going on at the school and thing?' He said the principal's murder replaced the fund-raiser as the latest big news in the place."

I sipped my tea and searched my mind for details of the fund-raiser. "I remember reading about the fund-raiser. It was for the school's library." I looked at my parents and grandmother. I was sure they'd remember that news as well. "It was last month, remember? The *Beacon* ran an article announcing it. Then there was a follow-up article that stated the school had raised something like sixty thousand dollars."

The cloud of confusion cleared from my mother's eyes. "Oh, yes. It was a lot of money. The school made a big push to reach out to the community, including former staff. I sent them some money."

Granny nodded. "Yes, it was a monthlong event with activities: a book swap, presentations, and such. We went to an author signing, remember? I sent money, too. But what does that have to do with our investigation?"

Uncle Roman looked at each of us before settling his attention on Mommy. "You remember hearing about it? Good. What you didn't hear because it wasn't in the news is that three days after the fund-raiser ended, the money, it disappeared."

A collective gasp came from the four of us and rose up in the bakery. In my peripheral vision, I noticed our guests in the dining room glance at us, then look away.

Uncle Roman smiled. His eyes gleamed with satisfaction at our reactions. "Just as Lynds had said, the fund-raising started April Fool's Day. It ended the twenty-second of April. By the twenty-fifth of April, the money was gone, *oui*."

My jaw dropped. "Sixty thousand dollars is a lot of money. Why wasn't it in the news?"

Uncle Roman shook his head as though he still couldn't believe it himself. "The money was gone, but the school board didn't want the negative publicity so they didn't tell the police. They wanted to handle it hush-hush. So instead they told Principal Smith to handle it internally. She was under a lot of pressure to catch the thief."

This was bombshell information, but could we trust our source? "Uncle Roman, how does Mr. Bertie know this?"

Uncle Roman shrugged. "Bertie, he's been delivering mail to the school for a good number of years now. He knows everybody in the place, from teachers, to staff, to security guards, to janitors. He knows some of the students, too. They're all comfortable talking with him."

I frowned. "Who was in charge of the money?"

Uncle Roman sat back, nodding his approval of my question. "Emily Smith said she was determined to find the thief, eh? She was certain it had to be one of the committee members."

"Oh, oh." Mommy covered her mouth in dismay. "One of them would've had to have been June. But she wouldn't have taken the money. No, sir. She's too honest. You'll never make me believe it."

The librarian had been Mommy's friend for more than ten years. They still kept in touch even though Mommy had retired. She knew June better than we did, but could she be unbiased?

I returned my attention to Uncle Roman. "Do you know who the other committee members were?"

His expression was more somber now as though he'd realized the significance of the information he was giving us. "The assistant principal, the admin, and the guidance counselor."

This was overwhelming. "Now we know why she'd invited those people to her retirement dinner. She'd suspected one of them had taken the money. Maybe she'd even figured out which one. But why had she invited Meera?"

Daddy ran his hand over his hair. "Do you think she was going to reveal the thief during her dinner before telling the board?"

Mommy wrapped her arms around her waist. "I'm sure she was. If she'd announced the name beforehand, they'd already have been arrested. She must have been waiting for the dinner."

My sigh lifted my shoulders. "Uncle Roman, you just gave us the motive and cleared Mommy. We have to figure out how the poison was administered; then we'll know who the killer is."

"Look who walked through my door." A smile lifted my cheeks and filled my heart as Dev entered the bakery Thursday night. But the smile he offered me in return was as fake as the colorful tissue paper butterflies Granny had packed into the two-gallon acrylic jug that stood on the customer counter.

"It's good to see you, too." He turned the Closed sign in the front door and secured the lock.

When he turned back, I saw the lines of fatigue scoring his features. Tension bracketed his lips. His movements were stiff as he crossed the blue-tiled flooring to meet me in the middle of the room. His royal blue tie lay loosely against his limp cloud-white shirt. His iron gray suit jacket, a match to his pants, hung in the crook of the arm that carried his black combination lock briefcase.

I wrapped my arms around his back, giving him a hard hug. He gave me a one-armed embrace, almost folding himself in half since he was almost a foot taller than me. Seriously, if it weren't for Granny, I'd be the shortest one in the entire family. And I only had about half an inch on her.

His back muscles were knotted beneath my palms. Whatever trouble weighed on him was heavy. My smile wavered as I felt myself taking on his burden. I couldn't help it. My connection with my brother was as natural and effortless as breathing.

I stepped back and searched his face for a hint of what could be bothering him. "How's everything with Joymarie?"

He smiled and my heart sighed with relief. "Everything's good. She's great. We wish we could spend more time together, though."

"I'm glad." He and Joymarie had only been dating a few weeks. But if his love life was fine, then work must be the cause of his problems. "Are you hungry? I could heat up some leftovers."

Gratitude flashed in the depths of his dark eyes. "I don't want to put you to trouble, though. You've probably already cleaned the kitchen."

"Oh, brother." I led him into the kitchen. "While I fix you a plate, I'll give you the latest update on the investigation."

I told Dev about Uncle Roman's visit that afternoon as I prepared a couple of pieces of jerk chicken and a serving of macaroni-and-cheese pie for him. Dev put his jacket and briefcase in the storage closet at the back of the kitchen before returning to the blond wood center island. While his main course heated in the microwave, I placed a small bowl of our garden salad in front of him.

He pulled out one of the barstools we kept beneath the island. "Thanks, Sis. And the chicken and macaroni-and-cheese pie smell wonderful."

"Not wonderful. Exceptional." I smiled at him and breathed another sigh of relief when he grinned back. "Anyway, whoever stole the money from the library's fund-raiser may have poisoned Emily to keep her from revealing their identity."

Dev washed down his salad with the sorrel juice I'd given him. Some of the tension eased from his face and shoulders. "It makes sense. And it's a much stronger motive than the ones the detectives have given Mom. Have you told them about it?"

I poured myself a glass of sorrel juice on ice and joined

Dev, sitting across the island from him. "Not yet. I want to talk with the school's librarian, June Min-ho, first."

Dev paused with a forkful of salad halfway to his mouth. "The detectives should interview her, not you. That's their job."

I took a sip of the juice. "I'm sick of hearing: 'I'm sorry, Ms. Murray, but we can't discuss ongoing investigations.' Seriously? I have questions that need answers. I'll tell the detectives about the stolen money once I get them. Then if they feel like it, they can do their own interview."

I sensed his opposition to my plan and braced to defend my decision. His tension was on the rise again. The microwave's sensor put our discussion on pause. As I crossed the kitchen to collect his main course, I mentally prepared one argument after another to pull out as needed: Someone with Mommy's best interest at heart needed to make sure the right questions were asked; we needed to know what was going on with the investigation to protect our family and our business; if the detectives were doing their due diligence, they would've found out about the missing money themselves. For that last reason alone, I wasn't prepared to give the detectives this information until after I'd spoken with June.

Dev murmured his thanks as he took the hot plate of food. "Lynds, I'm concerned about you questioning *murder* suspects on your own. The killer's already threatened you. We can't act as though that didn't happen—even if the detectives are ignoring it."

"I'm not ignoring the threat." I took another drink to ease my dry throat. It bothered me that Bryce and Stan thought I'd written the note to draw suspicion away from my mother. "Yes, it scared me. Yes, I'm afraid. But I won't allow fear to keep me from helping Mommy."

"And I don't want you or Mom in danger." His frustration crashed over me like a cold wave.

"We have a lot in common." I finished the sorrel. Should I pour myself another glass? I decided against it.

Dev reached across the center island and laid his warm hand over my forearm. His restlessness reached out to me. "Lynds, please give the lead to the detectives and let them follow up. I'm only asking because I'm worried about you. You've been threatened, stalked, and shot at."

I tried to suppress a shiver of fear but failed. "You don't need to remind me."

"Apparently, I do." He took a bite of the jerk chicken. The hot, spicy aroma burst free and leaped across the table to me.

I still hesitated. "They don't take our leads seriously, Dev."

"They'll take this one seriously. It could change the direction of the investigation."

"All right." I sighed. "But if they don't jump on it, I'm going to speak with the committee members myself."

"And I'll go with you." He finished the plate of food.

My brow furrowed in confusion. "You'll be at work."

"No." His voice was strained. "I won't."

A chill of foreboding swept over me. "Why not?" But I already knew the answer.

He took my empty glass and carried it and his dishes to our industrial sink. "I quit my job."

My jaw dropped. "What?"

CHAPTER 22

A dozen questions rushed into my mind as I mentally replayed Dev's announcement Thursday night. I waited until he'd washed his dishes and placed them on the drainboard before asking them.

"Why did you leave the firm?" I stood from the kitchen's center island.

Dev seemed tired, almost drained. He shoved his fists into his front pant pockets. "Ever since the papers reported Emily Smith's murder, the partners have treated me differently. They seemed cold, curt, impatient. When I asked if I'd done something to upset them, they denied it. This afternoon, they called me into one of the conference rooms."

I dropped back onto my barstool and lowered my head into my hands. "Oh, that doesn't sound good."

"It wasn't." Dev began to pace the length of the kitchen. "The senior partners are concerned about the negative press the bakery's been receiving. It doesn't look good for a member of the firm—especially a partner—to be connected to a business that's been at the center of one, much less two, murder investigations."

I tracked his long, agitated strides from the sink at the front of the kitchen to the storage closet in the back. "And

I don't suppose it matters that I was cleared in the first case and Mommy will be cleared in this one?"

He gave me a humorless smile as he passed me on his way back to the sink. "No, it doesn't."

"But wasn't there something you could've done instead of quitting? Being a lawyer has been your dream since you were a child."

Dev stopped pacing. He turned to me. "Owning a bakery has been yours."

I stiffened. "What do you mean by that? Did they suggest we close the bakery?"

His jaw stiffened. "I told them that wasn't an option. When they couldn't offer another solution, I resigned."

My heart broke. My dream of opening a family-owned West Indian bakery had destroyed my brother's career. That realization brought me more pain than I could ever remember feeling. And there was nothing I could do about it. The events that were happening to us were out of our control. We had nothing to do with Claudio Fabrizi's or Emily Smith's murders. Yet the homicides had damaged our business and Dev's partnership.

I finally regained my voice. "Dev, I'm so, so sorry. I could look into arrangements to close the bakery. It would take some time, but maybe they'll give you your job back if they know the bakery will be closing." It hurt to say the words, but being the cause of my brother's pain was worse.

"Don't." His eyes glittered with anger. His voice was firm. "You love running this bakery. You're good at it and it's good for you. Lynds, you've grown so much since opening the shop, personally and professionally. You're much more confident, assertive, and courageous. I didn't think I could be more proud of you, but I am every day. This place is your passion. Don't close it."

I blinked back tears. "But what about your passion, the law? Your career with the firm. You were doing so well. What about *your* dream?"

Dev sighed and returned to the barstool across from me. "It's not my dream anymore. My work . . . It hasn't made me happy for a long time. And lately, things have been getting worse."

This was news to me. "How?"

"It's getting in the way of my family." He swung out his arm. "Because of the long hours I'm forced to work, I'm not here when my family needs me. Instead, I'm sitting behind a desk. Meanwhile, Mom's under suspicion for a murder she couldn't possibly have committed. The bakery's suffering because of the hit to its reputation. And your life's being threatened—again."

"You're so ridiculous, Dev." I unclenched my teeth. "You came to the precinct when the detectives brought Mommy in for questioning and before that when they brought me in. You've come to every family meeting to share your insights on our investigations. We know that if we need you, you're just a phone call away."

"That's not good enough anymore, Lynds."

"Then what are you going to do?"

"I wish I knew." He expelled an impatient breath. "Whatever it is, I want more time with my family. And with Joymarie."

I studied his tense features, tight lips, and turbulent eyes. His frustration weighed on me as though it was my own. He was my brother. I wanted to carry this burden for him, but I knew I couldn't. He'd have to get this one on his own.

I stood, but depression made my body feel heavy. "I'll drive you home."

"Thanks." Dev followed me to the rear door, where he collected his briefcase and jacket from the closet.

"Sure." I glanced at him from over my shoulder. "But you're on your own to tell Mommy and Daddy about quitting your job."

His groan of discomfort made me smile.

"What're you doing here?" I suppose I could've been more diplomatic, but I was so surprised to see Dev in the bakery's kitchen Friday morning with Granny, Mommy, and Daddy. He was dressed in the black chef's hat and smock and dark gray slacks.

He smiled at me from his spot on the left side of the center island as he combined the ingredients for the hard dough bread. "I need something to do until I find a new job."

"And we can use the extra hands." Granny stood across from him, slicing the currant rolls.

Mommy and Daddy murmured their agreement. On a closer look, I saw the concern that darkened their eyes.

Happiness replaced my surprise. It felt right to have him here with us, and not just because we could use the help. Now our whole family was together. It was going to be a good day. I took a deep breath, enjoying the scent of warm, buttery breads; fresh, sweet pastries; and strong bush teas. Harry Belafonte's "Matilda, Matilda" swung from the speakers connected to the CD player. I took my position at the island and helped my family prepare for our breakfast customers. When Granny opened the door promptly at 7:00 AM, Dev and I took our positions behind the counter.

The morning traffic still wasn't quite back to the volume we'd had before Emily's murder. Frustration twisted deep in my gut. We needed to focus on growing our customer base. Instead, because of this case, we were struggling to get back to where we'd started.

Tanya and Benny were the first at the counter. My smile felt warm and natural. "Good morning, Ms. Nevis. Mr. Parsons. Would you like your usual?" The couple especially enjoyed our fish bakes and fried plantains for breakfast.

Tanya nodded to the line behind her. "Look who's made it here early, yes."

I followed her gaze to Bryce. He stood alone in the line, looking somewhat uncomfortable. My smile disappeared.

Other customers had noticed our attention shift to the homicide detective.

Grace Parke grunted. Her long-sleeved banana yellow dress flowed over her full figure to her calves. "Where's your partner, Detective?"

Bryce's smile seemed forced. "We're meeting at the precinct. I told him I'd pick up our favorite currant rolls."

I turned away. Did he think he could get on my good side by praising our food while investigating each member of my family for murder? If so, that was another reason for me to question his judgement.

The Knicks Fan spoke over his shoulder to Bryce. "Have you found any actual leads on Principal Smith's murder?"

Bryce spread his arms. "I can't discuss an ongoing investigation. I'm sorry." He was beginning to sound like a parrot.

A sharp crack came from the end of the line. The Bubble-Gum-Chewing College Student shifted a wad of gum to her left cheek. "We know Cedella Murray didn't kill anyone. So you might as well move on."

Bryce was stubbornly silent. I exchanged a look with Dev. His eyes were warm with the same almost suffocating gratitude I felt toward our patrons' support. It meant a lot to have the community behind us.

I pulled off my gloves and called to my grandmother

at her table, "Granny, could you take my place for a moment, please?"

She set aside the hat she was crocheting and rose. "Of course, love."

I circled the counter and pulled Bryce from the line. Knowing we had a live audience, I lowered my voice. "Did you get my message?"

Bryce whispered back, "That's why I'm here. Well, that and your currant rolls." His smile was crooked. He really was very handsome. Too bad he had poor judgement.

Focus, Lynds. Your mother's freedom's at stake. "Have you checked into it? Have you taken my mother off of your suspect list?"

His hesitation spoke volumes. "Lyndsay, I agree the theft of the money from the school library's fund-raiser gives members of the fund-raising committee a motive, but it doesn't clear your mother."

"Why not?" I struggled to keep my voice down. "Have you questioned the committee members?"

"Not yet. We—"

"What?" I unclenched my teeth. "I didn't give you that information for you to tuck it into your back pocket for a rainy day." I counted my fingers. "Every member of the committee was at that event. It was a *retirement* dinner, which means Emily's retirement was approved, which means Emily had identified the thief. And that thief had the strongest motive to kill Emily. Most importantly, my mother was not involved in any way."

"I agree, and so does Stan." Bryce raised his hands as though trying to calm me. Good luck with that. "But my lieutenant doesn't think that gets rid of your mother's motive."

"She doesn't *have* a motive. And what about that threat

I found in my gym locker? Doesn't that prove someone other than my mother killed Emily Smith? And now that person's after me."

Bryce stared at me in silence. "Lyndsay, we only found your prints on the paper."

I fisted my hands. "I was afraid of that. The killer must've worn gloves."

"That's one possibility."

I frowned. "What other—" I saw the question in his eyes. Unbelievable. "You still think *I* wrote that note to take suspicion off my mother?"

He spread his arms. "Lyndsay, my lieutenant thinks it looks—"

I cut him off. "What do I have to do to convince you my mother's innocent? Catch the killer for you?" I turned to stomp back to the counter.

Bryce caught my arm. "Lyndsay, I'm sorry. I'm just asking the questions my lieutenant asks Stan and me. The same questions the prosecutor will ask. We know your mother's innocent, but our gut instincts don't mean anything to them. We *have* to clear her before taking her off our list or the prosecutor could put her back on it."

I jerked my arm free and fisted my hands at my sides. "Then show more urgency in getting my mother off your list. I don't like having suspicion hanging over her head."

This time, I managed to get away from him. I pushed my way into the kitchen. I needed time and space to calm down before returning to the customer counter.

"Everything all right, Lynds?" Beneath Daddy's easy words I heard several notes of concern.

I forced a smile into my voice. "It will be. Thank you, Daddy."

I ducked into the office and closed the door behind me

without slamming it. Small victories. The office didn't offer enough room to pace. It was more like wandering in place.

Why had I bothered to give Bryce information on the library fund-raiser theft? I should've known he wouldn't take it seriously. At the very least, he and Stan should be at the school, interviewing the committee members right now. I ground my teeth.

I'd told Dev we couldn't depend on the detectives to follow up. They were wasting our time. We'd have to continue our investigation on our own.

CHAPTER 23

"Thank you for coming with me." I glanced at Dev beside me as we approached Kings County Early College High School's library late Friday morning. Sunlight streamed in through the window at the end of the hall. We'd left Granny in charge of the customer service counter while we dropped in on June.

"You've made good progress on your own, more than the detectives." Dev's sneakers squeaked against the gray vinyl flooring. "I asked Bryce yesterday about the threat that was left for you. They still haven't found anything."

"Really?" Why did high school hallways smell like sweaty socks? I took shallow breaths. "He said they only found my prints on the paper. He thinks I faked the letter."

Dev came to a sudden stop. "Are you serious? That's outrageous."

I kept walking. "I know. It's maddening."

Mommy had given us directions to the school's library. *Turn right at the end of the main hall.* I led Dev around the corner and into the library. The smells of musty old books and fresh periodicals greeted me as we crossed the threshold. June was seated at the circulation desk. Her eyes lifted from her computer as we entered.

"Good morning, Ms. Min-ho." I smiled as Dev and I approached the desk.

"It's good to see you again." Dev stopped at the counter beside me.

June's cool green coatdress emphasized the edgy lime green streaks in her raven hair. The heavy mass was twisted into a knot on the crown of her head. Her smile warmed her angular features as she rose to her feet. "Devon. Lyndsay. This is a nice surprise. Please call me June. How's your mother?"

"She sends her regards. Thank you." I inclined my head toward Dev. "We were wondering if you had a few moments to speak with us?"

"Of course." Curiosity sparkled in her black opal eyes. "How can I help you?"

I hesitated. My questions weren't going to win any friendships. "Could you tell us about the library fundraiser?"

June's brow furrowed as though she was puzzled. "What do you want to know?"

I locked my knees. "We want to know about the stolen money and who you think might have taken it."

June's dark eyes flew to Dev's before returning to mine. She circled the library's desk and gestured for us to join her at the nearby study table. Lowering her voice, she settled onto a chair. "Who told you about the missing money?"

"That's not important." I took the matching blond wood chair on the other side of the table from her. "The stolen money could be the reason someone killed Principal Smith."

Dev sat beside me. "How was someone able to take the money?"

June hesitated. "I didn't take that money. Why would

I?" She swept her arms to draw attention to her surroundings. "That money was to go toward new books, periodicals, updated software, basic supplies. The school's budget doesn't extend very far. Who do you think has been supplementing those expenses? Me. Stealing that money would've been stealing from myself."

I exchanged a look with Dev. June had a point. "From where was the money stolen?"

Frustration flashed in June's eyes. "I'd kept it in a locked drawer in my desk."

Incredulous, I pointed toward the circulation desk, which stood in the middle of the floor. "That desk?" It was out in the open. Locked or not, it seemed like an easy target.

"No, my office is through that door." June pointed to a closed sturdy-looking dark wood door behind the circulation desk.

Relieved that the money wasn't kept out in the open, I nodded. "Why wasn't it taken to the bank at the end of each day?"

"That was Emily's decision." June split her gaze between me and Dev. "The bank that holds the school's account charges a fee for transactions over a certain amount each month. Emily wanted to avoid the charge by making just one deposit at the end of the fund-raiser. I didn't like that idea. No one on the committee did, especially when we were bringing in so many donations. We were supposed to make the deposit the next day, but then the money was stolen." She fisted her hand on the desk. "I wish I'd followed my instincts."

"Don't be so hard on yourself." Dev shook his head. "As you said, Principal Smith made the decision to keep the money here. Wasn't she also the one held ultimately responsible?"

June rolled her eyes. "She should've been, but she found a way to throw the rest of us under the bus. Now we're under pressure to either find the money or repay it."

I frowned. "Daniel, Guy, and Miguel also were on the committee. What about Meera?"

She looked puzzled. "No, Meera wasn't involved. And Emily was on it in name only, but when she learned how much money we'd raised she swooped down like a vulture to take all the credit. Typical."

I was restless as though there was more to this burglary than we were considering. But what? What was I missing? "The donations the committee received, weren't those paid in checks and credit cards? There couldn't have been much cash."

June closed her eyes and shook her head. "That's the most upsetting part." She opened her eyes. "We'd collected almost twenty thousand dollars in cash donations."

"What?" I gasped.

"How?" Dev spoke at the same time.

June shifted on her seat. "The final night of the fundraiser, we hosted a book discussion by a local author, an alumna. It was put together at the last minute. Everything was a rush. That was actually the only event Emily helped us promote."

I turned to Dev. "You remember that event, don't you? We all attended. Even Uncle Roman."

June continued. "We sold tickets at the door for cash and money orders only. We weren't set up for credit cards and Emily didn't want to accept checks."

The more I learned about the stolen money, the more convinced I became that there was more to this story. "Emily didn't want to put the cash in the bank immediately?"

"She insisted on one deposit." June shook her head. "So I brought my jewelry box from home. After the event, I locked the cash in the box, locked the box in my drawer, and hoped for the best. The next day, my jewelry box was gone."

Dev broke the heavy silence. "Did everyone on the committee know where you'd kept the money?"

"It's not as though I shouted, 'Hey, there's money in my desk drawer!'" June waved her hands. "But, yeah, I'm sure the others saw me putting the money in there. I kept everything related to the fund-raiser in that drawer: my project folder, expense receipts, marketing samples. And I kept the drawer *locked* at all times."

Dev gave June's office a considering look. "Could any of the members have gotten a key to the drawer?"

June shook her head. "I don't think so. Besides, the thief didn't use a key. The lock had been broken."

I shrugged. "Playing devil's advocate, perhaps the thief wanted to make it look like a break-in."

"That's a good point." A new voice joined our meeting. I was irritated to realize I would've recognized it anywhere.

Startled, I shifted on my seat to face the doorway behind me. Bryce stood there with Stan. Neither of them looked happy to see me or Dev. Bryce motioned with his hand for me to join them in the hallway. I tugged Dev along to join me.

"What're you doing?" Bryce looked from Dev to me as we joined him and Stan in the high school's hallway late Friday morning.

"We're doing what *you* should've done." I planted my feet and locked my knees.

"We're following a new lead in the investigation," Dev answered at the same time I did. His tone was much less belligerent than mine.

Bryce glanced at Stan before returning his attention to me. "You gave *us* this information for *us* to investigate. Let *us* investigate." His hazel eyes were hard with purpose and bright with irritation.

My skin heated as my temper rose to match his. For that moment in time, it seemed as though Bryce and I were the only ones in the hallway. I'd forgotten about Dev and Stan. All I could think about was clearing my mother's name and getting these two knucklehead detectives to treat their investigation with more urgency.

"You're not moving fast enough." I forced the words through clenched teeth.

"Ms. Murray. Mr. Murray." Stan's dark gray suit looked loose and shapeless as though he'd machine washed clothing that was marked dry clean only. "We appreciate that you're worried about your mother. We are as well. Like I told my wife, she's a great lady. You're also concerned about your bakery. We understand that. It's your livelihood. This is ours." He gestured toward the library behind him. "Why don't you go back and look after your bakery? We'll handle the investigation and make sure that justice is served for your family and Principal Smith."

Stan's words seemed so reasonable and comforting. But both he and Bryce were missing the point.

My voice trembled with anger and tears. "We're not stopping you from investigating, but while you're taking your time, our mother's under a lot of pressure. You don't understand how devastating it is to have your name in the paper as a person of interest in a murder investigation. I do. I've lived through that. It's *incredibly* stressful."

A flash of pain swept through Bryce's deep-set eyes. "We're not taking our time with the investigation. I promise. But we have to be thorough."

June watched from her seat at the library's blond wood table. I felt her curiosity across the few feet that separated us in the hallway. I pulled my eyes from her and glanced at Dev. He shook his head. He was warning me not to further antagonize the detectives.

I turned back to them. "I'll leave you to your investigation." *But I'm* not *giving up on mine.*

Dev kept pace beside me. "You did a good job, interviewing June. You asked good questions."

"Thank you." Long strides helped exercise my irritation after our confrontation with Bryce and Stan. "I'm convinced the stolen money is the motive for Emily's murder."

"So am I." Dev sounded as frustrated as I felt. "And, Lynds, you were right. We need to get our own answers. We can't rely on the detectives."

"No, unfortunately, we can't." That was disappointing. I shoved at the heavy gray metal door, pushing my way out of the school. It was several degrees cooler outside than it had been indoors. "But I'll need to figure out who among the four suspects—Daniel, Guy, June, and Miguel—would have the greatest motivation to risk their careers by stealing the money."

"Why did Emily want Meera at the dinner if this was only about the missing money, though?" Dev's question faded into the background.

I hesitated when my car came into view at the front of the parking lot. A cool breath of foreboding rustled the hairs at the back of my neck. The driver's side wiper pinned a white sheet of paper to my windshield. I approached it with cautious steps and tugged it free.

"What is it?" Dev stood behind me, looking over my shoulder.

I had a pretty good idea of its message but read it anyway: *This is your final warning. You see I can get to you wherever you are. Stop investigating—or else.*

"Lynds!" Dev caught my waist as my knees failed me. "We have to do something." His voice was gruff with anger.

"Yes." I swallowed to ease my throat and took a breath to settle myself. I smelled the warm asphalt beneath us and the gas from the traffic yards away. "We have to solve this case." I gestured back toward the school. My voice shook almost as much as my hand. "That's a security camera. Let's see if Bryce and Stan can convince the guards to let us watch it. Maybe this time they'll believe me when I tell them I didn't write the note."

CHAPTER 24

"There! You see!" I stabbed an index finger toward the security monitor as the head of Kings County Early College High School's security played the tape. The video showed someone pinning the threatening message against my windshield late Friday morning. "I told you I wasn't threatening myself."

The school's chief security officer, who was helping us review the camera footage, looked from me to Bryce. "You thought she'd left that paper on her own car?" His lyrical cadence gave a hint of his Jamaican roots. "That doesn't even look like her. They're too tall."

The officer's name tag read: "Campbell," and he was my new best friend. His brown head was bald, but the sprinkles of gray in the heavy beard and thick moustache that masked his rounded cheeks made me think he was in his mid- to late sixties.

Mr. Campbell was right. The person in the video was average height, but still taller than me. There was no way to identify gender, age, or ethnicity. An oversized red sweat suit masked their build. The white towel they'd draped over their head and shoulders covered their face, and they'd kept their back to the camera the entire time.

"We didn't think she'd left *that* note for herself." Bryce sounded impatient.

"My sister didn't write *either* of these threats." Dev's tone lowered the temperature in the room by at least ten degrees.

Mr. Campbell's thick shoulders bounced up and down as he laughed. "What foolishness."

I would've laughed, too, if the situation weren't so frightening. I drew my cell phone from the front right pocket of my navy jeans. Lining up the camera app with the security monitor, I recorded the video on-screen.

"What're you doing?" Bryce asked.

"Copying the video." Just as I'd photographed the threatening note that I hoped they'd take seriously this time. I could feel him looking over my shoulder. I could smell his cologne, subtle and woodsy. "I know the figure's unrecognizable, but I want a copy anyway. I might notice something later." I glanced at him behind me. "You're going to ask for a copy, aren't you?"

"Of course." He exchanged a look with Stan before turning back to Mr. Campbell. "Could we get a copy of the footage, please?"

Oh, brother.

The officer laughed again. "You have she tellin' you how to do your job? You have to get an early start if you want to keep up with Genevieve Bains's people."

Dev and I exchanged a wide-eyed look. I turned to Mr. Campbell. "You know our grandmother?"

He nodded. "You look just like she. Very pretty." He jerked his head toward Bryce. "Maybe that's why he's having so much trouble concentrating on the job. He's too busy staring at you."

My face burned with embarrassment. I glanced back at Bryce, but he looked away. A blush climbed from his neck into his cheeks. If Mr. Campbell was right . . . Well, I was flattered, but we had to focus on my mother for now. After we cleared her of even a hint of suspicion in Emily Smith's murder, then I could decide whether I had a future with Bryce. But I'll tell you, right now, it wasn't looking good.

I saved the video file, then pocketed my cell phone. "Thank you for your help, Mr. Campbell."

The officer smiled. "You be careful, nuh? And tell your granny hello for me."

"Yes, sir." I inclined my head toward Bryce and Stan. I felt their eyes on me as I led Dev from the room.

What were the detectives thinking? Were they finally convinced I wasn't fabricating evidence to clear my mother's name? Or did they think today's threat was an example of my doubling down on some plot to make my mother seem innocent?

"How're you holding up?" Dev's voice was soft and low with concern.

"To be honest, it wasn't any easier reading the hatred in that note than it was reading the first one." I couldn't suppress a shiver. "I need to know who's threatening my life. But I'll tell you one thing: I won't allow them to intimidate me into giving up on clearing Mommy's name."

Dev matched his strides to mine and put his arm around my shoulders. "My baby sister's turned into the Equalizer."

"Oh, brother." We pushed through the school's side doors that led to the parking lot.

"I'm serious." He gave me a half hug as we approached my twelve-year-old compact sedan. "Even when you were in college, you were like a turtle. If people looked at you wrong or spoke to you harshly, you'd shrink into your shell. Now you're standing up and speaking up for yourself. I'm proud of you."

My skin warmed under his praise. "Thanks, Dev. That means a lot to me. I'm proud of you, too." Using my remote car opener, I unlocked my car and slipped in behind the steering wheel.

Dev folded his long, lean frame onto the passenger seat. "Even though I'm unemployed?"

I started the car and shifted it into gear to reverse out of the parking space. "You'll find another job, soon. Hopefully, you'll love the next one more than the one you just left."

"Thanks. I hope so, too." Dev sighed. "In the meantime, I'd like to continue helping out in the bakery."

I looked at him in surprise. "Of course. We love having you there."

"And I want to help with the investigation."

"You already are." I exited the parking lot, merging into traffic. "Thanks to the video, we can rule out June as the murderer. According to the timecode, we were meeting with her when the killer put the message on my car."

"Since she and Mom are friends, I'm glad about that."

"So am I." I braked to protect a jaywalker. "That still leaves us with Daniel, Miguel, and Guy. Which one of them was desperate enough to steal the fund-raiser money and poison Emily to cover it up?"

The young singer on the dark wood stage had started her set at the nightclub late Friday night, covering some of British-Jamaican reggae singer June Lodge's greatest hits, including "Someone Loves You, Honey" and "More Than I Can Say." Now she was performing original reggae songs. Or at least ones I didn't recognize. Her voice was full, haunting, and captivating. Flowers crowned her upswept ebony hair. She wore a figure-hugging, sparkling turquoise dress that was more green than blue, depending on how she stood.

I took a closer look at the drummer. I was pretty sure he was Rocky's boyfriend. He was handsome, and all of the musicians were as talented as their lead singer. It wouldn't surprise me to read an announcement in next week's paper about their signing a big recording contract. Nutmeg's was well-known for launching up-and-coming musicians, singers, and other artists. Their last song of the night brought Reena, Alfonso, me, and the rest of the audience to our feet in a thunderous ovation. The singer's smile was surprised, pleased, and proud. The group bowed, waved, and blew kisses to the audience before packing up their instruments and exiting the stage.

I settled onto my seat at the round dark wood table. "They were amazing."

"They should be performing at bigger venues." Alfonso Lester, Reena's new boyfriend, flashed a smile.

Reena was seated between me and Alfonso. "We'll be downloading their music soon. I'm sure of it. Manny's been raving about them, especially the singer. I think he has a crush on her." She winked at me.

Lighting around the nightclub's circular space, including the bar toward the back, was just bright enough to make out the club's gold-and-crimson décor, our drinks, and the appetizers we'd ordered for our table.

The venue was always crowded, but tonight it was packed. Not surprising for a Friday. However, Reena knew someone who knew someone, yada yada. That's how we managed to find ourselves seated at a table near the stage. My joining my cousin and her boyfriend at this Little Caribbean hot spot had been Reena's idea. She'd insisted the atmosphere would help clear my mind. Her last attempt to distract me from an investigation hadn't ended well, though.

I'd been surprised when she'd invited me to join her and Alfonso. They'd been dating less than a month and had only gone out a couple of times. I felt weird being the third wheel when they were still getting to know each other. But in typical Reena style, she didn't care about the awkwardness of my situation. She knew what was best for me and that was my going to a nightclub with her and her new boyfriend. Whatever.

The master of ceremonies returned to the mic. "Our next performer is a very talented, very passionate spoken word poet. He's going to open your eyes and show you the truth. Ladies and gentlemen, it's my pleasure to introduce José Perez."

"What?" I gaped at the stage. Reena and Alfonso echoed my surprise.

José strode out from stage left. A wine red silk shirt flowed over his broad shoulders and lean torso. He'd paired it with sand-colored pants. He winked at me as he adjusted the microphone. We might be surprised to see him, but he must have known we were there. I shook off my amazement and gave the reporter/spoken word poet my full attention.

José's eyes left mine to take in the rest of the crowded room. His voice commanded attention. "Melting Pot. You tell me I must assimilate. But I say diversity's what makes this country great. If the many become one, who do the many become? This country was built on the backs of ethnics: Natives, Africans, Asians, Hispanics. You tell me to be just like you; then you take my food, my clothes, my music, and my hairdo. You want me to assimilate while you make bank as you appropriate. You say return from where I came. I tell you we both have rights to the claim."

The depth of emotion and power in his poetry stunned

me. The crime beat reporter had the soul of a poet. I hadn't realized I'd once again risen to my feet until I started to applaud. Reena and Alfonso stood with me. José had expressed my feelings so well. Judging by the loud applause and piercing whistles, his lyrics had had a similar effect on the rest of the audience. The MC returned to the stage to help José wrap up his performance. He walked offstage and strode straight to our table.

My eyes stretched wide with shock. I still couldn't close my mouth. "José, that was incredible." I waited while my companions congratulated him. "How long have you been writing poetry?"

"You would never have believed it, huh?" He took the empty seat at our table, which put his back to the stage. "Since I was little, but I've only been performing a few years."

"You're so talented." Reena stared at him as though she'd never seen him before. That's how I felt.

"Thank you." José lowered his eyes as though her praise made him uncomfortable.

I hunted for words to express how much his poem had affected me. "It's important to be good citizens to our adopted country, but I feel like your poem is also telling us it's important to remember the traditions and cultures of the countries we came from."

"Exactly." José turned to me. "The U.S. is a country of immigrants. One person's culture doesn't have more value than another."

"Do you want to be a poet?" Reena asked. "Is that what you really want to do?"

His smile was self-deprecating. "The crime beat pays the bills and I enjoy it. I'm good at it. But I enjoy writing poetry, too. One day, I'd like to publish a book of my poems. Maybe write some songs."

"You have a lot of talent. I look forward to hearing your songs." Who would've thought the irritatingly persistent newshound was such a sensitive and expressive soul?

"Thank you." His eyes twinkled with pleasure. "But for now, I'm a crime beat reporter. Speaking of which, have you learned anything new on Emily Smith's murder?"

"We found out all the money raised for the library's fund-raiser had been stolen from the high school at the end of April." I gestured toward Reena before turning back to José. "Did you know about it?"

José's thick dark eyebrows rose toward the wavy lock of hair that fell over his forehead. "Wait, at the end of April, I'd heard rumors about a break-in at the school, but when I'd asked the school board's media contact about it, she claimed it was vandalism. Do you think the break-in's connected to the murder?"

"We're sure of it." I brought him up-to-date. "We're focusing on the committee members."

José whistled. "I can understand why. I'll check with the education reporters, find out if they know anything." He rose. "For now, I'd better join my friends. They're probably wondering where I am. I'll be in touch."

An image of the threat I'd found on my windshield that morning settled on my mind. "The sooner the better, please. I have a feeling we're running out of time."

CHAPTER 25

"Looks like Detective Jackson has some competition." Reena sipped her planter's punch. Dark rum, syrup, grenadine, bitters, and pineapple and lime juices created the deep orange-red cocktail.

I frowned at her. "What're you talking about?"

Reena shook her head as though I'd brought her great pain and sorrow. "Girl, I saw the way that reporter was looking at you." She turned to Alfonso. "You noticed it, too, didn't you?"

He raised both hands, palms out. "I'm not in this."

Reena shook her head, a sign she was on her best behavior. The Reena I knew would roll her eyes at a response like that. I didn't know Alfonso well enough to tell whether, like Reena, he'd brought his representative to the club rather than his true self.

She turned her attention back to me. "I'm just saying. But speaking of the detective, has he come to his senses yet?"

"If by his coming to his senses you mean has he taken Mommy off his suspect list, the answer's no." I let my eyes move around the room as I sipped my bird of paradise. The drink contained pineapple and lime juices with rum. "And José's just as bad. By writing articles that refer to

Mommy as a 'person of interest,' he's keeping up the impression that she's guilty."

"Humph." Reena reached for a carrot slice. "You'd think the detective was smart enough to know this isn't the best way to win your affection."

"My affection? Reena, I'm not thinking about Bryce Jackson." That was a lie. "I have enough on my plate between the police investigation and rebuilding our customer base." That was the truth.

Alfonso dunked a celery slice into the blue cheese dressing. "How's your mother?"

I thought of the frown lines that had taken residence across her formerly smooth brow. Tension bracketed her full lips, which used to smile so easily. "She's under a lot of stress. The detectives keep saying they don't think she's guilty, but they won't take her off their list."

Reena scowled. "Why not?"

"They're doing their due diligence," Alfonso answered Reena. He was almost apologetic when he shifted his attention to me. "Your mother had an uneasy working relationship with Principal Smith. She also helped cater the event. If the prosecution doesn't have a solid case against another suspect, the defense could try to use those facts to introduce reasonable doubt for the jury. In the detectives' defense, the more information they have that clears your mother, the faster the prosecutor would be able to shut down that narrative."

"That's what Bryce said. I suppose it makes sense, but the longer she remains a person of interest, the more damage is being done to her reputation. I shouldn't have to solve the case to clear my mother's name." I absently wiped the cold, damp condensation from my cocktail glass with my thumb. "I even sent them dozens of photos from the event that proved Mommy and Daddy didn't spend time with the guests after the initial introduction. Bryce said just because they're not in the photo doesn't mean they weren't in the room."

"Ooh! You have photos?" Reena held her hands out, palms up, and wiggled her fingers. "Lemme see." She loved photos. I'm not sure why. If I had to guess, I'd say she loved seeing what people wore to various occasions.

I gave her my cell phone. "Granny used Dev's digital camera the day of the event. But I asked her to email the photos to me so I could get them to Bryce."

"Hmm." Reena was flipping through the photos with Alfonso when she made a puzzled sound.

"What is it?" I selected a carrot and dipped it in the bowl of blue cheese dressing.

She turned the phone's screen toward me. She'd manipulated one of the images to make Emily Smith look larger. "Look at her lipstick."

I leaned closer. "It's very red."

"That's right. It's a warm red. It looks good on her. At the wake, the lipstick the funeral parlor used for her was a cool red with a hint of blue. I remember thinking that shade wasn't right for her. I also remember thinking it looked a little janky."

Cheap or not, I didn't notice Emily's lipstick during the wake. I stared hard at the image. "Could it be the lighting that makes the lipstick look like a different color?"

Reena was shaking her head before I finished speaking. "I'm not looking at how the light affects the lipstick. I'm looking at how the lipstick affects Emily's skin tone. In these pictures, her lipstick complemented her. At the wake, the lipstick clashed with her coloring."

Alfonso leaned into the table. "Maybe the funeral parlor used a lipstick they had on hand."

"Maybe." Reena didn't sound convinced.

My pulse quickened. "I'll call the funeral parlor in the morning and ask whether they used Emily's lipstick. If they did, we'll know something's wrong." I met Reena's eyes. "We may have figured out how the poison was administered."

Reena's eyes sparkled with excitement. "You think the killer put the strychnine on Emily's lipstick?"

I rubbed my arms, trying to ward off a sudden chill. "Right before we served dinner, Emily went to the restroom to refresh her makeup."

Alfonso's eyebrows leaped up his forehead. "Emily administered the poison herself without knowing it."

"Then the killer switched the doctored lipstick with one they'd bought." My shoulders rose and fell with a sigh. "I need to speak with Bryce. The killer's prints might be on that lipstick."

"No one answered at the funeral home when I called this morning, so I had to leave a message." I joined Reena at Granny's table beside the checkout counter the next morning.

Reena gave me a sideways look. "Well, it is Saturday. They might be busy. You'll probably have to call again. Where's Granny?"

"She and Uncle Al had an errand." And Dev was with Joymarie. He was going to tell her about quitting his job. I was certain she'd support my brother's decision, but I couldn't relax until I had confirmation of that from him.

Reena frowned. "That's strange. Daddy didn't say anything about an errand."

That brought me up short. It wasn't like Uncle Al to not share his appointments with his family. Like my parents, Granny, Dev, and me, they told one another everything.

Someone always knew where and how to get in touch with us.

Then I remembered how secretive Granny had seemed. I smiled. "Maybe they're planning something to help cheer Mommy up."

Reena hummed her excitement. "Ooh, shoes. Shoes are always a good idea. But why wouldn't they have asked me to go with them?"

"The mind boggles." I held her eyes without expression.

Reena rolled her eyes. "So, did you tell Detective Fine about our lipstick theory?"

Just like that, every burden known to humankind landed on my shoulders. "No, I want to speak with the funeral home first. If they used lipstick they had in their inventory, then our theory will have fallen apart and I'll have even less credibility with him."

"You don't have a credibility issue with him." Reena arched a well-shaped eyebrow. "If he didn't trust you, he wouldn't be so into you."

I was speechless. First Mr. Campbell, the chief security officer at Kings County Early College High School, and now Reena were implying my high school crush was crushing on me. Bryce was crushing on me—when he should be focusing on finding Emily's murderer so we could clear my mother's name.

Temper loosened my vocal cords. "I'd rather he was *into* the fact that my mother isn't a killer. I can't see myself with someone who could so easily imagine me and my family as murderers. What would we tell our children? 'Before Mommy and Daddy got married, your daddy tried to throw your mommy and your mommy's mommy in jail.' Could you imagine how that would affect them?"

Reena raised her eyebrows. "I'm still trying to wrap my

head around your going from avoiding Detective Fine to raising a family with him in like two sentences."

Sometimes my cousin drove me insane. I think it was deliberate.

"I still can't believe Bryce remembers me from high school." I hadn't meant to say that part out loud.

"Are you kidding? *I* can." Reena leaned into the table for emphasis. "You were a very attractive teenager and you've grown into a beautiful woman. Now that you're more confident, you're even more beautiful."

I laughed. "You're only saying that because people say we look alike."

Reena tossed me a grin. "True. True. But it's not the only reason."

"Lynds." Mommy's voice carried across the pass-through window behind the customer counter. "Sheryl Cross's on the line for you."

Sheryl Cross, the president of the Caribbean American Heritage Festival Association. My throat went dry. "Thank you, Mommy. I'm coming."

Reena stood. "That's my cue to go. Good luck with the dragon lady."

I watched Reena leave, then scanned the dining area. Our half-dozen or so customers seemed fine. I headed back to the bakery's office and picked up the phone.

"Good morning, Ms. Cross. I wasn't expecting to hear from you on a Saturday." I thought I sounded somewhat self-assured.

"With the festival next month, committee members are working night and day, seven days a week, to make sure everything's perfect." Her voice was brisk and cool.

"It always is." I hoped she heard the smile in my voice.

Sheryl grunted. "Ms. Murray, flattery has no bearing on the committee's decision." I started to correct her, but she spoke over me. "We're meeting Tuesday morning at eight o'clock sharp to discuss Spice Isle Bakery's status with our festival. If you're still insistent on addressing the committee, that will be your only chance to do so."

My palms were sweating. The telephone receiver was slick in my grasp. "Thank you, Ms. Cross. I'll be there."

She gave another grunt. "Eight o'clock. Sharp. *Do not* keep us waiting. And come alone. We don't have time to hear from each member of your entire family."

I didn't like the idea of not having my family with me, but she didn't seem to be in a negotiating mood. "I'll be there on time and alone, Ms. Cross. I won't keep the committee waiting."

"Be sure that you don't." She disconnected the call.

I cradled the receiver and turned to find my parents staring at me from the doorway. "I have an appointment to plead our case at eight o'clock Tuesday morning. I'd better work on my speech. Heaven knows what I'm going to say to change their minds, but I'll only have this one chance."

CHAPTER 26

A little more than an hour later, I returned to the kitchen. "I hadn't expected Granny to be gone so long." I shared a look between my parents. "Have either of you heard from her?"

Daddy looked up from the vegetables he was chopping at the center island. "I haven't." He looked to Mommy. His voice was gentle. "Have you, Della?"

Mommy didn't seem to hear him. She stood at the stove, deep in thought, as she prepared the rice and peas for our Saturday lunch crowd. Salty, buttery steam drifted up from the boiling pot. Waves of anguish and agitation rolled from her. This wasn't about Granny. I closed my eyes briefly as I acknowledged what troubled her.

I cupped her shoulder with my hand. The knots of tension I felt against my palm shocked me. "Mommy, tell me what're you thinking."

"I don't know what I'm thinking." Her voice was sharp with frustration. "I don't know what to think." She turned, pinning me with her eyes. The emotions battling in their dark depths—fear, anger, sorrow, shame—pierced my heart. "We didn't do anything. The police tests came back, confirming we didn't do anything. Then why are you still catching problems. It's not right."

"No, it's not." I wrapped my arms around her, trying to give her the same comfort I'd found in her embraces all my life. She smelled of vanilla and powder, with a hit of the salt and butter from the boiling rice and peas.

Her arms squeezed me back. Daddy joined us, making it a family hug. It was something we all needed. The embrace told us we weren't alone. We'd get through this together. The suspicion and distrust weren't burdens we had to carry on our own.

Mommy stepped back. She cleared her throat. "Monday will be two weeks. And they're still watching me as though I'm the murderer. I don't understand why."

I took her hands. They were soft and warm in mine. "Mommy, I'm so sorry for the strain you're under. I wish I could make it go away."

She smiled, though the look in her eyes remained troubled. "You're doing so much with your investigation."

I shook my head. "I couldn't do it without you and the rest of the family."

Daddy put his arm around Mommy's shoulders and looked to me. "Lynds, how did you keep from going mad when the detectives suspected you of killing Fabrizi?"

"I got through it because of our family." I gestured toward Mommy and Daddy. "You all kept me sane. That's what we're going to do now. We'll get through this the same way we've gotten through other challenges, together as a family."

The office phone rang before I'd finished my sentence. I squeezed Mommy's hand again before releasing her and hurrying to answer the call. The ID screen displayed the local precinct's phone number. It was becoming too familiar.

I braced myself before answering. "Spice Isle Bakery. May I help you?"

"Lyndsay, it's Bryce." His voice was grim.

The back of my neck tingled. Something was wrong. "What can I do for you, Detective?"

His deep sigh rushed across the phone line. "You can come get your grandmother. She and your uncle have been detained for breaking and entering Kings County Early."

I collapsed against my desk. Unbelievable. "I'm on my way."

I shook with anger. My face burned with shame. Bryce led my grandmother and uncle from one of the precinct's holding cells like common criminals late Saturday morning. What made it even more galling was that this time he had good reason to. They'd acted like common criminals. What had they been thinking?

He studied me with caution as he stopped in front of me. "Good morning, Lyndsay."

I was too humiliated to meet his eyes. Instead, my gaze landed on his squared chin. He really did have handsome features. "Detective."

"You can call me Bryce." He paused. I was too annoyed with Granny and Uncle Al to reply. He continued. "Your grandmother and uncle didn't do any actual damage and they didn't take anything, so I was able to convince the arresting officers to let them off with a warning."

I unlocked my jaw and drew a breath. The stench of burned coffee and old pastries rushed up my nose. "Thank you. Does that mean we can leave now?"

What a nightmare. Before today, no one in my family had ever been on the wrong side of the law: no parking tickets, no speeding tickets, very few overdue library books. How do we explain today? Were Granny and Uncle Al under a spell? Had they vexed some duppies? I scowled first at Granny, then at Uncle Al. Their innocent expressions would be laughable, if we weren't in a police precinct.

Bryce hesitated again. "Yes. You're free to go." He turned to Granny and Uncle Al. "I got the officers to drop the charges this time. I won't be able to do that again. I understand you're concerned about Ms. Murray, but that doesn't mean you can break the law. Stay out of trouble. OK?"

They both enthusiastically agreed.

Oh, brother.

The top of my head was ready to pop off. I felt compelled to show respect to my elders, though. So I held my tongue and led Granny and Uncle Al out of the building. I'd parked my compact yellow sedan in the parking lot adjacent to the precinct.

Uncle Al kept pace beside Granny behind me. "Lynds—"

Taking a breath, I managed to keep my voice even. "Let's wait until we're in the car, please, Uncle Al."

I activated my keyless entry and settled behind the steering wheel. Granny took the passenger seat. Uncle Al folded his longer form at an angle on the back seat.

I locked the doors and cracked the automatic windows. "Did you find anything?"

Granny settled her red handbag on her lap and folded her hands on top of it. "We didn't even get a chance to look before the bo-bo showed up."

Somehow coming out of this empty-handed made this situation so much worse. I closed my eyes briefly. "How did your actions help our situation?"

Granny sighed. She glanced at me, then let her eyes drift away. "Lynds, I know you're angry, but your uncle and I wanted to search our suspects' offices. We need to find evidence that one of them killed Emily and get the bo-bo off Della, right?"

I turned to her. "We're investigating Principal Smith's murder as a group. I don't investigate people or question suspects without letting the family know what I'm doing. You shouldn't either."

Granny tightened her grip on her handbag. "Not only is someone threatening my granddaughter—"

"My niece," Uncle Al interrupted.

"They're also framing my daughter." Granny's expression was defensive.

"My sister," Uncle Al added.

"My mother." I tipped back my head and took a breath. "But breaking into a building, Granny? How does breaking the law help anything?"

"I'm sorry, Lynds." She sounded sincere.

"So am I." Uncle Al cleared his throat.

"I understand you're impatient. So am I." I shared a look between them. "But you wanted me to lead this investigation because of my experience with my own case. Then let me lead. Don't go rogue."

"You're right." Granny glanced over her shoulder at Uncle Al before turning back to me. "We're sorry. In the future, we'll speak with you first."

I still felt grumpy. I gave Granny the side eye. "Besides, do you really think the person who stole the money would keep it in the school? Come on."

Granny and Uncle Al exchanged a look before he spoke. "We didn't think about that. But there could be other clues at the school."

I shifted on my seat to better meet his gaze. "Like what?"

Granny shrugged. "We'll know it when we see it."

All right, then. I started my car and backed it out of the parking space. "Next time, please run your ideas by me. Or at the very least, wait until after the lunch rush before breaking into buildings."

CHAPTER 27

"My grandmother took this photo with Dev's camera during Emily Smith's retirement dinner." I gave Bryce my cell phone. On its screen was an image of Emily with June and Meera. They were seated at the table we'd set up for the event in the bakery's dining area, close to where I was sitting with Bryce now. It was a disconcerting thought.

It was late Saturday afternoon. I'd called to ask Bryce to meet with me at the bakery. Technically, Saturdays were his days off, but he'd been at the precinct, since he'd somehow gotten word about my grandmother being detained. I'd heard back from the funeral home and wanted to share our lipstick theory with him. There were a handful of guests in the dining area with us. I could smell the spices and savory sauces from their meals. But for the most part, Bryce and I had enough privacy to discuss the case, especially if we kept our voices low.

"All right." He shifted his attention from the cell phone to me. His hazel eyes were intense. "What do you want me to notice?"

"Emily's lipstick. See the way it looks in this picture?" I tapped my cell phone. "You were at Emily's wake. Did you look at her?"

"Yes." He met my eyes again.

"Do you remember the shade of her lipstick?"

He frowned at the image on my cell phone. He was silent for several moments as he combed through his memories. "Her lipstick hadn't been this red. It was darker."

"That's right." I was so excited he'd remembered. I wanted to jump up from my chair and hug him. "I called the funeral home. The lipstick they used on Emily was the one they found in her purse. But as you can see, that's not the shade Emily wore."

Bryce set my cell phone on the table in front of him and pinned me with his gaze. "What are you saying?"

I could tell he already knew but wanted me to spell it out for him. I didn't have a problem with that. "We've been wondering how the killer administered the poison. There weren't any traces of the strychnine in the food, drink, dishware, silverware, or glassware. Everything tested clean. We—my family and I—believe the killer put the strychnine on Emily's lipstick."

Bryce frowned at my cell phone. He seemed deep in thought. "That's possible. The killer tampers with her lipstick. She applies it—"

"Which was the first thing she did when she arrived at the bakery. She went to the restroom to refresh her makeup."

Bryce continued. "Then once the poison took effect, they switched the lipsticks."

"Emily's purse had fallen from her chair and the contents had spilled out."

He pounced on that. "Do you remember who'd repacked her purse?"

I frowned. "They all did—Daniel, Guy, Miguel, Meera, and June. I remember thinking it was weird that they all got involved as though they each wanted credit for helping. But the funeral home still has the lipstick. You could get it from them and dust for prints."

He spread his hands. "The killer probably used gloves. Or they could plausibly claim their prints got on the lipstick tube when they were helping to repack Emily's purse."

Frustration stirred within me. "Or they could've slipped up and forgotten to have used gloves. Or if their prints are on the lipstick but not Emily's, wouldn't that give you additional evidence you could use to dig deeper into them to see if there are other links to Emily's murder?"

"It's a long shot, Lyndsay." He rested his hand on the back of mine where I'd placed it on the table. "I just don't want you to get your hopes up."

I snatched my hand away. It was a struggle to keep my voice low. "You don't seem to understand, *Detective*. Hope is all I have right now. Hope and leads you don't seem to be taking seriously."

His eyes widened with surprise. He whispered back, "I am taking your leads seriously."

"You keep talking about removing all traces of suspicion from my mother so the killer can't point to her in order to cast doubt on their guilt. Well, here's an idea: How about you help me prove my mother's innocence by proving the real killer's guilt?" I stood from the table with as much poise as I could gather and strode out of the dining area.

Bryce and I obviously had different approaches to this investigation. He wanted to go on defense. I wanted to go on the attack. I believed my way was better and I was prepared to go it without him.

I checked my cell phone screen again. The time passed over to 8:31 AM Tuesday as I watched. *Urgh!* After getting all over me about being on time, the festival committee members were more than half an hour late for their own meeting. Outrageous. And this was after I'd arrived early. I took a calming breath to ease the screaming in my head. I caught the scent of frankincense. Lavender incense with its soothing properties would've been a better choice if the committee was going to keep people waiting.

I sank farther into the overstuffed navy armchair and looked around the Caribbean American Heritage Festival Association's small dark wood and eggshell waiting area. Wooden frames of colorful maps of the more than thirty independent West Indian countries and dependencies lined the walls. Souvenirs from all over the Caribbean— baskets, pottery, paintings, and statuary—were arranged on desks, tables, and cabinets around the room.

The receptionist sat at the dark wood desk at the front of the room. Her workstation was positioned beneath one of the office's fluorescent lights. I'd already approached her twice about the delay. Each time she'd insisted the committee knew I was here. Now I sensed her straining to avoid my eyes as though she was embarrassed I was being detained for so long.

I checked my cell phone again. Another two minutes had passed. My eyes strayed to the dark wood conference door. It remained condescendingly closed. *Urgh!* Granted the bakery wasn't open today. I didn't have to worry about helping my family and being available to customers. That didn't mean I didn't have anything to do, though. Instead, I'd spent the past thirty-three-plus minutes building up a huge reserve of panic.

Irritation weighed down my facial muscles. If my grandmother were in my position, she would've marched to the door and pushed it open. So would Reena. Mommy would've knocked first. Daddy would've charmed his way into the room, and Dev would've found an argument that would've convinced them to stop playing games with him.

Why was I the only pushover in the family? What was my superpower?

Before I could answer that, the conference room door opened. Gina Good, the association's secretary, stood in the threshold. "Ms. Murray, you can come in now."

It was about time. I squared my shoulders and marched into the room behind her. Gina joined President Sheryl Cross and Vice President Sean Baptiste at the mid-sized rectangular honey wood table. I struggled not to let my irritation show, although it would've helped if someone had acknowledged their lateness.

Sheryl was writing notes on a plain sheet of white paper on the desk in front of her. She spoke without looking up. "You know Vice President Baptiste and Secretary Good. You can speak now."

Seated on Sheryl's right, Gina kept looking at me, then glancing away. To Sheryl's left, Sean was texting someone. They were piling on the discourtesy pretty thick. Was that because their minds were already made up? Then why was I here?

I put the brakes on my straining temper. Unclenching my hands at my sides, I took one large step forward. It brought me to the opposite side of the table from the committee members. I slapped my palms against the warm laminate surface. They jumped on their seats. Three sets of eyes rocketed to meet mine. They obviously hadn't expected my reaction. That made four of us. But if they'd already made up their minds, I didn't have anything to lose.

My lips curved into a cool smile. "I know your parents would expect you to give me your undivided attention during this meeting."

Invoking parental expectations was a sure way to get a response. No one wanted to bring shame to their family. Blood drained from Gina's face. Sean's lips tightened with disdain as he set aside his cell phone. Sheryl's dark eyes flashed with temper, but she lowered her pen.

I straightened and met each of their eyes in turn, Gina, Sheryl, then Sean. "My family and I appreciate the committee has a difficult task in selecting vendors from among the large pool of small business owners who request a spot at the Caribbean American Heritage Festival each year. We were thrilled and honored to be selected this year. We've only been open a little more than two months, but in that short amount of time we've been fortunate to obtain a base of regular customers, and new customers are discovering us every day. Our bakery has received rave reviews for the exceptional quality of our food, our reasonable prices, and our exemplary customer service."

Sheryl rolled her eyes, interrupting me. "All of that—reviews, customer loyalty, income—is window dressing. The festival is about much more than appearances. It's about character, morality. We want upstanding vendors with unimpeachable reputations to represent the community during the festival. You and your bakery have been involved in not one, but two murders since the day you opened your doors. That is why you're not qualified to appear at the festival."

Her words stole my breath. Never before had anyone ever accused my family of having poor character, low morals, or impeachable reputations. My pulse pounded in my ears. I was speechless. How could I defend us? Sheryl was right. We had been involved in multiple homicide investigations. It didn't matter that we were the victim of circumstances beyond our control. The police and the media had involved us.

Gina continued to look uncomfortable with the proceeding. Sheryl stared at me as though I was her nemesis, and Sean seemed distracted.

I swallowed to ease my dry throat. "Yes, my family and our bakery have been mentioned in two homicide investigations for murders that have taken place in the Little Caribbean community. But that's not surprising. When you're part of the community, you're going to be affected by the events that happen in it, whether directly or indirectly. There's no escaping that and we wouldn't want to. We deliberately chose to open our bakery in the heart of Little Caribbean because we *want* to be part of our community. It's also one of the reasons my family has attended every festival since we immigrated to the United States. For almost twenty years, it's been my goal and a dream to participate in the festival as a vendor. The day you approved our application was one of the proudest days of my life."

Sheryl glanced at her gold wristwatch. "All right, Ms. Murray. That's all we need to hear from you. I'll reconvene the committee to vote on the matter."

Her dismissive tone confirmed my fear that she'd already made up her mind. Gina's and Sean's blank expressions didn't give anything away. I doubt they'd ever oppose Sheryl anyway. "When do you think you'll have your decision?"

Sheryl's lips tightened as though my question annoyed her. "By the end of the week."

That seemed a long time to wait. "Thank you."

I paused, but none of the committee members responded. I did my best. At the end of the day, that's all that mattered. All I could do now was wait and hope for a miracle. Turning, I let myself out of the conference room.

I was in this situation for two reasons: Claudio Fabrizi's and Emily Smith's murders. I'd been able to successfully close the first case. If I wanted another chance to change the festival committee members' minds, I had to close this one—and soon.

Miguel was seated behind his desk when I arrived at Kings County Early College High School late Tuesday morning. I'd come here straight from my meeting with the festival organizers. He seemed so intent on his work, I almost hated to interrupt him. Almost. I couldn't be timid if I wanted to clear my mother's name and remove my family's bakery from this latest scandal. As Granny said, "Beat the iron while it's hot." In other words, act while the moment is fresh.

I tapped my knuckles twice on his office's partially opened faux wood door. "Excuse me, Mr. Morales. May I speak with you, please?"

"Of course." He rose and gestured toward one of the two guest chairs in front of his bulky wood desk. "Please call me Miguel."

"And I'm Lyndsay." Returning his smile, I closed his office door and settled onto one of the aging navy visitor's chairs. The office smelled of strong coffee and a lavender cologne. "Thank you for your time. A few questions have been puzzling me about Principal Smith's death. I was hoping you could help clear them up for me."

"I'll do my best, but I'm not a medical professional." The guidance counselor's eyes were patient and curious.

The counselor's outfit—charcoal gray slacks with a matching tie against a black dress shirt—made it seem like he was still in mourning for Emily.

Miguel's office was a comfortable size. It included a bookcase and a circular blond wood conference table that sat four. A small rotating fan on the file cabinet across from his desk made a faint whirring noise as it struggled to keep the room cool. The window beside his desk had a nice view of the front of the school, but at this time of day it took the brunt of the sun's power. It must be a perk in the winter, but as summer approached, the heat became oppressive.

"My family and I were surprised that Principal Smith had such a short guest list for her retirement dinner." I watched him closely for any reaction he might have to my question. "Why do you think she only invited the five of you?"

"I really couldn't tell you." He shook his head. "Anything I'd say would just be speculation."

"Even that would be helpful."

"All right." He shrugged. "I think she invited us because we were the ones who worked most closely with her. A lot of people didn't like Emily. She had the best intentions for the school. She just expressed herself badly."

I blinked. Well, that was a generous way of putting it. "Can you give me an example?"

Miguel spread his arms. "Everything she did was for the welfare of this school. She hired people who really cared about the students. She supported events that would benefit them. She was completely committed to the school, the students, and their parents."

Maybe it was the skeptic in me, but he sounded like he was reciting a script he'd memorized during his new employee orientation. Too many people had corroborated my mother's memories of her as angry and unreasonable. So why was Miguel trying to rewrite history?

"You're the only person who's said anything positive about her. Other people have said she was verbally abusive to teachers, staff, and students equally. Why's your perspective so different?"

Miguel's eyes twinkled with amusement. "Maybe I have more patience than most people. Or maybe it's that

I hadn't worked with her as long. I started after the new year." His smile faded and he became serious. "I don't like to speak ill of the dead. Most people didn't like Emily, but I can't imagine any of them—including your mother—killing her."

"Neither can I, but someone did." I watched for his reaction.

He shook his head with a sigh. "I know. I still can't believe it. It's crazy, but I'm sure the police will figure it out."

I paused a moment before switching subjects. "You were a member of the library's fund-raiser committee."

His eyes flared in surprise. My sudden change of topic caught him off guard. I'd hoped it would.

"Yes, I was." He smiled as though the project held good memories for him. "So were June Min-ho, Dan Rawson, and Guy Law. Why're you asking?"

I frowned. "Haven't the detectives talked with you about it?"

He shook his head again. "Not about the fund-raiser, no."

Oh, for pity's sake. If Bryce and Stan wanted me to give up my investigation, they had to follow up on the good information I gave them with more urgency. *Much* more urgency.

I pushed aside my anger and disappointment. "The event raised sixty thousand dollars, right? As a committee member, what did you think about the board's decision not to report that some of the money had been stolen?"

He hesitated. I sensed him debating the pros and cons of different answers. "How do you know so much about the fund-raiser?"

I tossed him a smile, trying to put him at ease. "We both live and work in very nosy neighborhoods."

My answer didn't seem to satisfy Miguel, but he didn't

challenge it. "It was the board's decision not to report the theft. It wasn't my place to second-guess them. But I understood their decision. It wasn't our finest moment. In fact, the whole event was a horrible black eye for the school."

I sat straighter on the chair, leaning forward. "Who do you think took the money?"

He shrugged. "I have no idea. But I have a better question: Why would the thief still be here?"

That was the million-dollar—or twenty-thousand-dollar—question, wasn't it? I felt more confident than ever that if we followed the money we'd find the killer.

CHAPTER 28

The clock was ticking, but my conversation with Miguel hadn't brought me any closer to identifying Emily's killer. I left his office late Tuesday morning. My thoughts tumbled over themselves, adding to my confusion. Emily must have been poisoned by one of the people she'd invited to her retirement dinner—the same people who'd served on the committee—and their motive for murder had to be the missing money. But how could I prove that?

I turned toward Daniel's office. The soon-to-be high school principal had expensive tastes. Twenty thousand dollars could buy a lot of new Italian suits.

Guy looked up as I approached his desk. He puffed out his chest as a flicker of irritation wrinkled his freckled face. "Principal Rawson doesn't have time to speak with you today."

I glanced at the open office door behind Guy's desk before returning my attention to him. "Shouldn't that be '*Assistant* Principal'? Or has the announcement already been made? I didn't see anything in the papers."

He scowled, extending his neck toward me. "How could they fit the announcement in the paper with all those articles about your family and the bakery in there?"

That was mean. I wanted to pinch him so hard. But I'd

learned how to ignore bullies a long time ago. I circled his desk and marched toward Daniel's office.

"Wait." Guy stood. "I told you Principal Rawson's busy." He grabbed my upper arm.

I looked at his beefy, pale hand, then locked eyes with him. "You have three choices. You could get your hand off me. You could be humiliated when I pin you under your desk. Or you could be charged with assault, and believe me when I tell you I have a direct line to the local precinct."

His Adam's apple worked as he swallowed, but he released me. "You can't go in there."

I shrugged and stepped into Daniel's office. "Good morning, Daniel. May I—"

Guy rushed in at my heels. He pitched his voice above mine. "Principal Rawson, I told her you weren't to be disturbed."

Daniel saved the computer document he'd been working on, then spun his chair to face us. "Lyndsay, common courtesy demands you make an appointment if you want to see someone. Your barging into my office shows you don't respect my time. So tell me why I should give you any of it."

I crossed the room to stand on the other side of his desk, staring him down. "Because my mother isn't the only suspect on the detectives' list." I spared a look toward Guy. "If you're both innocent, you should want to find out who killed Emily just as badly as I do."

Daniel's eyes wavered as he considered my words. Finally, he broke the silence. "Guy, come in and shut the door."

"You were on the library fund-raiser committee." I sat on one of the faded navy visitor's chairs in front of Daniel's desk without waiting for an invitation I didn't think was coming. Guy took the seat beside me.

Daniel shrugged his broad shoulders under a champagne shirt. Was it silk? "Guy and I both were. Along with Miguel and, of course, June."

Guy nodded enthusiastically. "And Principal Smith. She was sort of an honorary member. She didn't come to the meetings, but I gave her regular updates on the committee's progress."

Daniel's features tightened with disapproval. He didn't seem impressed by Emily's honorary membership status. Perhaps he saw it as another example of her taking credit for other people's hard work. "My role was to be the liaison between the school and the community. I brought in several big donors for the event, both in terms of money and items to be auctioned."

The pride in his voice was understandable, considering all the money he'd single-handedly brought in for the fund-raiser. Then again, the more money the committee brought in, the more there would be to steal.

How did he feel about the theft? "It's been reported that of the sixty thousand dollars raised for the library, almost twenty thousand dollars in cash was stolen right out of the school."

"*Sixty* thousand?" Guy looked from me to Daniel and back. "It wasn't sixty. It was almost eighty thousand."

I sat up straighter. "The newspaper claimed the school had raised sixty thousand dollars for the library."

Guy shook his head. "I know the number the media reported, but I was on the committee. I know how much money we raised and it was closer to eighty."

"Guy's correct." Daniel sipped his coffee. "We worked hard to raise that money and we were just shy of eighty. Emily insisted she'd told the reporter the correct amount, but the newspaper had made an error."

What was going on? The newspapers reported the

fund-raiser had brought in sixty thousand dollars, but the amount was closer to eighty thousand. Was it a coincidence that the difference was almost twenty thousand—the same as the amount that had been stolen?

"What were your roles for the project?" I shared a look between Daniel and Guy.

The question seemed to make Guy angrier. "I took the meeting notes, kept the project on track, and kept Principal Smith informed. *June* was supposed to keep the money safe. Why aren't you questioning her?"

"I already have." And I knew June wasn't the killer. She couldn't have left the threatening note on my car because Dev and I had been speaking with her at the time. I turned to Daniel. "You were in charge of getting the donations?"

"That's right." Daniel inclined his head. "And Miguel created the internal and external communication plans to promote the fund-raiser to staff, students, and teachers, as well as alumni, parents, and the greater community."

"June took care of the budget and coordinated the events." Guy gestured toward the door. "If I'd taken the money, you can bet I wouldn't have stuck around. I'd have had a plan to leave before anyone even realized the money was missing."

Miguel had made the same point. Yet none of the committee members had made a move to disappear. The only one with an exit strategy was Emily. She was going to retire.

I gestured toward Guy and Daniel. "Everyone at Emily's retirement dinner had been on the committee except Meera. Why was she there?"

Guy shrugged. "Principal Smith told me to add her at the last minute. Meera hadn't wanted to come, but Principal Smith was adamant, so she came."

But why? Was it because Meera was a nurse? Had

Emily had a premonition that something would happen? Is that the reason she wanted someone with medical training at her event?

The thought gave me chills. "The lock had been broken. Is it possible the thief was someone outside of the school?"

"I'd wondered the same thing." Daniel's shrug was restless. "But how would someone from the outside have known we had the money on-site?"

Frustrated, I sat back against the chair. "Or where it was being kept: the office, desk, or drawer."

Daniel spread his arms. "All of the evidence points to us, but I assure you, none of us took that money."

Guy cut in. "We were all under suspicion. It was one of the worst times in my life."

I knew how he felt. It was horrible being suspected of a crime you hadn't committed. "I understand it was Emily's idea to hold on to the money until the end of the fund-raiser. Why didn't the board hold her accountable for losing the money?"

"But it did." Guy frowned as though he thought I was losing it. "And she was enraged."

"That's a good way to describe her." Daniel nodded his approval. "They told her she couldn't retire with her full pension until she'd either recovered the money or found the thief."

Guy expelled a breath. "That made her even angrier."

I looked from Guy to Daniel. "Do you think she found out who the thief was?"

"She was retiring, wasn't she?" Daniel's tone was dry.

"And the dinner was her finale." In more ways than one.

Almost twenty thousand dollars was still missing from the donations, but the board had approved Emily's retirement. What if Emily had taken the money? Her retirement would allow her to disappear with it. The plan seemed too easy, but sometimes the simplest solution was the correct one. Emily had been setting up one of the committee members to take the fall for the theft she'd planned. To do that, she'd have to choose someone who trusted her, someone she'd be able to take advantage of.

My knees were shaking, but I pushed myself to my feet and used one of the arms of the chair to steady myself. I considered Daniel. "Did you believe Emily had sent a correction about the fund-raising donations to the newspapers?"

Daniel's eyes were steady on mine. "No, I did not. Time and again, Emily had proven herself to have a troubled relationship with the truth."

Fair enough. I turned to Guy. "Did you?"

He lowered his eyes. "I wanted to believe her, but the papers never printed a retraction."

"Thank you, gentlemen."

I called Granny on my cell as I hurried through the school to the visitors' parking lot. "Granny, I think I know who killed Emily. Can you help me prove it?"

CHAPTER 29

Granny's name and number popped onto my cell phone screen Tuesday afternoon. I straightened on the desk chair in the bakery's office. "Is everything set?"

"Yes, we'll be able to get into the school this evening." Her voice was low, emphasizing our need for secrecy. The fewer people who knew what we were planning, the better. Deniability was key. "Although I don't understand why it's OK to break in when *you* want to, but wrong when Al and I do it."

I saved the inventory file on the computer, shaking my head in disbelief. "You two were caught."

"Oh-ho!" Her sarcasm was unmistakable.

I chose to ignore it. "We'll leave a little before the sun sets at eight."

"I'll be ready, love." She ended the call and I went back to work.

Minutes later, the office phone rang. It was someone from the Caribbean American Heritage Festival Association. I cleared my throat before taking the call. "Spice Isle Bakery. May I help you?"

"Lyndsay Murray?" It was the association's president, Sheryl Cross.

I squared my shoulders, refusing to let go of hope. "Good afternoon, Ms. Cross."

"The committee has come to a decision." She sounded even more officious than she had four hours ago. I squeezed my eyes shut and waited for her to continue. "We're pulling your bakery from the schedule of event vendors."

My eyes popped open. My heart punched against my chest. The thump reverberated in my ears. It was the decision I'd expected. Still, I was speechless.

"Ms. Murray?" Sheryl snapped across the phone line. "Ms. Murray, are you still there?"

My eyes swept the office, but nothing registered, not the silver metal filing cabinets that housed most of our important documents; or the cherrywood bookcase packed with industry magazines, and tomes of city, county, and state regulations; or the grass green cushioned visitor's chair right in front of me.

They locked onto the sterling silver framed family photo beside the computer. Daddy, Mommy, Granny, Dev, and I stood together in front of the bakery. Our arms were around one another as we laughed toward the camera. Reena had taken the picture with her cell phone days before we'd opened.

"My family hasn't done anything wrong." My voice was a thin, breathless whisper. "Our customers don't believe we're guilty. Why do you?"

An angry breath pushed its way down the phone and into my ear. "We've been through all this already."

"Then explain it to me again, please, Ms. Cross." I fisted my free hand.

Sheryl gasped as though I'd struck her. "Well, if you insist, Ms. Murray. I will spell it out for you. Again. It's been more than two weeks. Principal Smith's murder is still unsolved. This murder's on everyone's mind. Your family and bakery are in the middle of it, and your mother's been named a person of interest."

I drew in the scents of the sweet pastries and seasoned entrées that were baked into the office's walls. "So are the five guests who were here for the dinner. Are you going to bar them from attending the festival?"

A ripping sound came through the phone as though Sheryl had kissed her teeth. "What foolishness."

"It's not foolishness." My voice grew stronger. "We need your support. By removing us from the event, people will think you believe we're guilty. Do the right thing, Ms. Cross. Stand with what you know to be the truth and let us participate in the festival."

"We can't help what people think." Beneath Sheryl's dismissive words, I heard a tapping sound as though she was working on a computer. She wasn't even giving me her attention any longer. "As association president, the right thing for me to do is whatever I have to, to protect our brand and image. We're a family-friendly event. As such, we can't have even a whiff of scandal attached to the festival."

What more could I possibly say to try to change her mind, especially since she wasn't paying attention to me? "What was the committee vote?"

"That doesn't matter."

"I have a right to know. Was it unanimous to have us pulled?"

Sheryl was quiet for so long, I'd begun to wonder if she'd hung up on me. But I could hear her fingers drumming against her desk in the background. Finally, she spoke. "The vote was two-to-one to remove you. You made quite an impressive speech, Ms. Murray. Unfortunately, it wasn't impressive enough, not this year. Reapply next year. Hopefully, you won't be involved in any more murders."

The line went dead. I cradled my receiver and stared at the phone for what felt like hours. What had just happened? My God-fearing, law-abiding, well-respected family was dropped from the festival because its organizing committee believed we were too scandalous to appear at their event. It sounded like a bad joke, but no one was laughing.

I balanced my elbows on the arms of my chair and covered my face with my hands. *What* am I supposed to tell my parents, my grandmother, my brother, my other relatives? I'd let them down. I'd let them all down. How could I have let this happen? I should *never* have agreed to cater Emily's retirement dinner. Why hadn't I followed my instincts?

Anger propelled me from my seat and out of the office. I needed room to pace. Because of my bad decision, the bakery's business still wasn't back to the levels we'd had before Emily's murder. I circled the kitchen's center island. I'd hoped the festival would help with that, perhaps even push us to greater sales. That wasn't going to happen now. *Urgh!*

My shoulders dropped. I couldn't put off telling my family the bad news any longer. The sooner I told them, the sooner we could make a plan to move past it.

"Here's the hard dough bread, two loaves." Granny handed the paper bag to Mr. Campbell, the Kings County Early College High School's chief security officer.

He'd let us into the school after the sun set Tuesday night and was giving us access to the administrative office suite.

The older man opened the bag and inhaled. "Mmm, they smell fresh."

Granny had gathered her long gray hair in a knot at the crown of her head. She was dressed in what I guessed was her burglar clothes: black, straight-legged pants, a lightweight, long-sleeved black jersey, and black canvas shoes. Her dangling sterling silver earrings and matching necklace ruined the impression of stealth. The outfit looked new, though. Had she gone shopping for an outfit to wear to break into the school? *Oh, brother.*

Granny gestured toward the bag. "I just baked them. As we agreed, that's your payment for letting us into the school."

Mr. Campbell frowned. "And remember, no one can know I let you in."

Granny rolled her eyes. "Of course not."

I put my hand on Granny's shoulder. "We should probably get going. We need to be quick. Do you have your gloves and flashlight?"

Mr. Campbell jerked his head toward me. "Your girl's right. I'll go watch the monitors to make sure no one spots you. But be quick or we'll all get in trouble, eh."

Granny and I whispered our thanks. As I watched him amble down the main hallway, I pulled on one of the pairs of black chef's nitrile gloves that I'd taken from the bakery's supply for Granny and myself. I'd also taken two of the industrial flashlights we kept in the supply closet for emergencies.

I turned to Granny. "Are you ready?"

She turned on her flashlight. "Ready."

"This way." I gestured for her to follow me to Miguel's office. "How do you know Mr. Campbell?"

"Wilson and I've been members of CAAS for years." Granny's stage whisper sounded from close behind me.

"How do you think Al and I were able to get into the school last time?"

Just feet away from Miguel's office, I stiffened. I turned to face her, pointing my flashlight to the floor so the light didn't strain her. "Granny, you and Uncle Al were caught last time."

She waved a dismissive hand. "That won't happen again."

That didn't exactly flood me with confidence. "I hope not." Turning, I led us the rest of the way down the narrow aisle to Miguel's office. "This is it."

"What're we looking for?" Granny followed me across the threshold.

I made a beeline for his desk. She opened his file cabinet.

"I don't really know." I settled onto Miguel's black-cushioned desk chair and waved the flashlight over the contents of his center drawer. There was nothing out of the ordinary: pens, pencils, paper clips, rubber bands, an open packet of hard candies.

Granny rifled through the folders in the cabinet's top drawer. "Then how do you know we should be going through his things?"

I opened his top right drawer and found more office supplies: sticky notes, staples, tape, glue, index cards. "Because I think he . . . Hold on. What do we have here?"

The bottom right drawer wasn't properly closed. I pushed against it, but something pushed back. I tried again. The obstruction wasn't my imagination. Propelling the chair farther away from the desk, I pulled the drawer from the hinges and set it out of the way.

I slid off the chair and onto my knees. Angling my

flashlight, I peered into the open space. "Granny, I think we've found June's jewelry box."

Granny hurried to join me behind the desk. Kneeling beside me, she focused her flashlight on the drawer space. *"Bonjay."*

The office's overhead light turned on. Granny and I called out in surprise, our voices sounding in stereo. I blinked in the sudden bright light.

"Put that back. It isn't yours." Miguel stood framed in the threshold of his office. He held a flathead screwdriver like a knife.

Oh, Lord.

I rose to my feet beside Granny. "Something tells me it's not yours, either."

I caught Granny's attention. *Why hadn't Wilson warned us?*

Her eyes grew wide. *I have no idea.*

I turned back to Miguel, positioning myself closer to Granny. "How'd you know we were here?"

He arched an eyebrow, shaking his head. "I didn't. This was just your bad luck."

"You can say that again," Granny muttered.

I frowned at her, warning her not to draw attention to herself.

Miguel turned his attention from Granny back to me. "For the past two weeks, the cops have seemed more interested in your mother, Dan, Guy, and Meera. No one was looking at me." He cocked his head, crossing into the office. "Except you. You were asking dangerous questions. I started thinking it might be time for me to disappear. Looks like I was right."

My eyes shifted to his screwdriver. Had he planned to open June's jewelry box with it? How lucky that he'd brought it; lucky for *him*, since it could double as a weapon.

"It looks like I was right, too." I stepped closer to Granny, partially blocking her. "Emily convinced you to steal the money, didn't she? Right after she'd talked June into keeping it locked in her drawer until after the fund-raiser."

His voice was sharp. "How'd you know?"

Keep his attention on you. I prayed Granny would keep silent. I wanted him to forget she was there. "You believed her when she said she'd fix it so no one would notice the money was missing. She said the two of you could split it."

"But she lied!" His shout was like an explosion.

Granny and I jumped back. My heart was galloping in my throat. Granny reached for my hand. I gave hers a comforting squeeze, then released it. I needed to keep both hands free. My mind raced with possible ways to get out of this situation, even as I tried to distract Miguel with a long, protracted conversation. But he had the screwdriver. I didn't want to do something that would prompt him to charge at us, not when Granny was the one closest to him.

I took a steadying breath. "When did you know she'd been lying to you?"

His hand holding the screwdriver jerked with anger. "When the school board president walked into our fund-raiser committee meeting and told us we'd have to find the missing money. I told Emily I was going to return it. But she said if I did, she'd tell them I'd acted on my own and they'd believe her."

Granny kissed her teeth. "It took you that long to real-ize she'd treated you like a *bababooy*?"

I winced. Granny was incapable of keeping her thoughts

to herself. Taking another step to my right brought me out from behind the table, letting me block her from Miguel's view. "Is that when you decided to kill her?"

"Yes." He gave a clipped response. "Poisoning her lipstick was an easy decision. She cared more about her *appearance* than the *school*. She couldn't go three minutes without that lipstick and a mirror. I thought she'd put it on *before* she left the school, though. I hadn't intended to involve your bakery."

My blood ran cold. Miguel was being very free with his confession. What made him think Granny and I wouldn't go straight to the police? My eyes fell to the screwdriver in his hand. My knees shook. I balanced my hand on the desk beside me to steady myself. I needed to keep him talking until I figured out how to get Granny and me safely out of this situation.

I cleared my throat. "Emily's collapsing right next to you allowed you to switch her tampered lipstick with the one you'd bought."

Miguel narrowed his eyes in confusion. "You're very smart. That's one of the things that impressed Emily about you after she read the article about how you'd solved Claudio Fabrizi's murder. I thought you'd let the police investigate but you didn't. That's why I left those threatening messages. But you don't scare easily, do you?"

Granny spoke up behind me. "No, she— Ouch!"

I'd stepped back onto Granny's foot to get her to hush up and pretend to be invisible. "The police know about the lipstick, too. They know we're here."

Miguel's smile transformed his appearance from stressed to amused. "No, they don't. If they did, *they'd* be here instead of *you*."

So I wasn't going to bluff my way out of this.

"*Weh yuh deh pon?* You want us get caught?" Wilson's

voice carried down the hallway, asking what we were doing.

Miguel spun in its direction. Wilson froze in the doorway—eyes wide, mouth slack—as he came face-to-face with an armed Miguel.

I raced around the desk. Grabbing Miguel's arm, I pulled it back and up, forcing him to drop the screwdriver. I kicked the tool out of the way, then punched him in the face with enough force to propel him across the narrow hallway. He landed against the wall and slid to the floor. Rolling Miguel facedown, I collected his arms behind his back and straddled him.

I turned to Wilson. "Please get us something to restrain him with. Quickly." I didn't know how long he'd be compliant. As Wilson jogged off, I looked over my shoulder at my grandmother. I was so grateful she was OK. Some of the tension in my neck and shoulders eased. "Granny, could you call Bryce, please?"

Wilson jogged back with a length of silver braided nylon rope. "I found this in the maintenance room."

"Thank you." I took it from him and quickly tied Miguel's hands. Behind us, Granny was speaking urgently with someone on the other end of the call, presumably Bryce.

She ended her conversation. "The bo-bo are on their way."

"How did you know how to do all them fancy moves?" Wilson looked at me as though he wasn't certain I was real.

"I've been kickboxing for years." My muscles were shaking in reaction to the stress, fear, and adrenaline. I didn't think I could stand. I'd been more afraid tonight with my grandmother in danger than I'd been the last time I'd had to use my skills in self-defense.

Wilson scratched his head. "You were amazing."

"Of course she is." Granny helped me to my feet. "She's my granddaughter."

I smiled at her. "We'd better let the family know what we've been up to."

CHAPTER 30

"One of the questions that kept coming up was why now?" I sat in the bakery's dining area with Granny, Mommy, Daddy, Dev, and José late Tuesday night. Once again, we'd combined two tables so we could sit as a group. "If you disliked your boss so much, why wait until days before she retired to kill her? That made me think the motive wasn't connected to whatever would happen if she *stayed*. It was about what would happen if she *left*."

Bryce and Stan had answered Granny's call for help after we'd subdued Miguel. They'd driven us along with Wilson to the police department to take our statements. That's where we'd run into José. He'd caught news of the arrest on his police scanner and had rushed to the precinct, hoping to be the first reporter on the scene. I'd been so overjoyed the investigation was over I'd invited him back to the bakery to sit in on the family debriefing—provided he omitted some parts, like Granny and me accessing Miguel's office without proper authorization.

Daddy's arm rested along the back of Mommy's chair as they sat together at the head of the table. "When Roman told us about the missing donations from the school's library fund-raiser, we thought that seemed like a stronger motive."

My parents had been getting ready for bed when Granny had called to let them know we'd solved the case but would be late getting home.

Granny sat at my right. "From the beginning, we'd wondered why she'd invited so few people to her retirement dinner. With the exception of Meera, all of them were on the committee."

I turned to her. "We think she'd invited the school nurse because she was afraid Miguel was going to hurt her." I gestured toward Mommy. "Guy said one of the reasons Emily admired Mommy was that she was always able to defuse tense situations. But if you weren't able to resolve this one, she wanted Meera at the dinner to provide medical care."

"Woi." Mommy shook her head. "That dinner wasn't to celebrate her retirement. It was about setting Miguel up to take the fall for the theft in a public way. She'd hoped he wouldn't make a scene in front of his colleagues, but if he did try to hurt her she'd have witnesses."

Dev sat diagonally across the table from me. He looked more relaxed than he had in weeks. "It's a good thing June told one of the board members how much money the committee had raised. If she hadn't, when Emily reported the donations at sixty thousand dollars the board may not have realized it was almost twenty thousand short and she would've gotten away with her scheme."

I held up a hand toward José. "Don't print that part. June shared it in confidence. But everything the committee members told me pointed toward Emily being the thief."

"But how did suspecting Emily as the mastermind of the theft lead you to Miguel as the murderer?" José was seated on my left, typing his notes into his tablet. He planned to write and file his story before leaving the bakery tonight.

I looked to one of the five large windows in the dining area as I collected my thoughts. The red, yellow, and green valance Granny had sewn topped it. A metal gate protected the bakery's facade. Semi-sheer alabaster cellular shades covered the windows. Still, I could make out the hint of shadows as pedestrians walked up and down the block past our shop, even this late at night.

"People kept saying Emily always took credit for other people's hard work." I turned back to José. "Then she'd blame everyone *but* herself if something went wrong."

Granny harrumphed. "She only had mouth."

"Exactly." I smiled at the West Indian wisdom that meant, basically, Emily was all talk but no action. "She'd wanted as much of the donations as she could get, but she didn't want to get caught. She needed a fall guy. That's where Miguel came in."

Mommy nodded, catching José's eyes. "June, Daniel, and even Guy had worked for Emily for years. They didn't trust her and she knew that. Miguel had worked for her the least amount of time. He wouldn't've known she was setting him up to take the fall until it was too late."

"I don't feel sorry for him." Dev folded his arms and settled back against his seat. "He stole money from a library, killed someone to cover it up, was planning to let my mother be charged with the murder he committed, and threatened my sister."

All eyes turned toward me as murmurs of agreement circled the table.

Granny put her hand on my shoulder. "Lynds, love, we're really proud of you. You took charge of this investigation. You led us, and once again solved a murder case. You proved our family's innocence."

"Thank you, darling." Mommy's eyes were swimming in happy tears. "You have a real talent for investigation, you know."

Daddy chuckled. "Yeah, man. But it's a good thing we enrolled her in those kickboxing classes, *oui*."

"I don't know." Dev ran a hand over his close-cropped hair. "I think I've gotten some gray hairs, thinking about you being confronted by people holding first a gun and now a screwdriver."

"I'm feeling some kind of way about that, too." I pressed a hand to my heart. "The really terrifying part was having Granny in the mix."

"You're an impressive lady, Lyndsay." José's eyes shone with admiration. "How 'bout a quote to wrap up my story?"

My mind went blank. Then I looked at my family. "I'm glad we've been proven innocent. And I want to thank the community for believing in us during this *really* difficult time."

"Yes," Mommy murmured. "We're really thankful."

"Justice has prevailed." Dev inclined his head toward me. "And you made it happen, li'l sis."

I nodded, lowering my eyes to the table as disappointment washed over me. Don't get me wrong. I was grateful Mommy wouldn't be charged with murder and that our customers were returning. But I wished I could've solved the case sooner; then we'd still be part of the

Caribbean American Heritage Festival. Now we'll have to wait another year to reapply—and hope we wouldn't be connected to any more homicides in the meantime. Easy enough.

"You're like the Grenadian Nancy Drew," the Knicks Fan called out from near the middle of the bakery's customer order line early Wednesday morning.

José flashed a grin. "I wish I'd thought of that. I could've used that description in the article."

"Nah, she's more like a Dora Milaje warrior, ready to do combat." The Bubble-Gum-Chewing College Student cracked a bubble as she referenced the female warriors from the Black Panther comics.

"I don't know about all that." I exchanged a look with Dev beside me.

His lips trembled and his throat worked as he fought against laughter. I rolled my eyes. *Oh, brother.* But it was good to see him happy again.

We worked together behind the counter in perfect sync. Dev cashed out customers while I prepared their orders. Patrice Roberts's "Mind My Business" bounced out of the speakers. Every now and then, we'd do a shoulder roll, dancing a little as we served our guests. Our breakfast crowd had returned to the robust numbers we'd enjoyed before the tragedy of Emily's murder. Maybe we had even more business. I was thrilled and so relieved.

Our patrons had been boisterous in celebrating our family being cleared in the case. Mommy's and Daddy's laughter carried from the pass-through behind me as they contributed to the free-flowing group conversation. Granny retold our mission—with some poetic license— from her table while our guests hung on her every word.

Customers wanted to know details that hadn't been in the newspaper.

Had I used my kickboxing skills? *Yes*.

Was I using the bakery as a cover for my crime fighting? *No*.

Did I have an inside person at the school to help us get into the building? *No comment*.

"The committee was wrong to pull you from the festival." The Bubble-Gum-Chewing College Student adjusted her overstuffed backpack on her shoulders. "This is the most exciting shop in Little Caribbean."

"We won't enjoy the festival as much without all you there," Tanya called from the table she shared with Benny in the dining area.

"We should boycott the festival." This suggestion came from a young lady who was becoming our newest regular. A few customers murmured their agreement.

Irritation pinched me. "It's not a good idea to boycott an event by us that celebrates us. The festival is too important to the community. We should show our support. Spice Isle Bakery will be there next year, please God."

Joymarie came to the counter. She was lovely in a figure-hugging cream skirt suit and matching stilettos. "Good morning, Lyndsay." She turned to my brother. "Good morning, Dev."

He smiled at his girlfriend. "It is now."

She blushed as she handed him some money. "My usual, please."

"But wait," Grace Parke called from the line. The tall, big-boned woman was formidable in a navy pantsuit with a shimmering crimson blouse. "How're you going to charge your girlfriend?"

Granny glanced up from her crocheting. "So, Grace, you're a relationship counselor now?"

Joymarie gave the older woman a tight smile. "It was my decision to use my money to pay for my purchases."

Grace grunted her displeasure, then looked away. Dev had asked Joymarie not to pay, but she wasn't comfortable being treated differently from the other customers despite Dev's efforts to get her to see she was different. Granny, Mommy, Daddy, and I were staying out of it.

Joymarie turned her smile back to Dev. "I like seeing you in the mornings. Are you thinking of making the bakery a permanent change?"

"I'm hoping to." He looked at me.

My eyes widened. Excitement made my voice breathy. "Are you saying you don't want to work for a law firm? You'd rather work here?"

"If that's all right with you." He extended his arms. "You'd still be in charge. But I'd like to work here. This is where I'm happiest. This is where I belong." He shrugged. "I love baking, and I love being here with you, Grandma, Mom, and Dad."

"Of course it's all right with me." My heart was ready to burst. I threw my arms around him. "This is a family bakery."

"About time," Granny grumbled from her table.

The customers' applause nearly drowned out the sound of the bell above the door. My shopkeeper's ears were always attuned to new guests, though. I released Dev, stepping back to see who'd joined us: Sheryl, Sean, and Gina from the Caribbean American Heritage Festival Association. Silence descended in the bakery. The temperature dropped at least twenty degrees. Our guests must be more upset about the bakery being pulled from the festival than I'd realized.

A low rumble of discontent rose from our patrons as Sheryl led her group past them to the counter. Mommy and Daddy joined us from the kitchen.

Frowning, I gestured toward the other customers. "Ms. Cross, there's a line. You can't just walk to the counter."

She waved a dismissive hand. "I'm not here to buy anything."

I glanced at Sean and Gina, who flanked her. Their expressions were unreadable. I caught Granny's eyes. She stood from her table to take my place at the counter. I led the representatives to Granny's table. "How can I help you?"

Sheryl's eyes sparked with annoyance. She stood straighter. "We want you to call off your army."

The bakery became even quieter. I felt like I was on stage for our patrons' benefit. I frowned my confusion. "My *army*? What're you talking about?"

"Your fan club then." She set her hands on her full hips. "Your cousin, Serena Bain, has spread the word that Spice Isle Bakery won't be at the festival."

She had? I turned my head to seek my family. Daddy, Mommy, Dev, and Granny shrugged. They looked as puzzled as I felt. I turned back to the association members. "We weren't aware of that. Is there a problem?"

"Yes, there is. Since yesterday afternoon, our phones have been ringing off the hook and we've received scores of emails. People are very upset. They're demanding we reinstate Spice Isle Bakery."

My lips parted. Surprise cleared my confusion. I looked at our customers—our friends—and once again, my heart felt like it was going to burst. They were smiling and nudging one another, unapologetic for what they'd done. Their actions probably wouldn't change the association's mind. Sheryl was as stubborn as a rock. But I was so grateful for their support.

It took a moment for me to be able to speak. "I told you our customers supported us, and they have a right to express their opinion."

"Yes, I know. Even if their opinion is wrong." Sheryl wrinkled her nose and puckered her mouth. She looked like she'd eaten bad fish. "But in light of this overwhelming and unprecedented support by the community for your bakery being at the event, we've decided to reinstate you to the festival."

A shiver of excitement raced up my spine. I gasped. Was this really happening? I covered my mouth with both hands and screamed with relief and happiness. The bakery went from silence to celebration in an instant. Shouts of victory and applause exploded in the space. Granny and Mommy jumped for joy. Daddy and Dev raised both fists in the air, triumphant.

"Thank you." I extended my hand to Sheryl.

She took it without hesitation. "I understand congratulations are in order. You caught the murderer and proved your mother's innocence. Very impressive. Again."

"It was a family effort." I glanced over at the counter. Mommy, Daddy, Granny, and Dev were laughing, dancing, and hugging one another. I stepped away from the association members and clapped my hands to get everyone's attention. "Thank you so much for your support. To show our appreciation, currant rolls and mauby tea are on the house."

The cheers grew even louder. Daddy and Mommy hurried back to the kitchen. Shortly thereafter Eddy Grant's "Caribbean Queen" was bumping through the speakers.

Mommy reemerged with a tray of currant rolls to distribute to the line.

Looking back at Sheryl, Sean, and Gina, I shrugged. "Any excuse for a party." I gestured toward the line. "Join us."

RECIPES

Hard Dough Bread

Dry ingredients

- ¾ ounce instant yeast
- 4 tablespoons butter, softened
- 4 cups all-purpose flour
- 3 tablespoons sugar
- 2 teaspoons iodized salt

Wet ingredients

- 1 cup water
- ½ cup almond milk
- 2 tablespoons olive oil

Utensils

- Large mixing bowl
- Fork
- Spoon, wooden preferred, but metal will do in a pinch
- Clean, dry hand towel
- Rolling pin
- 9″ × 5″ loaf pan

Instructions

Add yeast to cup of water and leave to rise.

In a large bowl, using a fork, combine the butter into the flour.

Add sugar and salt. Mix well.

Slowly stir in almond milk and yeast mixture until the flour is completely moistened and the dough begins to lift from the mixing bowl.

Remove and rub the entire surface of the dough and sides of the bowl with olive oil. Return the dough to the bowl and cover it with a clean, dry towel. Leave the dough to rise for 30 minutes.

Flour a smooth clean surface of your counter or table. Remove the dough from bowl and knead it on the floured surface for about 3 minutes, to release air bubbles.

Using a rolling pin, roll dough into a flat rectangular shape, approximately 9″ × 12″.

From the 9″ side, roll dough into a tight log shape and put it inside the 9″ × 5″ greased loaf pan.

Cover the pan with the towel and allow the dough to rise for another 30 minutes.

After 20 minutes, preheat the oven to 350 degrees Fahrenheit.

Bake bread on center rack of oven for 40 minutes.

Note: Because the hard dough bread does not use preservatives, store in an airtight container for up to 3 days at room temperature or up to 7 days in the refrigerator.

Coconut Drops

Dry ingredients
    1 cup flour
    4 tablespoons unsalted butter, softened
    ½ cup sugar
    ¼ teaspoon iodized salt
    ¼ teaspoon nutmeg
    2 teaspoons cinnamon
    1 teaspoon baking powder
    2 cups grated coconut
    2 tablespoons ginger
    ½ cup raisins

Wet ingredients
    1 egg
    2 teaspoons vanilla extract

Utensils
    13″ × 18″ baking sheet
    Large mixing bowl
    Fork
    Tablespoon
    Cooling rack

Instructions
Preheat oven to 350 degrees Fahrenheit.
Lightly grease a 13″ × 18″ baking sheet
In a large bowl, using a fork, combine the butter into the flour.

Add sugar, salt, nutmeg, cinnamon, and baking powder. Combine thoroughly.

Add the egg and vanilla extract. Mix well.

Added grated coconut, ginger, and raisins. Mix well.

Using a tablespoon, scoop spoonfuls of the coconut drop batter onto the previously prepared baking sheet.

Bake the coconut drops for 12 minutes until golden brown.

Remove the coconut drops from the oven and place them on a cooling rack for 20 minutes.